Praise for Mic
Child of

MW01026326

"*Michelle Adam has written a beautiful story that will take you into magical and mystical realms, and remind you, once again, of your connection with the earth. Child of Duende is a rich and inspiring story filled with love.*"

—Sandra Ingerman, award-winning author of
ten books, including *Walking in Light: The Everyday
Empowerment of Shamanic Life*

"*Child of Duende takes us on a voyage where the earth speaks about our immense power and responsibility as humans to be agents of change for a better world. We discover, through Michelle Adam's magical storytelling, who we are capable of being, and must be, at this unsustainable time in history, if we are to come home to the heaven on earth that our indigenous ancestors have known this place to be.*"

—John Perkins, New York Times bestselling author
of *Confessions of an Economic Hit Man* and other books,
including *Shapeshifting, The World Is As You Dream It,
Psychonavigation*, and *Spirit of the Shuar*

"*Michelle Adam is masterful writer. Artfully weaving together Spanish culture and Gypsy mysticism, Child of Duende is a provocative tale that will bring you home to yourself—and to what is truly possible for our relationship with nature, and all of life, on our collective journey here on Earth.*"

—Llyn Roberts, MA, award-winning author of
Shapeshifting into Higher Consciousness, and co-author
with Sandra Ingerman of *Speaking with Nature*

"Our Mother Earth has dreamed into life all that grows, flies, swims, or crawls upon Her. For much of our brief human history, we knew how to repay the gift and replenish her fruitfulness. Child of Duende is a tale of one woman's magical odyssey to the edge where human spirits and the soul of nature dance. Through a page-turning whorl of half-remembered promises, buried emotions, and visionary dreams, Michelle Adam takes us on our own shamanic journey to discover the sweet promise of renewal."

—Evelyn C. Rysdyk, author of *Spirit Walking: A Course in Shamanic Power* and *A Spirit Walker's Guide to Shamanic Tools*

Child of Duende

A Journey of the Spirit

MICHELLE ADAM

Published by Pachamor Publishing

www.michelleadam.net

www.childofduende.com

print: 978-0-9972471-0-7

kindle: 978-0-9972471-1-4

ePub: 978-0-9972471-2-1

Cover design by Damonza

Back cover head shot by Caren Phillips

Cover painting by Michelle Adam

Interior Illustrations by Jenna Kass

Printed in Albuquerque, NM

*Dedicated to the spirit of the Earth,
my grandmother Oma Erica,
and to my ancestors.*

DUENDE:

A goblin, an imp, a spirit, a quality of passion and inspiration.

—Oxford Spanish Dictionary

Elf, ghost.

—Webster's New World Spanish Dictionary

"The spirit of the earth... one must awaken... in the remotest mansions of the blood."

—from Spanish poet Federico García Lorca's lecture
Theory and Play of the Duende, 1933

A Spanish word whose origin is...
A contraction of duen de casa, from dueño de casa, "owner of the house."

PROLOGUE

Paco's voice slid deep into the smoke-filled room. Silence sifted into the space between his breaths. Crying with the anguish of a people who had left their homeland centuries ago, he carried a song that still knew its way inside the heartbeat of the earth. Eight-year-old Duende listened. Twenty-eight-year-old Ingrid barely remembered this mysterious melody that came from within.

In the small village of Málaga, on the coast of Spain, where the Mediterranean Sea separated Europe from Africa, from the Arabic cries of "Allah," and from the Jews' search for their homeland, Paco and his Gypsy song remained. Duende, raised in this culture, knew this song and its origin, yet Ingrid, tossed into the modern reality of separation, had yet to find her way back.

This is the story of both, woven together by magical vines carrying the blood of the earth and a forgotten way of living.

INGRID

INGRID

Munich, Germany, 2003

At times, Ingrid heard the song from somewhere deep within her.

It was faint, though, as her mind was a chatter of to-do's and a determination to be someone she had yet to become.

This moment was no exception as she listened to the crackling on the telephone line.

"*¿Hola?*" she said in a Spanish she hadn't used in years. Her boss watched from inside his glass-walled office of their magazine, *Die Kelter*, called *The Wine Press* in its British edition.

"Franz!" Ingrid called to him. "Are you sure I'm not connecting to some remote place in the Congo?"

With piles of paper stacked in front of him, Franz grinned, the sides of his moustache inching up toward his eyes. Ingrid tried again, her voice louder.

"Hola?" she said with some force.

"Señora." A man's voice finally broke through the static on the line.

"Señorita," Ingrid corrected him as she stood hunched over her immaculate desk.

"*Perdón,* señorita. Can you hear me now?"

"I hear you. Proceed."

"I'm sure your editor told you—"

"Nothing. He told me nothing."

"It's a disaster here," he said. "I've never experienced anything like this. It's my vineyard. My vines have grown wild. Every day they grow several feet. They're out of control."

Ingrid pulled the phone away from her ear. She tried to be as professional as possible, even though Franz had transferred the call to her without explanation.

"They've taken over the house and the fields."

Not only could she still hear Señor Ramos, apparently everyone else in their Munich office could as well. Their desks were cramped together tightly in a small room with big windows.

"Why don't you cut back the vines?"Ingrid asked.

Franz, listening, nodded his approval.

"Señorita. Of course, we do, every day, but they grow too fast. Right before my eyes. Every day. You wouldn't believe it, but it's true."

There was no doubt in Ingrid's mind that this was his reality, but what he wanted from her wasn't clear.

"When did this start?" she asked.

"It's been about a week, I'd say. Maybe two. Hard to tell."

"What do you mean?"

"Well, it started slowly, and I didn't think much of it. But then…"

Señor Ramos's voice faded.

"Señor?" Ingrid hoped she hadn't lost him.

"Señorita. You have to come down here."

Hearing him clearly again, she realized there was no way of avoiding this curious conversation. If Franz had wanted to take over, he would have.

Ingrid looked at her editor again. Did he have any idea about the nature of this potential story?

"Where are you located?" she asked.

"Málaga, in the hills. Can't see…"

It seemed the man kept talking, but all Ingrid could hear was the word "Málaga" repeating over and over in her mind. She pulled herself upright from her hunched position over her desk. *Málaga?*

She swallowed deeply as the old songs drifted into her memory. In her mind's eye, she saw a little girl who stood alone by the sea. Lost. In pain. Ingrid put her hand on her chest and held it there. She would have preferred to keep all this locked away. Málaga?

"Your magazine has the best wine coverage in Europe," the man said. Ingrid stared at the poster of *Die Kelter* on the wall. The warmth of her hand pressed against her fast-beating heart.

"The others would make a sensation out of it," he continued. "They might invent some story that I'm trying to sell out to the olive industry. I know your magazine—"

"We've never covered anything like this, Señor Ramos." Ingrid pulled herself back to the present moment.

"I know. But you'll tell the truth. The real story."

Franz stood in the doorway to his office. Surely, Ingrid thought, he knew Señor Ramos's story and had heard the whole thing before passing the call to her.

"Can you give me your number?" Ingrid said. She dropped her hand from her chest to write. "I must talk to my boss. I'll call you back."

As soon as the call was over, she joined Franz, who closed the door behind her and threw himself into his desk chair. He twisted the edge of his moustache.

"Why'd you give *me* the call?" Ingrid asked, surprising herself with her sudden change in demeanor. "We don't cover sensational stories—and why me? I'm an editor, not a reporter."

"No, we don't write these kinds of stories," he agreed, leaning back in his chair. "But I owe a vintner friend a favor. He's good friends with Señor Ramos, and he asked me to look into this. Let's just say I need you to write this story. Plus, you speak Spanish and you've lived in Spain."

Ingrid sat down, crossed her arms over her chest. "Am I not doing a good job editing?"

"You're doing a great job. A bit stressed lately, I must say, but doing a great job."

"Sending me off on some sensational story feels like a demotion." Ingrid tilted her head to the side.

Franz leaned forward. "It's not. You're just perfect for the job."

A rush of memories engulfed her. She saw the girl again, this time inside a tall building. No one but Ingrid could know what she had left behind in Spain.

"Glad you're ready for this one," he said, clearly unconcerned with her unease. "As a matter of fact, I already have your train ticket."

"Train ticket?"

"I know, it's a long trip. But there were no decent last-minute plane tickets and I got a great deal on the train."

Franz, who appeared tall even when sitting, opened his drawer and pulled out an envelope. The desk lamp flickered as the late-afternoon sunlight shone on him, creating a halo on his bald spot, although, at that moment, he looked far from angelic.

Scheisse, Ingrid swore to herself, wishing she could wipe that grin off his face. He was always so cheap and she had no interest in going anyway. She settled for a deep breath.

"You leave tomorrow," Franz said. "You will meet the photographer, a man named Roger, in France, actually in Cerbère, near the border. He's been bugging me to let him take photographs for the magazine. Plus, he's been traveling through Europe and is willing to work gratis. Señor Ramos has agreed to pick you up at the station and take you out to his place. It will cost less if you both stay with him, and you can take a vacation while you're at it."

"Who'll do my editing?" Ingrid asked, hoping to dissuade him from sending her to Spain.

"You know we've got other editors. They'll work a bit harder." He stood up and handed her the ticket. "Look. Think of it as a favor. You can enjoy a few days on the beach afterward. What German wouldn't want to do that? Either way you look at it, you don't have much time. You'll need to instruct Gitta on the loose ends to be taken care of."

Ingrid's apprehension and shock had turned to confusion because everything was moving so quickly. She felt trapped. *Málaga. Málaga.* She stared at Franz on her way to the door.

"You'll thank me later," he said to her back.

She wanted to tell him he was wrong, that she needed to stay, not go. But instead, she gathered her things and left the office, after filling Gitta in on what to do in her absence.

Once outside, Ingrid walked aimlessly, past the butcher's and the bakery. She usually loved the smell of bread straight from the oven, but not now. Something followed her—and it wasn't the old songs, although they found their way back to her in gentle ways. It was what lay behind them.

She walked toward the park. Stood under a tree. She longed to hit it and let out the tension gaining strength inside her. She didn't have it in her, though, to hit anything. What good would it do?

All she wanted was a real night's sleep. Not an assignment in Spain—and of all places, not in Málaga—just a good night's sleep. Anxiety had visited her these past few months.

Ingrid tried to avoid weeping, without success. The ripped bark of the tree looked like skin. She hated the way she was feeling.

She told herself to be strong, not to let Franz get to her.

After all, it was only a trip to Spain. Her heart skipped a beat. To Spain.

Ingrid sighed. The tree hadn't moved, nor had she.

She had to gather herself. She was a professional. Ingrid was good at whatever she did. She would do a good job on this, as well.

The Munich sun descended behind a group of tall buildings as Ingrid walked home, past two honking cars, and ascended the flight of steps to her apartment, surprised to be out of breath upon reaching her flat.

Her cat, Mookie, greeted her at the door. Ingrid smiled briefly and held her tight. She'd have to find someone to take care of the cat, and then exercise so she'd sleep well enough to face tomorrow's journey... to Málaga.

≪⑤

Ingrid watched passengers hurrying in either direction through a smeared café window. It was two the next afternoon, almost half an hour before she'd need to board the train.

She was finally at the station after a night of poor sleep and a morning working out her anxiety on her exercise equipment. Ingrid noticed her wrists, how they seemed to be getting thinner by the week, as she checked the time every few minutes.

Franz had just called her, making sure she was on her way. Where, she wondered, did he think she would be? Ingrid kept it short, told him everything was fine—she had Señor Ramos's information and Roger's—and not to worry. She hoped he wouldn't be calling too often.

She ordered a refill on her coffee. Her third cup. She was sipping it, savoring the aroma and the warmth of the cup that calmed her cool hands, when she heard a familiar voice calling her name.

As Ingrid looked up to see who it was, she spilled her coffee on the table. It was her father.

Her look of surprise replaced any words that may have come out of her mouth.

"Your mom said you'd be here, so I thought I'd see you off on your trip." Her father sat down in the seat across from her.

Ingrid suddenly wished she hadn't called her mom, hadn't told her she'd be here, or that she was going on the trip to Spain.

"You should be glad to see your father," he said and gave the waitress his order as Ingrid played with the napkin now soaked in coffee.

She grinned and glanced back down at her watch. Two ten.

"So," she said, looking at her father. Conversations with him were never comfortable, and it was unusual for him to just show up like this, unannounced. Typically, her mother was the one who made the effort to reach out, to insist that Ingrid come over once a week for dinner with them. "Why... why'd you come?"

Her father rarely minced words. "I have something for you," he said, handing her a cream-colored book the size of her two hands. "Your grandmother wanted you to have this. And since you're going to Spain, I fig—"

His words landed on closed ears. Ingrid was elsewhere, her eyes on the book, which was all too familiar to her. *Why now?* she thought, although she knew the answer to her own question.

"I'm going on assignment, Dad. I'm not carrying some book with me just because—"

"I know you're going on assignment. But you're also going to Málaga, your birthplace."

Ingrid squeezed the warmth out of the cup in her hands before lifting it to her mouth. He didn't have to tell her the obvious.

"I can look at it when I get back," she said.

Her father—a good-looking man with premature gray hair and crystal-blue eyes raised in World War II Germany—looked down at his watch now. "It's two twenty. You ought to get out there. I'll walk you to the train."

Ingrid took her eyes off the book. She knew her father wouldn't give up on handing it to her, but hoped maybe if she could distract him, he'd forget.

"I'll pay," he said, reaching for his wallet. "You just get your stuff together."

❧

On the station platform, they stood silently, waiting, their eyes on the clock that hung high above their heads. Two twenty-nine.

"Ingrid, I insist you take this," her father finally said, holding out the slim volume.

She resisted, her bag hanging full on her shoulder, and her suitcase below her, on the ground. "I've got no room. Can't you see?"

"If not for me, or you, take it for your grandmother," her father said gently. "Plus, it's not that big."

Ingrid felt a sudden tingling sensation, thought she heard a whisper, ever so slight, in her left ear, but quickly discounted it as she heard her father's next words. "You meant the world to her."

His change in demeanor and softer way caught Ingrid by surprise as her train, destined for Paris—and ultimately Spain—came to a full halt in the station. She looked toward the train, its doors now open and passengers getting off. "I've got to go."

Her father leaned forward, placed the book in Ingrid's hand, and gave her a kiss on the cheek.

He's so stubborn, she thought as her father leaned back again and held her gaze, seemingly wanting to tell her something.

She waited briefly, but the moment left them, and she entered the train with book in hand through the closest door.

Once on board, Ingrid claimed three seats as hers, determined to sleep the journey away, as her father stood on the platform. He remained there until the whistle blew, passengers scrambled to board, and the wheels of the locomotive began inching forward.

Through her broken reflection in the window, Ingrid watched him walk away, a small figure in the distance. She loved him, she sensed. But now she was alone and her stomach suddenly knotted into a fist of fright, which spread into waves that rocked any sense of solid ground out of her.

Ingrid forced herself out of her seat and quickly walked through the train's sway to the nearest bathroom. Pushing the door open, she vomited into a small sink. *It's just a quick trip,* she told herself. *Get yourself together.*

Looking in the mirror, she saw how pale she was. The anxiety of the past months, the sleepless nights that seemed to only get worse after her ex-boyfriend, Kazik, broke up with her—was this more of the same, or was this the residue of something that had happened much earlier?

Staring at her reflection, Ingrid saw a frightened girl looking back at her, a girl who carried a pain that now bubbled up inside her, raw and uncontrollable. She had vomited like this back then, in their bathroom at home in Málaga, only days before her family had left Spain and moved to Germany. Now, at twenty-eight, she was returning to her hometown with an identical feeling in the pit of her stomach.

Her desire to get off the train and return to Munich paralyzed her as Franz's words—"You'll thank me later"—echoed in her mind. There was no thank-you in this one. Ingrid should have convinced him somehow to send someone else, so that she could have avoided all of this.

She splashed water on her face. Her eyes looked so distant. Where had she gone? Who was she? And that little girl, where had *she* gone? It was as if her life in Germany—twenty years of going to school, then college, and working as a journalist—suddenly seemed like nothing compared to the knot she held inside her.

Ingrid walked back to her place on the train and looked blankly at the back of the seat in front of her. There was nowhere to go. No one to call on—no close friends to tell her all would be okay. She wished she were at home with Mookie and in bed, under the down comforter she saved for colder seasons.

Ingrid fumbled through her bag for sleeping pills. She had packed them for her trip earlier this morning after she had called her mother, hoping for some consolation she never got. Not that she should have been surprised, since her mother had never really been able to understand her. And Ingrid didn't share her struggles with her anyway—although Mom had expressed concern about her weight loss.

Contacting her ex, Kazik, wouldn't have done much good either. He would just have told her that she needed to get out of town, relax for a bit on the Spanish beaches.

No. There was no use reaching out to anyone, she thought, as she took two sleeping pills and reminded herself that the trip would take a while—into France and past Paris and the Pyrenees bordering Spain—before she'd arrive in Málaga.

DUENDE

DUENDE

Málaga, Spain, 1983

In her small home in Málaga, an eight-year-old girl listened intently. The voice of her grandmother's spirit, ethereal as a violin's last cry, whispered her name, Duende.

From the family couch, the girl smiled. Her grandmother's image stared at her from inside the picture frames on top of the piano, the kitchen table, and three coffee tables throughout their apartment. As Duende used mere thought to move the picture on the piano toward her, warmth filled her body. Her grandmother, whom she had always called *Oma*, grinned from inside the frame at Duende's magic-making.

The girl had never known her grandmother. She had never met her, unless her Oma's one visit at her birth counted. She merely knew that her grandmother had insisted on her name. No one else she knew was named Duende; no one else would give a child that name.

"Your grandmother named you Duende for a reason, you know that," her father said. He sat on the other end of the partially faded white couch no one was allowed to sit on without his permission. "I'll never forget those days."

He looked more solemn than usual, having just returned from Germany, where he had attended a funeral for his mother, Duende's grandmother. His wife, the girl's mother, Mutti, was busy emptying his suitcase in their bedroom as the two sat awkwardly on the couch in the dim late-afternoon light.

Duende had a hard time seeing her father so sad, yet she felt consoled by her grandmother's spirit, which had become especially strong since her passing.

"It was strange how your Oma was so determined to name you Duende," her father said. "She was such a powerful a lady. And she always got what she wanted, including your name."

He looked blankly toward the window in front of him and nodded. "A shame you were too young to know her."

"I know." Duende peered out the window at her neighbor, Latia, who was waving at her from her porch.

Latia danced with her hair blowing around her, twirling and twirling her dark-brown curls for the whole neighborhood to see. Duende waved back, slightly, so as not to upset her father.

Oblivious of their neighbor, her father cracked a smile. It was probably the first time he had done so since returning from Oma's funeral. "Your grandmother traveled thirty-eight hours from Germany to the Spanish coastline here, carrying your name inside a book."

Duende straightened her back and looked directly at him. *Thirty-eight hours holding a book? All for me? Why?*

"My mother hadn't slept in days," her father added, speaking more fiercely. "Your birth meant so much to Oma. You were the beginning of a new generation for our family. She used to say you would make right by our family name, although I'm not sure what she meant by that."

Oma's spirit stood behind Duende now, her presence brushing against the girl's back and producing a delightful shiver. "Our family name means 'vine,'" her spirit whispered.

Duende turned toward the sound, surprised to hear her

grandmother speak, and so clearly, as if she were really there. "Don't forget that," the ethereal voice said.

Forget? Forget what? The girl suddenly felt trapped between two conversations—one of which her father was completely unaware of.

"Your grandmother was so eager to get here that she even packed her bags weeks before boarding the train, everything neatly cleaned and ready inside her suitcase," he said.

Duende turned back toward her father. "But that's crazy," she blurted out before feeling somehow embarrassed and sinking into the sofa. She was sure Oma was listening now.

"Duende!" Her father's mouth twitched.

She turned her gaze toward the window and took her cue to be quiet. Latia was gone now, her porch empty, and Duende found herself wishing that her father would stop trying so hard to mold her memory of a woman she had never really met. She preferred to make up her own stories of her grandmother.

"Maybe she passed a bit of that wisdom down to you, through your name," her father said.

Duende looked at her reflection. Why had Oma shown herself to her? Did she want something?

Her father pointed out the window. "When your grandmother arrived here in Málaga, your mother was there, greeting her with full belly. You were late, you know, and Oma didn't like to wait. She only had 'so many days' before she had to return to Germany."

Duende listened intently with a growing sense of resentment. It wasn't her fault she was late.

"We rushed you along, all right," her father told her. "Your mother took heavy doses of castor oil after three days of not eating. You were finally born, on November 20, 1975, the same day that General Franco, the old dictator, was pronounced dead."

Duende didn't understand what castor oil was or what it had to do with General Franco, about whom she knew very little.

"Your birth was about that freedom, your Oma used to say," her father said earnestly. He sat up taller on the couch. "Your grandmother felt it. That's why she insisted on your name, Duende. Your mother wanted to give you a nice German name, but in your hospital room, Oma declared, 'This child will be Duende. There is no better name for her than this.' And that was that."

"What name did Mutti want to give me?" Duende couldn't help but ask as she relaxed into the story.

"That's not important now, is it?"

The girl's jaw tightened.

"Your mother didn't have the strength to resist your grandmother," he said as Mutti walked into the room, a shadow in the background. "She never did."

"Heinrich!" Duende's mother seemed upset by his remarks, yet walked right back out of the room before he could respond.

Her father was too absorbed in his recollections to take notice of her remarks anyway.

"So why did grandmother pick my name?" Duende stayed focused. "I mean, why *that* word from some book?"

"You may not understand yet," he said, "but your name is a word that means ghost, goblin, or earth spirit. It means the spirit of the earth."

Duende looked at her father, puzzled. Was she a ghost? Was she like her grandmother, this sudden spirit following her? Or was she more like her furry, small friend who came from the sea and was so different from anyone else she knew, yet seemed much more than a spirit to her?

The girl smiled as she recollected the times she'd seen this little man who'd come to her when she stood alongside the sea's edge. He had danced for her the last time she had seen him, appearing so thrilled to see her.

"Don't forget who you are," he had told her. "Don't forget that you are an earth spirit like me."

How could Duende forget something she had never understood to begin with? She didn't get half the things he'd say, just like she didn't understand her father's comments about her name. But she didn't care. She loved seeing the little man. He carried the smell of the sea with him.

"Well," her father said, suddenly pulling Duende out of her trance. She could smell the salt water in her mind. "Time to get ready for dinner."

Her mother was back again, in the kitchen, overriding any sea smells with her cooking. Her father had already joined Mutti as Duende stood up and looked toward the window, where, instead of seeing her own reflection, she saw that of her grandmother's spirit watching her through an unusual veil of vines.

Oma returned to Duende nights later, her spirit's breath tickling the girl's neck and waking her. "Follow the sound of the Gypsy children," she said. The girl slowly opened her eyes to a small blue-gray cloud above her bed. The cloud became a dancing, twisting ball of light, out of which Oma's face appeared.

Duende had never felt her grandmother's spirit so close, so full. But now she lay in bed, opening, closing, and then opening her eyes again to confirm the apparition. Because she knew that it was only that.

"Go now. I'll watch over you, but go, follow the Gypsies." Oma spoke without moving her lips. "It's time for you to learn about freedom."

Oma—or Oma's spirit—was so insistent that without asking a single question Duende slipped out of bed. She wasn't sure how to escape from her second-story bedroom without waking her parents. But, less worried about being caught and more interested in following her grandmother's urgings and her own, she tiptoed to a utility closet. She held her breath and found some clothesline rope she had seen there before, and tied it to the solid metal leg of her bed, all the time listening for any movement from her parents' bedroom.

Her blue-and-white-striped pajamas hung loosely from her frame. She changed into brown pants, a dark T-shirt, and a pair of sneakers so her pajamas wouldn't get tangled in the rope. Then she climbed down.

Upon landing on the sidewalk, Duende couldn't find her grandmother's spirit. Where had Oma gone? Had it simply been a dream? Duende hesitated, wondering if she should return to her room, avoid the possibility of her father's wrath.

But her momentary fear faded, and her impulse to follow her grandmother's urgings and the sound of the Gypsies overcame any hesitation. She stepped forward into dimly lit streets lined with small, tightly packed homes where, under the streetlights that danced down the narrow road, the Gypsy kids played. They ran past cars on Avenida San Sebastian toward Las Cuevas, an old Gypsy neighborhood named after the caves that once dotted the hills.

Duende noticed everything: a small furry animal running along the side of the wall, dragging its thin white tail; a line of ants nestling their bodies into a crack in a beige wall; under the shadow of a flower, broken pieces of a pot resting between the sidewalk and wall.

The Gypsies' cries sounded up ahead as Duende crossed the big street carefully on a green light and ascended a hill. She followed the kids who entered a doorway that released a mouthful of light below the words *El Carbonero*. As Duende approached the tavern, she heard the sounds of Flamenco, shouting, clapping, and hard heels tapping against the ground, riding along a mist of smoke that pushed through the arched doorway and into the light of a streetlamp. Small spirits rode along the smoke and surrounded Duende, inviting her to walk through the doorway to a mystical realm.

She had never seen so much smoke in a room. It filled the

spaces where dark-haired women danced, their hands clench-
ing turbulent rivers of skirts stained shameless red, solid black,
sun-drenched yellow and orange. They flirted with the darkness
as an audience stood pressed against the walls and sat at small
tables with low-hanging lights that created restless circles around
the dancers.

Duende stepped reluctantly deeper into the tavern. A short,
stocky Gypsy man began to sing in Spanish. He called out the
anguish of a people who swore they would never forget the beating of their hearts. One, two, three. One, two, three.

"I am Gypsy, and this port carries the tears of my people…
aya… aya…"

His voice elbowed its way through the room. "*Aya… aya…
aya…* my warm tears fall in a cold sea." The man sang from the
deepest part of his throat, producing a sound like the bow off
the strings of a reverberating cello.

"Paquito, Paquito," the crowd cheered, but Duende
remained still, watching at least a dozen spirits dancing fiercely
in a circle around her, almost dizzying her by the time Paquito
ended his song and broke the spell she was under.

"Come here, darling," the singer said, his voice as full as the
ocean.

Duende looked to the left, then right, then behind her. Who
was he talking to? The other kids were running in and out of the
bar, unresponsive to Paquito's request.

"Let's dance the Gypsy rhythm!"

The man now looked directly at Duende. Her eyes caught
his gaze. The spirits vanished as her knees began to shake. *Me?*

Paquito nodded.

Duende could hear her grandmother's words now, telling
her to follow these people, to learn about freedom. Did that
mean following this man?

He waited. The room silent. The dancers still.

Duende exhaled a deep breath. *Oma? Where are you?*

Timidly, she stepped toward Paquito, who took her hand and introduced her to Graciela, the dancer. "Show her how to dance Gypsy," he told her, releasing Duende's hand. His sweat remained in her palm and thickened with her own. All eyes were on her.

Graciela stepped forward with her masklike face—black eyebrows, blood red lips; her wrists wrapped in multiple colorful bracelets resting on her waist. With her hair pulled back in a ponytail, stretching her mouth into a broad smile, she lifted her arms as her hands hit each other, making a loud, clanging sound. The woman smiled through her missing teeth.

Graciela's eyes held Duende's gaze. The girl stared, frozen, waiting for some signal to call her into action. The woman nodded a subtle invitation to begin and lifted her skirt to her knees. Duende looked down at her pants, her little fingers grabbing what material she could. The room remained quiet. The other dancers had stopped moving, their eyes on the girl who now watched Graciela intently.

Tap. The dancer pressed the toe of her foot to the ground. *Tap.* Her heel lifted. *Tap.* She looked at Duende. Nodded.

Duende felt the stiffness of the pants she wore. Her hands shook as she noticed her sneakers. She shrunk in front of this queen and her black-heeled shoes. The room broke into laughter, the crowd clapping, calling out in a clatter of exclamations: "How adorable." "Look at the little one." "Look at those shoes."

But then a loud clap broke the noise. Duende's heart thumped. Her eyes darted back to Graciela, who directed fierce concentration toward her. *Clap.* Graciela commanded the room. The girl's feet pressed forward against the floor, her heels, one at a time, lifted. She fumbled for balance as she looked up at her hands attempting to come together. *Clap.* She raised her hands to the left, slightly above her, imitating Graciela.

Duende didn't dare take her eyes off the woman.

Again, she clapped, but this time the flats of her palms met like discs of rusted metal. *Smack*.

Graciela's eyes turned to fire. *Look*, her eyes insisted. *Clap*. Her hands cupped slightly to produce a fearless sound. Hollow on the inside. Solid on the outside. The lines of her hands found each other like suction cups.

Duende followed suit, this time producing a sound that echoed the dancer's. *Clap*. The corner of Graciela's mouth revealed a quick grin. Duende let her thin lips stretch across her face, while cupping her palms to clap in time with her feet.

Point, *clap*. Point, *clap*. Graciela added more. Duende's eyes remained fixed on Graciela's. The dancer approved. *Never lose your partner's eyes*, she seemed to tell the girl. That night Duende knew at least this. Point, *clap*. Point, *clap*. The crowd picked up its pace, becoming louder and louder, cheering olé, before others joined in the dance. Paquito sang and Duende became lost in other people's movement, and inside a bubble of spirits encircling her in dance and celebration.

As Duende walked home a little before dawn, she was aware of a new lightness, as though a string dangling from heaven was holding her up. There was, perhaps, a God.

The rules. She knew them well. They shadowed her daily life, despite her attempts to break them. Her father was God, constantly watching her, judging her imperfections. Until tonight.

Duende didn't feel the shadow of her father tonight. He had not been there with the Gypsies, in those final moments when she danced with curling, spiraling hands moving outward toward Graciela, hands and feet unafraid, familiar with their own grace as they submitted to the spirit living inside themselves.

Duende danced down the empty streets with her new angel wings all the way home. As the skies lightened to shades of soft gray and purple, and white lines of cotton clouds moved toward Málaga's ocean, Duende heard a voice. Her grandmother's, but this time soft and tender. "Duende."

Oma's face appeared as gently as her voice, but for a brief moment she looked like Graciela, wild and untamed, and unrecognizable.

Is that you, Oma? Duende wanted to say before her grandmother disappeared into a thin layer of white mist. By the time she reached out to her, though, it was too late. Duende's hands remained empty, her heart full.

Was this it? Was this night a taste of what her grandmother had felt before leaving this world—when she had named the girl?

The green shutters of several homes clapped against their windows as the sun slowly lifted its face into the sky. Duende, sensing her grandmother's approval, made her way home.

INGRID

INGRID

T he little girl stands in a field of vines, the earth trembling below her. Ingrid watches. Wants to save her, but it seems the girl is making it all happen.

Everything is moving, including the vines, deep green vines that crawl out of the thinned-out soil and cover the little girl. She becomes the ground, entwined by masses of green, the pieces of sand and clay bubbling up around her, consuming her.

The little one is surrounded by spirits, by these elf-like beings that dance into the ground with her, dropping deeper into a sea of tentacles.

Ingrid wants to save the girl as she calls to her and runs toward her, but the earth is now caving in below Ingrid, the verdure wrapping its arms around her, pulling her in as well. She screams out a name that is lost in the rumble. "Can't you stop this?"

She knows the girl can.

Now Ingrid's hands reach for the sky to keep from drowning. She sees her life leaving her—sees images of those she's hurt, nightmares of her power, her capacity to harm everyone she's ever cared about. She pushes the images away. They leave her as she sinks, alone, into the belly of the earth.

Ingrid startled awake with her fingers clawing onto the seat in front of her. She tried to cling onto the little bit of life she had left in her, even though it had taken the form of a nightmare.

When the train came to a screeching halt, the momentum rolled her forward, and she opened her eyes to the breeze of passengers and their bags moving through the corridor.

"Cerbère" broadcast through the station. "Cerbère."

"Scheisse." Ingrid raised her head and sat upright. Already? What happened? It seemed only hours ago she had been in Paris, and now she needed to get off the train quickly.

Ingrid rubbed the sleep from her eyes and pushed back the strands of hair that now hung in her face. She got up and brushed past passengers trying to leave.

In front of the bathroom mirror, she looked at herself again. Tension still aged her face. At least she had slept well.

She pulled her long brown hair out of the loose bind of her hair tie and put it back together neatly and firmly before straightening the white blouse that stretched to her clavicle and tightly covered her small breasts.

Deciding that this would have to do, Ingrid returned to her seat, pulled her bags together, and pushed her way out of the train and onto the platform.

The concrete felt surprisingly soft below her feet as she walked catatonically across the platform through the station noise, the density of her nightmare sifting through her body. Ashen skies covered green mountains in either direction in the early morning haze that carried the smell of the sea. She approached the station house and its light-ochre walls. Despite her exhaustion, she spotted the photographer at once. His orange outfit glowed inside the dim morning, like a pumpkin in a field of weeds.

"Look for the man in tacky orange," Franz had told Ingrid when he called her yesterday on her cell phone. "That's what he told me to tell you. You won't miss him, he said."

Missing him was impossible, as the thirtysomething

Englishman leaned against the wall. His light-brown hair curled around the edges of a wide-brimmed straw hat, and at six foot six, wearing bright-orange overalls, he looked like someone who loved to draw attention to himself.

"Hello." Ingrid dropped her bag at his feet. "Are you the photographer Franz hired?"

"And you must be Ingrid." He grinned. "The orange worked well, did it not? Much better than a name tag or a ridiculous cardboard sign."

Ingrid nodded, examining the man before her, who looked like a walking neon sign. His colors were a far cry from what you'd normally see in Spain, or at least the Spain that she remembered.

"Well, it's a pleasure to meet you. I'm Roger Watts, but just plain old Roger will do."

"Nice to meet you." Ingrid feigned a smile. "Well, I suppose we should find the next train, then."

"Right. Just what I was thinking."

Roger had a huge backpack that looked like it had traveled through the jungle—this, compared to Ingrid's shoulder bag and her suitcase, into which she had stuffed her father's book.

Ingrid walked ahead of Roger, keeping some distance between her and the orange. They made their way to the next train to Spain. The rusted sides of the Renfe locomotive were painted in black and yellow lines, and the wheels had carried decades of weight.

Ingrid remembered. She had ridden on one of these types of trains as a kid. With a quickening heartbeat, she got on first. Roger followed, knocking his huge bag against the copper-stained hinges of the old Spanish locomotive, tucking his head to avoid hitting the low ceiling, and squeezing himself into one of the six worn leather seats in the small compartment. It occurred to Ingrid that it must be difficult being so tall.

"We've got ourselves a good old Spanish train." Roger

dropped the bags to the ground and leaned back to test his seat. "Good and old. They don't make them like this anymore. Probably one of the last of these in Spain. Surprised they still use them."

Ingrid placed her bags above the window seat before sitting down across from Roger. She looked beyond his enthusiasm and outside, where a little girl with a country hat strapped around her neck held onto her mother's hand as they walked. Two teenagers kissed while an elegant man dressed in a black suit and shiny leather shoes glanced up at the departure sign and then back at his watch with furrowed eyebrows and pursed lips.

Inside the compartment, passengers seemed so calm and comfortable, unlike Ingrid, who was still feeling slightly nauseous. She tried to settle her nerves by focusing on the ordinary—the smell of the seats, tinged with the raw and musty odor of fumes filling their compartment; the sheen of sweat on passengers' faces; and the sweat spots under their arms.

Ingrid had just started to relax when a full-bodied woman wearing a bright-orange and light-blue skirt and peacock feather hat settled herself beside Roger and said loudly, "Good afternoon, *Meine Damen und Herren*. My name is Maria Maria."

Without pausing, she proceeded to share that her real name was Margareta—Margareta from Austria. But ever since she had seen *The Sound of Music* as a little girl, she had called herself Maria—twice—for the musicality of it.

"You see, I am a *vaitress* at night, but during the day an actress. A very good actress. But you see, I am a singer as *vell*." Her hands moved up and down her robust body. "And now I go to Spain to sing opera in the Zarzuelas. All my life I have *vanted* this, and now…" Maria Maria grinned widely, her chest projecting pride through her suspenders.

As Ingrid watched, images of bold, fearless dancing flashed before her, and that voice, that deep resonating voice she had heard as a child, returned, if only for a moment, before she began wondering how anyone with a voice as shrill as Maria Maria's could sing professionally, especially opera.

"I love to sing opera. It is like heaven, you know," Maria Maria said. Her multicolored dress fell across Roger's lap, the bright colors blending well with Roger's neon outfit. One would have thought they were traveling together.

"So sorry." Maria Maria tucked the edges of her dress closer to her thighs, brushing Roger's knee in the process.

"No apology necessary," Roger said, grinning.

Meanwhile, Ingrid looked outside, to a more familiar world. It had been a long time since she had seen a sea like that of Cerbère outside her window. It calmed her. She closed her eyes to her dreams. She could still feel the vines that remained inside her, and a nervousness that had intensified in the past months before this trip.

What had happened to her?

Ingrid had been fine—uptight maybe, but fine—until she'd become increasingly agitated and on edge for months before Kazik finally broke up with her, saying he couldn't take it anymore. At times, she'd wake up in the middle of the night, shaking, sweating, her sheets soaked in fright.

"What the hell's the matter with you?" Kazik would say. He had always seemed so fearless to her. The dancer she had met in a café who made her feel, for the first time it seemed, alive—sexually, physically alive. Not the kind of workout alive she experienced at the gym or at home, but alive, as though there was more to life than making things happen. She'd even gone dancing with him, partied with his friends instead of just going home at night, following her usual routine.

But then she started sleeping poorly and would quarrel with Kazik over the silliest things. Calm escaped her, and she sought solace in more workouts and longer hours at the magazine, fine-tuning articles that didn't need further work.

"You'll thank me later," Ingrid could hear Franz saying now through the sound of the compartment door moving.

She opened her eyes and saw a young couple, who, unlike Maria Maria, quietly took their seats.

Roger looked at his watch and then back outside. "Five o'clock," he said.

Ingrid clenched her hands together. They would soon be in Spain—the image of the little girl was with her now, and the vines that awaited them.

The conductor blew a drawn-out whistle, and the metal of the train's wheels brushed like sandpaper against the tracks. The late-August sun rose slowly over the sea as the old locomotive inched its way into the tunnel of the Pyrenees Mountains.

✧

It didn't take long before the country that Ingrid had once loved appeared beyond the tunnel that separated Spain from France. The old train—breath by breath—rode through another town and its emerald-green waters with lines of multicolored boats docked on its shores. Birds rose into the sky to announce a new day as low-lying trees on hillsides waited to be greeted by the morning sun.

"España," Ingrid mumbled as her heart beat faster. Was she really here? Was it possible, after all these years? *What had happened to... Where did... Don't go there, Ingrid! Don't—*

Roger rose from his seat and formally announced that yes, they were in Spain.

I'll be okay. I'll be okay. Ingrid held her hand steady on her heart.

"I have the perfect—" Roger began and then, looking down at Ingrid, said, "You look rather pale there. Are you okay?"

Ingrid lifted her chin and nodded.

"Well, I've brought along something special to celebrate this occasion." Roger extracted a bottle of rioja from his bag, along with several plastic wine cups and a corkscrew. "Imagine if the whole of Spain were steeped in disaster, the vineyards no longer cultivating this extravagance, and the English becoming a major exporter of wine," he said to everyone seated. "Imagine that! What a shame that would be. We must toast to Spain! And her wine!"

Ingrid barely listened. She wanted to be anywhere but here. She pictured her father handing her her grandmother's book. She had never seen him so tender, except during that time after her grandmother had died and later when he had taken her to his childhood home in Germany. In the attic, her father had proudly shown off his stamp collection, pulled together from bombed-out homes during World War II. He had also opened a volume of their family lineage and history. "Don't ever forget where we come from," he had said.

Ingrid was wondering what he meant by that, when Maria Maria, and her loud voice, brought her attention back into the room.

"Don't be such a pessimist about Spain and her wine, my dear," she said to Roger. "All *vill* be all right. Just a little song from me and all *vill* be all right."

To Ingrid's surprise, the woman cleared her throat and pulled her shrill voice at least four octaves lower than usual to produce a sound that was smooth as chocolate. "Mi tierra querida... ," she began in a tender Spanish.

Maria Maria was good—actually really good. But Ingrid had her eyes on Roger, who stood mesmerized, clearly entranced by the big woman's beautiful voice until she concluded with a "Now open the bottle, *mach schnell.*"

"All right," Roger said, releasing the cork from the bottle's grip and, with eyes closed, smelling its bloodied end. "Ah... Now that—"

"Enough with smelling there, Mr. Englishman," Maria Maria told him. "Give us those cups and let's have a drink."

Roger released himself from his trance and grabbed the cups, passing them around as he poured everyone a generous helping of rioja before lifting his cup toward Ingrid. "Cheers. I expect we'll make a good trip out of this one," he said. She wished she could be so sanguine.

Still, Ingrid appreciated a good rioja, made from Tempranillo grapes that had soaked up the oak from the wine barrels. She had first learned about it, and pretty much every other kind of wine, from her uncle, whom she had visited at his vineyard in Italy shortly after obtaining her degree in journalism. It was her uncle, well connected in the business, who had known of a job opening at *Die Kelter* and suggested she apply for it.

Now, Ingrid sipped her rioja, less for its taste and more to alleviate unease. How many drinks, she wondered, would it take?

It didn't take long before she and everyone else in the compartment fell in and out of sleep. Many hours passed traveling under dark clouds, their gray-black masses releasing a loud, torrential rain, which pounded the metal roof of the train. Hills of dark-green intoxicating lushness rolled in every direction until the sun broke through and the fields turned a fluorescent green.

Bit by bit, everyone woke up. Ingrid looked out the window. This was different from the Spain she remembered, the Spain in which the land was dry and held the guilt and shame of her childhood.

Roger pulled a camera bag down from the overhead compartment, being careful not to awaken Maria Maria, who was now asleep, her mouth half-ajar as if ready to sing again. He took out a large lens, dusted it tenderly with a soft rag before fitting it on his camera. "A seventy-to-three-hundred-millimeter lens and a macro as well. Makes for beautiful photographs."

Pointing the camera at Ingrid, he managed to take a picture before she had time to turn away, absorbed as she suddenly was in the memory of the snow that had covered Munich the day she and her family had moved there from Málaga twenty years ago. She recalled her father photographing her and her mother in the snow when they had arrived after a long car ride. She had been mute the whole way. The soft, white drops that had fallen from the sky and into her mouth had felt like magic that could clean away the past and offer a new beginning.

"Ingrid." Roger brought her back. "You look beautiful. Why hide?"

She covered her face with her hand. "Please don't."

"My dear, he's right," Maria Maria said, awakening. "You are quite beautiful."

Ingrid faced Maria with pursed lips while Roger stuffed the camera back in its bag, ready to change the subject.

"Now, I'm not a full-time photographer, you know," he said, returning his green backpack to the overhead rack. "You see, I'm an adjunct professor of anthropology at Oxford. But don't worry. I take good photographs."

Ingrid didn't bother to hide the fact that she was surprised and not particularly pleased. She considered herself a professional and figured Franz would have at least paired her up with another professional, even if this was an unusual assignment.

"I've been doing this summers for about five years," Roger said, settling himself beside her, "mostly in England, although I've done some work in Wales and Ireland."

If he had hoped to reassure Ingrid with this, he had failed.

"But I must say, this is my first time photographing outside the UK, and for an actual magazine," he went on. "I sent your editor my work several years ago. Then last June, I decided, forget it. I want out of the cold, stuffy north—to travel some, see the world, at least in southern Europe to start, break out of the same old routine."

So what he was saying, basically, was that photography was his hobby. Ingrid began to worry that this whole trip was going to be a disaster.

"I was getting bored, you know. Other than my photographic treks in the summers, my life felt so predictable. The girlfriend, the same boring meals every night, the subway rides where everyone's so wrapped up in their little controlled world—including me. Now I've been through France, just got back from Corsica. My favorite." Roger rolled his eyes up toward some heaven. "And now, here I am."

He was here all right, Ingrid thought.

"Oh, and don't worry," Roger added. "I'll do a good job photographing. You'll see. And we'll have a jolly good time."

Roger looked at Ingrid, seemingly puzzled by her silence. "How long have you been with your wine magazine anyway?"

This guy doesn't know when to stop. She took a moment to think about her answer. "Six years."

"A bit more than my time photographing."

Ingrid cringed at the comparison.

"Your editor told me you speak Spanish, lived in Spain some years back," Roger said, incorrigibly.

Was this, she wondered, how it was going to be? Constant question time? How could she convey to him the fact that, for complicated personal reasons, the last place she wanted to be was Spain?

"Must be great being back. I've wanted to visit Spain for a long time now."

Ingrid pictured herself in her old home, boxes everywhere, only days before her family had moved to Germany.

"How long has it been, or do you always come back to visit?"

"Twenty years," she said with great effort.

"Twenty. Wow! I imagine you were fairly young when you lived there. I wish I had grown up in a place like this. Quite exciting to return, yeah?"

"No," Ingrid said abruptly. "I have no interest in returning. I'm just here to do this assignment."

Roger leaned forward, apparently noticing Ingrid's discomfort at last. "Ingrid. You look really pale. Did I say something?"

She felt as if she had been placed in a corner she hadn't wanted to be in. "Excuse me," she said, and rushed out of the compartment.

Ingrid held her stomach to the sway of the train as she stood in the narrow hallway. Fresh air entered through open windows that shook furiously. She was determined to avoid the bathroom this time.

Ingrid felt tears threatening. Where was her strength? She had focused on her work and being the perfect daughter her father had wanted. But now she felt incredibly alone.

Get yourself together.

The train slowed and then came to a stop. The door to her compartment a few feet away opened, and Maria Maria boisterously expelled herself. Her bags billowed around her as she approached Ingrid.

"*Meine Schätzlein,*" she said while reaching out in a failed attempt to caress Ingrid's face. "All *vill* be all right."

The big lady stepped down off the train onto a lonely platform in the small village they had entered, filling it with her presence. A single cow appeared in the distance.

When Ingrid stepped back into the compartment, she was greeted with silence. The couple, and especially Roger, just looked at her, appearing concerned, although she felt better.

Ingrid sat down and leaned her head against the window. The sun pushed through a large white cross that marked the resting place of the late dictator Francisco Franco. His body lay inside this mountainside north of Madrid.

The train moved past renditions of Don Quixote's windmills spinning vigorously. Black silhouettes of bulls, once advertisements for sherry, but now emblems of Spain, stood boldly against the sky. In the distance, barely visible, were olive groves, their broad trees and long limbs standing ghostlike, as if waiting for Ingrid's return.

DUENDE

DUENDE

As a thin morning light returned to Málaga, Duende heard her father whistling an accompaniment to Maria Callas hitting one high note of *Madame Butterfly* after another on the scratchy record player.

It had been two months since his mother's funeral, and Duende could hear him stepping across the hard floor of the hallway and knocking on her door before throwing it open. "Wach auf!" he shouted. "Wake up!"

Duende's dreams, of riding a whale that swallowed the entire ocean below her and of her grandmother wrapped in a glittering cape of emerald-green vines, scrambled behind her mind's protective curtain at the sound of her father's voice. If only they could stay with her.

"Wake up!" he repeated.

At times Maria Callas was a surprising relief, breaking her father's display of self-importance. But most of the time, his insistent German words pierced her sleep like shovels pushing through piles of stones. He shoveled, shoveled, until every stone picked itself up like a soldier and marched through the last dark corridors of dawn.

This morning was no different than other ones—Duende

could smell her father's cologne, the sharp scent of Gold-Dachs as she made her way to the kitchen, uniform on, ready for school.

Mutti was boiling eggs and toasting bread. Meanwhile, Duende's father stood in front of the long mirror in the apartment's entrance, adjusting his perfectly ironed shirt, gray tie, and pinstriped jacket.

"This is an important day," he announced to Mutti as Duende set the table. "A good Spanish firm wants to buy the hotel we just finished building. After ten-some years of building and selling homes here, we're finally seeing it pay off."

Mutti nodded.

Duende sat down. Her mother brought eggs and toast to the dining-room table as her father leaned over her in customary fashion and demonstrated the subtleties of eating soft-boiled eggs—how to cup the yolk with the small round of her spoon and bring it to her mouth without moving her head forward or backward. He measured the portions, inspected the exact angle at which her thumb and forefinger held onto her spoon. She swallowed without taking a breath. This he followed by checking to see that her feet were planted firmly on the rung of the chair, and that her back was in upright position.

More than anything, Duende wanted to escape her father's usual fastidiousness on this cool spring morning that blew through windows designed for Málaga's milder weather. She would listen to him, once again, but was more interested in visiting her special friend from the sea before making it to school.

"There is one truth that *always* holds true," her father said matter-of-factly after taking a bite of his own egg. "Do you know what it is, Duende?"

He seemed to wait for Duende to say something, even though her mouth was full of food and she dared not speak for fear of being reprimanded for eating with her mouth open. She didn't want him to kick her or put his fork against her mouth, so she remained quiet.

"Well?"

Duende hurriedly put more food in her mouth while shaking her head.

Her father's lips stretched wide and narrow like a banana. "Change... life is *change*."

Duende nodded.

His eyebrows scolded her as he explained, not for the first time, the hypothesis he had spent his entire life proving, in a monologue she was all too familiar with, explaining how life is always about change in its most obvious manifestations—the birth and death of all life forms; the tree that grows each day taller, changing color, dropping and adding leaves.

"Change occurs even in lifeless forms, like the time my sister hid a loaf of bread under her bed during the war and I found it later as a mass of blue, powdery mold." Her father gained momentum in his speech as Duende's urge to flee grew.

"Even change changes." He leaned forward, doing what he told his daughter never to do at the dining room table, his head resting on his hands, propped up by his elbows.

Duende finished her bread, brushing a few additional crumbs together with her finger, before her mother took her plate to the kitchen.

"Unexpected variables influence the original course of something," her father continued. "A stone appears still, but it is changing all the time. Down to every molecule, it is changing. The clouds, they change all the time, dropping rain, which forms rainbows with the sun's rays."

Duende got caught on the word "rainbow." She imagined herself as the rainbow with the sun's warm rays dancing through her while Mutti washed dishes in the kitchen.

The sensation ended quickly, though, when her father

slammed his hands on the table in satisfaction. The rainbow's bright colors scuttled to the corners of her mind.

"It's time for Duende to go to school, Heinrich," Mutti called from the kitchen over the sound of running water.

"*Ja, ja.* I'm done. Go then, Duende. I've got to get to work as well." Her father returned to the mirror, wiped his mouth perfectly clean, and put on his coat.

As soon as he left, Duende donned the coat with the big blue buttons, placed her lunch in her satchel, and after kissing her mother good-bye, joined the other students and parents who were filling their narrow street of Málaga's fishing village with life.

Once Duende reached the corner of her street, though, her fast walk turned into a sprint to the sea. She wanted to greet that vast body of water that sprayed a mist of salt into the air in her sleep every night. She'd get to school on time if she went quickly.

The sun skimmed along the ever-changing crest of waves. Duende, with her crossed arms protecting her from the wind, watched the morning unravel itself. She listened for a familiar high-pitched sound, and then it came. It seemed to travel from far away, from way inside the sea. It somersaulted its way to her, a sudden whirlwind of sand and water encircling her.

Duende closed her eyes to the ensuing dust. She could feel it now. Inside an unusual calm slowly embracing her, a familiar furry hand touched her.

"Hello," a voice said. With eyes closed, Duende sensed her friend smiling. It was the same smile from other encounters that she now saw upon opening her eyes and turning to the sight of her strange friend.

He was no ordinary friend. His small eyes looked at her past his large, wide nose, and from under a head of tangled, furry hair. His skin was made of earth, covered in a taut, sand-covered hide, and he had backward feet—they faced away from Duende, although the rest of him looked right at her from slightly behind her and to the right.

"Good to see you again," the three-foot man said to her.

His thin, long hands touching her shoulder, or his narrow, weblike feet, would have scared her if she hadn't seen him before. But he was familiar. Very familiar.

"You are one of us," he had told her one time, although she hadn't understood what he had meant. "I am a duende, a nature spirit, like you. I just don't look like you because I change form when I want to. You, on the other hand, are learning to be a duende in human form for the first time."

Duende wondered if his words had something to do with what her father had told her about her name. Was he a ghost, even though he didn't look it? Was she really like him? Where did he come from?

Duende let the thoughts go, though. She relaxed inside the warmth of his presence. He was like a brother to her who announced himself with a whistling, wind-hurling sound. This man was also shorter than her, stood below her with his strange pointed ears and an unusual cone-shaped horn coming out of his furry head. But when he looked at Duende, his odd features didn't matter, for his eyes saw through her, all of her.

She smiled in a ticklish way, until it was time for her to go.

"See you," he said, and with that the wind picked up, encircling Duende, and that piercing whistle took off into the ocean again.

"See you," she said, breathing deep contentment. She knew they would visit again. "See you."

A week later, Duende sat on rocks that jutted out over the sea into the rising early morning mist. She waited for her furry friend to show himself as the sudden wind wrapping its arms around her, tapping her with its long, wiry fingers on her back.

Instead, hundreds of birds trilled their chorus of songs into the much louder waves that broke against the rocks, and Duende, wanting to make her presence known to her friend, joined her own whistle with nature's song.

Within seconds, the sea roared a fierce fountain of water toward the sky, releasing a haunting sound that made Duende jump back. A deep, wide, eternal longing, pulling its anchor into her heart and down toward the seafloor, enveloped her, then echoed against the rocks.

"Duende." She heard her name coming from the depths of the sound. "Duende."

She turned her head in either direction, trying to see or place this voice that resonated from another world.

Her friend was nowhere to be seen.

Instead she heard, "Come inside."

Where? Duende thought. *Inside where?*

By now the birds had stopped their chanting, or at least Duende could no longer hear them. She stood frozen, her hands clenched, her eyes wide with wonder and fright, inside the warm morning.

"Here," the voice responded, lifting itself into a high-pitched sound as a large hand rose from the sea's fountain.

Duende shook in shock.

"Come on," she heard again.

She continued to look around, smelling the air and sensing for that presence she had become used to. But there was nothing. Just this voice repeating the same request.

As the hand descended into the sea again, Duende closed her eyes, finally letting go of expecting the same as before, and summoned her knowing. She cleared any fear or doubt she may have had about this voice and hand, and let herself fall deep into the vast body of water. She knew how to let her spirit travel in ways most children or adults never understood.

When she arrived, he was there. Her friend was waiting.

"Duende, I like your name," he said slowly, through a gurgle of water and wind, as if he were the sea, but not the kind the girl was accustomed to. His voice came from a deep, dark place, like the longing of a whale's cry that Duende had heard echo against the rocks and reverberate inside her.

"Come with me," her earth spirit friend said as he faced away from her while turning his long weblike feet toward her, moving the opposite direction she expected him to go.

He was a strange one, but the girl didn't care. She stood in a bed of seaweed, of long, vinelike plants dancing, glittering a soft green inside the dark sea floor. She could make out her friend's outline more than his exact features, until he turned his feet, and a golden glow emanated from his bones.

Was it his hand that had come out of the sea? she suddenly wondered, as the little man extended his hand for her to take. How had he made it so big, when the hand she now grabbed was smaller than hers and gnarly and bony?

There was little time to answer her questions. He drew her toward him. She hesitated briefly. Where was she going? The dancing reeds on the seafloor surrounded them, wove around them, tickling Duende at first, but then pulling them down, into the earth.

Duende trembled at the idea of descending beneath these waters, but her friend held her hand firm, and the green grasses of the seafloor pulled them together and down with a force she couldn't resist. An eternal hole opened below them, clearing the soil and sand around them, as the center of the earth sucked them closer and closer, accelerating their journey.

Duende kept her eyes closed, too frightened to see what was happening to her. At one point, her body began burning, and increasingly so the further they went, until she was certain there was nothing left of her but ashes descending to the earth's core. She tightened her grip on the man's hand, determined to feel her own form, to somehow know that her body, her limbs, were still working. She could now sense her own form, feel her heart pulsing blood through her, yet she hoped beyond all hope she would not get stuck in this place of no return.

"You are going home," her friend suddenly whispered as they accelerated through the earth's layers.

Duende seemed jolted by his words, stepping momentarily out of her fear, although they were moving too quickly for her to have budged in any other direction but down. *Home?* She recalled her father's words. She was the spirit of the earth, he had said, or at least her name was. Was her home inside the earth? Where was she going?

Duende's final thoughts landed with a thump, her feet touching the ground she hadn't felt in a while, or so it seemed. She trembled, scared to open her eyes as her friend let go of her hand.

"Take a look. This is your home," he said.

Slowly, carefully, Duende opened her eyes to a place of eerie stillness, unlike anything she had ever felt. Another world.

"You came from here," her friend said.

I did? Duende thought as she absorbed the reality of this place. A permeating bright light illuminated a meandering river of golden-orange tentacles flowing in all directions under a tall cave of protruding crystal columns. In the distance, she could barely make out a city, or at least it looked like a city.

Where am I? Duende thought, realizing that she remained hot, scorching hot, yet her body seemed to have changed to accommodate the temperature. The heat pushed through her skin, opening her without dissolving her form.

"We are in the center of the earth, your original birthplace, and where you will one day return." Her friend seemed to get bigger as he spoke. Duende felt herself shrinking.

"You are your thoughts, and especially here," the man said As he took her two hands and invited her to become bigger with him. "See."

Duende expanded into this underground world, feeling her own form change into someone, something else. What was happening to her?

"You look more like me now."

Duende cringed as she felt for the top of her head. A cone-shaped surface lay where her hair had been. "Eeeee," she tried to say, yet she couldn't hear her own voice.

"There is no sound here," the man said, smiling. "What you hear is me speaking to your mind, and it's not quite your mind either. It's all of you, all of you that is changing and has no name, no beginning and end. It's the 'you' that is this place."

Duende listened carefully to his every word, as she did to the golden-orange waters that had no voice yet moved in familiar ways that should have produced sound.

The girl waited, waited for the water and everything else to make some kind of noise. But there was nothing.

"Listen deeper and longer," her friend said.

When he spoke this time, Duende noticed for the first time that his mouth hadn't moved when he talked. How was that possible?

"Listen," he said again without moving his lips.

Duende closed her eyes and listened. Quiet. Quiet. Quiet, and yet, as she waited, something like a kind of a subtle vibration arose from under the silence. It enveloped her, like an echo from far away that had yet to reach her, but she could feel it inside her whole being. If she waited long enough, she sensed she would hear more. And with that, she stayed still, sensing for the echo to make its way to her.

Bit by bit, the vibration increased, beginning with her fingers and feet, which, when she looked at them, kept growing bigger, stretching her now malleable and weblike skin outward. The more she listened and sensed in her body, the more she expanded to include this sensation. She was becoming this place; the edges of her form were slowly disappearing.

Duende wanted to speak but couldn't. The little man was now glowing like the river and its tributaries around her.

"Home is more than place," he said, backing up into a giant crystalline wall. He disappeared into it, leaving an imprint of his body on the outside, before it too faded away and all that was left was his voice, deeper still. "We are the keepers of the earth."

As Duende listened to him, the vibration she had heard as a far-distant echo was nearing, increasing in intensity. It became louder, and not just to her ears, but to her entire body, which had filled this new world she was inhabiting, and possibly more.

Had she expanded to meet the echo? It was hard to tell, yet the sound shook all of her with a discordant, screeching energy. Her body, in all its fullness, could hear or, more accurately, feel all the screaming and unease beyond this place of stillness.

She didn't like it. She didn't like it at all. It reminded her of her parents when they were upset with her, and of the children who were all alone, and of cars, and a kind of frenetic movement that had no pause, no space for something Duende had always wanted. No place for being heard.

"Few people have been listening to the earth," her friend, now invisible, said from a place behind or inside the crystalline wall. "It's gotten loud out there, and yet we try, we try to keep this life going, try to keep growing what sometimes doesn't want to grow with all this noise."

Tears filled Duende as he spoke, although she had no face for tears to run down. Only the sensation of water, or sadness from this kind of liquid, existed. Who was she now? She wasn't sure she liked this space she was in.

"You are much more than this place now," he said. "You are feeling what the earth feels because you are her."

The tears that had no face to claim as theirs rolled into the golden river, cooling the waters with Duende's sadness and her sudden desire to return to a place where life sung a sense of hope.

She wanted to leave this place, longed for the sound of water, for that ancient cry of the whale to return.

"Let's go," her friend said, and with a glow of embers he stepped out of the stone and reached out his hand.

Duende had become too big to touch his hand, so she focused her energy on becoming like him again. She closed her senses down and aimed her shrinking hand toward his glow.

When her hand met his, both the same size now, it warmed her to feel his touch, to know she could return to the smaller size she had once been.

"Let's go," he repeated.

Duende looked around her at this womblike world wrapped in an afterglow of eternal sun. How would they get out of this place?

"Follow me." Her friend turned around, his feet once again facing her, and invited Duende to melt into the dense but hot crystalline stone he had just emerged from. She followed, surprised that it received them easily.

Soon they were ascending through earth and subtle stone and sand and ever-decreasing levels of heat, until, at one point, Duende's body shook from the growing cold. Would she turn to ice before making it to the ocean floor?

Duende pressed down on her friend's hand again, extracting warmth and a feeling of trust from his presence. They continued to rise through layers of earth. The pressure in her head increased. Were they almost there?

Duende's head pushed through a final layer of soft sand. A gentle stream of water dripped down her. "Ahh," she gurgled through the water, relieved to hear her voice again.

The little man shook the sand off his head into the water, something Duende never thought of doing. She was too relieved to be alive, to be reminded by the familiar waters that she was still the little girl who came to visit this place almost every day from land.

"I want to go home," she said to him.

"You were home, but I understand." He led her to the sea's surface, where Duende rose, sprouting from a fountain of water into the air, and onto the rocks where she had earlier stood.

Duende felt for all she had ever been—for her hands, her feet, and her entire body. And then, slowly, she opened her eyes, looked in either direction. She was back.

The birds were once again calling out their song into the breaking waves, and a soft breeze caressed her face. Duende missed her friend's hands, could feel her own still holding a tingling sensation from his presence, but she was glad to be back.

She would soon make her way home as if nothing had happened. Just an ordinary morning for an eight-year-old girl who had stood in front of the sea long enough to let the smell of its salt water and a whistling wind carry her to another place and time.

INGRID

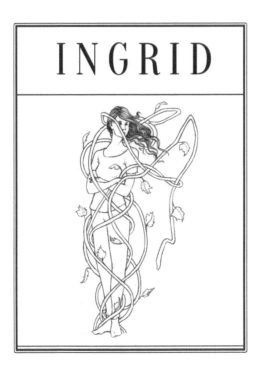

INGRID

By the time Ingrid and Roger arrived outside of Señor Ramos's estate, her dreams had crossed into reality. Grapevines upon grapevines crawled like long, coiled snakes across the road, growing so quickly that they could see them move and change form as Señor Ramos drove.

He must have been used to this all by now, but Roger and Ingrid kept leaning their heads out the window, Roger photographing with his mouth agape, exclaiming "Wow" every other breath. The vineyard looked as though it had been abandoned for years, green tendrils curling around fences, intertwining like long, dangling pieces of tangled rope. Twisting, crawling up and down poles and trees, and spreading their masses across the road, they remained without grapes. It was a world beyond Ingrid's dreams as she saw still more green, untamed masses invading the hills and threatening to take over this man's home.

After several hundred feet, Señor Ramos abruptly stopped the car and stepped out, ripping away the vines that clung to the ironwork before opening the gate to his estate.

The dirt driveway was framed by rows of trees that opened to the sight of a traditional two-story Andalusian house with a red-tiled roof. It looked as though a painter had rubbed the remains of his pink palette on its exterior, making what could be seen of the house through the tangle of vines appear worn and dirty.

Ingrid and Roger walked carefully along a narrow path that had apparently been cleared of vines only minutes before. They carried their bags—Señor Ramos helping with Ingrid's suitcase—past piles of cut vegetation that lay on either side as they approached the door. She grimaced at its ugliness, so reminiscent of her nightmares.

"Everyone asks the same question," Señor Ramos said while Roger rubbed his finger against the building's façade. "They want to know if the vines bleed."

"I don't understand, señor," Ingrid said. "Did you say 'bleed?'"

Roger brought his nose close to the rust-colored water stains on the wall near his finger and sniffed.

"*Sí*, señorita. I did say 'bleed.'" Señor Ramos stepped up to the wall next to Roger, touching what seemed to be a wet spot. "Every day they bleed and grow. They're still growing some now, but the blood is dry. It stopped about an hour ago, but it's there."

This is ridiculous. Franz hadn't told Ingrid about this, nor had Señor Ramos during the phone call. And how had Roger even known to check?

Señor Ramos laughed ruefully. "I know it is hard to believe. But it's true. Tomorrow you can ask the scientist who's been running tests. He—"

El dueño was interrupted when the door opened and a woman dressed in an apron and simple dress introduced herself as Amalia, Señor Ramos's cousin. She leaned forward to kiss the two guests on both cheeks, before pausing to examine Roger's outlandish outfit.

"Narinjee," he said, grinning as he attempted to say "orange" in Spanish.

His accent, Ingrid noted, was deplorable.

Amalia nodded a kind of "Yes, you *do* speak Spanish" and led them into the house.

Ingrid relaxed as they made their way inside. Roger, meanwhile, continued lifting his finger to his nose, sniffing its end.

They walked through a short hallway, past the kitchen with its smells of eggs and garlic, and into a large room with wooden beams across a high ceiling. Regal-looking paintings inside ornate silver and gold frames hung above an immense nonworking fireplace.

"Those are our ancestors," Señor Ramos explained. "Our bodega family has been making wine for 150 years. Imagine that. There's my grandfather's great-grandfather. Now you tell me how many generations that is."

Ingrid took care of his question—"Many"—and peered out one of the three long windows at vines crawling along the glass like in her dream, but here even the house was under attack.

How could Señor Ramos and Roger be so calm? she wondered.

"Señor… Raaaamos. Raaamos… means 'branches,' no?" she heard Roger say, pointing to a tree outside.

El dueño looked at Roger, clearly puzzled. Ingrid imagined he knew less English than the Englishman did Spanish—a bad formula for a conversation that was, Ingrid discovered, so muddled that she stopped listening. Didn't these two men realize that those vines could take over the house?

Obviously not.

Maybe she was overreacting, stuck in some dream. But the vines… And now they were bleeding…

Ingrid paced in place until the two men finally ended their scrambled conversation and they all walked through the house meeting other cousins, aunts, and uncles who, according to Señor Ramos, were all there for the birth of his baby girl, Isabel.

"She will be home soon, and you will see for yourself what a beautiful one she is," he told them proudly.

Because his baby girl had been born earlier than expected, Señor Ramos couldn't pick Ingrid and Roger up last night as planned. Profusely apologetic, he had insisted on paying for hotel rooms when they arrived in Málaga, and promised to get them to his place in the morning.

Ingrid was surprised to hear that the family had been expecting a child during her visit, just like she had been taken aback by the bleeding vines. But el dueño, with his bald head covered in sweat and his five-foot stature disappearing in front of Roger's towering presence, arrived at the hotel in an unusual hundred-degree dry heat to take them to his vineyard.

"God works that way. A disaster followed by a miracle," he had said, contrasting the vineyard to his newborn on their way to the car.

When they had driven past high-rise buildings, construction sites, and dried-out ditches in downtown Málaga, Ingrid was surprised to feel a sense of relief. Everything looked so different than the city and home she had once known, and she thought, maybe, this wouldn't be a trip into her past after all.

But now, Ingrid was more focused on the vines as she and Roger followed el dueño up a flight of stairs and into a small room with two beds. "Our place is small, and all we have is one guest room," said Señor Ramos as he turned to go downstairs and give his guests a moment to settle in. "My apologies."

"This is fine," Ingrid said politely, thinking back to how nice it had been to have her own room at the hotel. She had no interest in sleeping near Roger, or sharing a room with him, but in this house she somehow dreaded being alone—that is, until Roger walked toward the window covered in vines and opened it halfway.

"What are you doing, Roger?" Ingrid screamed impulsively.

"I'm just clearing the vines away a bit so we can see out," he told her. "Relax. Now we have ourselves a nice view."

Ingrid sat down on the bed farthest from the window. A nice view? Was he serious or did he have a sadistic streak?

"This is magnificent," said Roger. He peered outside. "I've never seen anything like this. So alive, don't you think?"

"No." Ingrid lay down on the bed and turned her back to the window. She closed her eyes, imagining snow falling on her lids, cooling her.

She had barely rested when she heard a knock on the half-ajar door. "Señorita. Señor."

Señor Ramos appeared, inviting them to join him in inspecting the vineyard. They soon followed el dueño outside, where, to Ingrid's great relief, the vines were growing more slowly than before.

Still, as they walked up the hillside between trellises that had become fortified walls of grapes, she felt the danger of stepping into the unknown.

Roger tried to help clear the way by trampling a path that was barely visible between the trellises with his big square shoes, but there was no controlling the mess that surrounded them.

Even the workers were unsuccessful in noticeably cutting back vines as they tried to manage the unmanageable this Sunday morning.

"Everything we do by hand here," said Señor Ramos as they followed him up the hill. They could barely make out men bent over near the top of the incline. "We have always been good to our vines, tending to them with love. It is important to know just when to cut back, when the crop is ripe, how long the wine must sit in the barrels, what the right temperature is."

Señor Ramos bent down and began clearing some of the verdure from his feet. He tore away at the tangled web of grapes. "It's taken us generations to create what we have here," he said. Ingrid carefully knelt near him, taking notes on a narrow pad of paper that rested on her knee. "Sometimes my family would work all night long here, on this land, after toiling from early morning until late afternoon for other *dueños*."

Standing tall, but a bit lower on the hill, Roger took photos of Señor Ramos speaking and forging a path through the green jungle.

"It's how we've kept the land and this business in the family," he went on. "My grandfather was out here, carrying bushels of grapes, separating the bad from the good, preparing the crop for wine, until he was seventy-five. His last breath was taken on this land. Now I carry all of my ancestors on my back. They're in the land, in every bit of the hard work that it takes to make this wine. We've all worked so hard, and yet I feel we're being punished, that God is punishing us and this land."

Roger clicked. Ingrid wrote. It took her full attention to keep up with Señor Ramos's words.

"But why? Why just me? Why here? What have I done to deserve this?" asked el dueño, his face full of anguish. "I cry out for help. I ask God to have pity on me so I can survive this… so I don't have to let my ancestors—and all their hard work—down. I can't do that. I can't."

Ingrid felt a tinge of compassion and the earth move below her. What the hell was she doing here?

Señor Ramos finally cleared enough vines to reveal a small patch of earth and asked Ingrid and Roger to come closer and feel the dirt.

"Can you see the blood, how dark the earth is?" he asked.

Roger's big hands dug in first. Ingrid was in no rush. The earth clung to his big right hand after he pulled it away. Then Ingrid, cautiously, touched the earth. With one finger, she rubbed the soil, and then curled a few other fingers under it to cup it in her hand.

Wet, moist, it slowly sifted through her fingers, some of it holding onto her with a gluelike quality. Of course it was wet, she told herself. It was morning. There was dew on the ground.

Ingrid was glad to be distracted by el dueño's talk as she rubbed any remaining earth from her hand.

"Where does this come from? I ask myself," Señor Ramos continued. "Where? The roots? Everything begins in the root. Everything... So what's in the root causing this shooting growth that's taking over my farm, my land, my house, my work? And this blood? What is it? I ask myself this every day. What else can I do?"

There he goes with the blood thing again. Ingrid wished he weren't so certain of what it was.

"I must go and see my daughter now," el dueño said, getting up and clapping his hands together, brushing the soil off.

Ingrid smiled, tiredness moving through her.

As they walked back, Señor Ramos continued to speak. "I am thirty-five, you know. This is my first child, although we had wanted to have more before now. She may be my only one, and I think, when she grows up, maybe there won't be this land anymore. It's bad enough that all the foreigners are buying up the land and letting the old vines rot. It's hard enough to make a living from the earth. But now this. What am I supposed to do?"

Ingrid had nothing to offer him as they returned to the house and she made her way back up the stairs to the closest thing she had to a temporary sanctuary. Here, without Roger or the vines, she would rest and shut out the world for a while, she thought. But much to her dismay, she was suddenly covering her ears, doing her best to block out a piercing whistle that tried to enter her room through the walls.

⁂

Ingrid wished she wasn't so tired when, later in the evening, Señor Ramos and his wife, María Juana, entered the living room with their newborn. Even she could sense how a renewal of hope filled the room where she and Roger sat.

"*Felicidades*," Ingrid said, forcing herself to stand. She gently placed her hand on the child's head and introduced herself to Señor Ramos's wife, a petite woman with wide hips. Roger followed suit.

María Juana, who had spent the night and early part of the day in the hospital to ensure her premature child's health, greeted the journalists with a feeble hug. She quickly retired to her room upstairs while the entire family—cousins, uncles, aunts—gathered around the baby.

When little Isabel suddenly opened her eyes and let out a cry, Amalia lifted the child from her father's arms and carried her into the kitchen. No one saw Isabel again until the next day.

What awaited Ingrid and Roger next was an elaborate meal with the family, a celebration of Isabel's birth. Señor Ramos began the festivities with the same reverence that Roger had displayed on the train, wrapping a napkin around the neck of a bottle of fine wine.

"Vino de España," he said reverently. "Spanish wine. This is our blood. We share with you. You who have come so far."

The wine was smooth, almost silky.

"Is this from your vineyard?" Ingrid said, realizing she hadn't done her research on Señor Ramos's wines prior to traveling. She could blame it on her concern for other matters this time, or the mere fact that this wasn't a real story, just a sensational one.

"Yes," el dueño said proudly. "Two thousand."

"Pedro Ximénez grapes?"

"Yes. We grow Pedro Ximénez grapes here, red ones, and Muscatel, for the sweet Málaga white wines. The Muscatel are considered the most ancient of grapes. The Phoenicians brought them to Egypt almost three thousand years ago. We've been growing them—"

Ingrid was very familiar with Muscatel grapes, having eaten them in Málaga as a child.

"Well, at least, until now." El dueño frowned.

A young woman carrying a tray on her shoulder served them chicken, rice, and red beets garnished with bright-green parsley. While she served Roger, he looked up at her, smiling. The woman nodded shyly and walked back to the kitchen.

"Josefina is her name," Amalia said in her best English.

Roger blushed as Amalia went on to ask him if Ingrid was his wife.

"No. No." Ingrid laughed and explained how they had only recently met.

The aroma of fresh herbs—rosemary, thyme, and oregano—reminded Ingrid of her childhood, but this time there was no bitterness. Every bite of food evoked memories. She washed the meal down with the mahogany wine that left its scent on her tongue.

By the time evening cast a shadow over the vineyard, the wine had lifted everyone's spirits and even Ingrid chatted like someone who actually wanted to be there. Despite the absurdity of everything, she began easing into the comfort of the Ramos family's welcome.

As for Roger, he didn't say anything about any changes he may have observed in Ingrid's behavior. Instead, he picked his way through the Spanish language, offering occasional words interspersed with English while Ingrid asked question after question in Spanish about their land and history. Although Señor Ramos answered everything he could, it was clear that his mind was elsewhere. At least every half hour he stood up, raising his glass and inviting all to toast to his daughter.

"*Mi hijita* Isabel," he said. "The miracle of God is with us every day."

The rest of the family was as excited by the newborn as he was and took every opportunity to add to each toast. Roger also seemed to feel right at home with all the celebration. "Este muy muy bene," he said in his fractured Spanish after Señor Ramos gave still another toast.

An awkward smile moved around the table when Roger spoke. The diners appeared to silently rally on his behalf, wanting to send him the words he needed, help him out, so he could finish his sentence.

While everyone looked at Roger endearingly, as though watching a child take his first steps, one of Señor Ramos's older cousins, José, who sat to Ingrid's right, asked her how it was she spoke Spanish so well. A silence fell over the room as she explained, reluctantly, that she had been born here.

"I lived in Málaga when I was a child," Ingrid added, before Roger, who seemed to be listening carefully, had a chance to say anything. "From 1975 to '84."

"Were you here when *El Caudillo*—our *sweet* dictator—was still alive?" José said.

"Actually, I was born the day he died," Ingrid replied.

"The day of Franco's death? What a day to be born." He lifted his hands toward the heavens. "Much has changed since. The day Franco died, my uncle left his wife and ran off with the next-door neighbor. He disappeared for months. They thought he was dead," he said, laughing. "But he returned… alone. Those were crazy times."

"Do you remember how we went out that night after they announced that Franco had died and the bars were packed? Everyone was out," José continued with enthusiasm.

José's older brother Pedro, who sat at the end of the table next to Señor Ramos, laughed. "I'll never forget how we walked from one bar to another, figuring there'd be more room in the next one. But no. Impossible. Remember, José? We were like cattle, all pressed together, holding our glasses filled with champagne high above our heads. It was like that no matter where we went. Well, until we ran out of champagne. Remember, they didn't have any more? All of Málaga—for that matter, all of Spain—ran out of champagne."

"A little exaggerated, don't you think?" said Señor Ramos, who Ingrid imagined must have been too young then to have gone out with the rest.

"I wouldn't be surprised if Pedro's right," said Amalia.

"But you stayed home like me. How would you know?" Señor Ramos said.

"I would have liked to have gone out and seen it for myself," she said. "But, you know, I was too young."

"What was so strange about that night is that we were too scared to say anything," José said. "I remember how I'd look at the macho next to me, or at all of you. We had these silly grins on our faces, but we didn't dare say anything. After all, what if Franco wasn't really dead?"

"Well, it sure took a long time for the *chaval* to die," Pedro concluded. "One day he was in the hospital, then the next they showed those films of him out fishing, as if he was completely fine. He was always fishing."

Josefina walked back into the room and cleared everyone's plates. From upstairs, Isabel cried.

"They say he was actually dead already, the night before they announced it," José said. "But, you know, they had to keep us waiting with the TVs playing some stupid documentary—like how hard it was to be a penguin and shit like that. The news was going to come out sooner or later, so what the hell."

"It's true," Pedro agreed. "The guy took a long time to die."

Pedro's final words produced nods of agreement. Everyone concurred that Franco had taken a long time to die.

Ingrid laughed heartily for what seemed the first time in months, amused that mentioning her birth date could have sparked all these stories of a dead dictator.

She wondered if Roger had understood what they were saying. She couldn't tell, but he did seem content to be watching

Josefina as she brought in dessert, a flan with caramel gently gliding down the side of the creamy custard, followed by raspberries in a thin brandy sauce.

By the time everyone had finished their meal, three hours had passed and the heat had softened into the evening.

⋘

Later that night, when Roger and Ingrid prepared for sleep, the baby's cries resumed. Then there was silence, a long period of quiet. Maybe she was being fed, drinking hungrily from her mother's breast. But then she started up again, emitting a cry with every breath. One more breath. One more cry for life.

Ingrid, in her light-blue nightgown, carefully covered with a short-sleeved button-down shirt, sat looking out the window. Everything seemed quiet, motionless, including the vines that had covered the windows and were now illuminated by the full moon.

Ingrid moved away from the window and tucked herself into bed. She was glad the day was finally over. She pulled her face close to the sheets and smelled their fragrance. It brought with it another childhood memory.

From her bed, Ingrid watched the moon through a liquid fog of tears until her eyes closed to the night. She felt the tightness she had been carrying in her stomach soften. *Must have been the wine,* she thought, and then realized she had made it through her first day in these hills of Málaga. Tonight she could briefly forget that she was here in Spain, and that its unruly supernatural world awaited her outside their window.

DUENDE

DUENDE

D uende stood outside her friend Lázaro's house, a shack near the ocean made of cane and metal. Málaga's waters drifted toward her on the dry riverbed where small pebbles blanketed a narrow strip of land separating itself from the Mediterranean. Water hadn't run down the mountains into this parched throat of earth for almost three years.

Duende knocked on Lázaro's door and then lowered her hand to her side. Her fingers held the warmth from the sun's daylong beating against the door, which had a small vine growing off to its side. Duende hadn't noticed it before.

"Who's there?" her friend called out. The old man's voice was neither rough nor soft. It was quiet and scratchy. "Who's there?"

"Duende."

She could see him peering at her out the dirt-stained window, much older than when she had seen him last, but with the same sparkle in his eyes.

"Not today." He sounded tired, as if he'd spent all day playing the air out of his lungs with his flute. "Go home."

Duende knew better than to listen to Lázaro's grumpy words when he was tired. Almost a year ago, she had become friends with him—having been drawn to him one day when he sat outside his home on a crisp fall afternoon. He'd felt like the kind of father she had always wanted. Since then, Duende had come to understand that if she just stood there long enough, he would open the door.

"Do you still see that friend of yours from the sea?" Lázaro finally asked Duende as he held his flimsy door ajar. "Does he still arrive with the wind and a whistle?"

Duende nodded. "I saw him last week before school."

"My, my. You amaze me, my little friend." Lázaro leaned into his doorframe. "What does he look like?"

Duende had to think about it for a minute. "He has big ears, and well, he's little, smaller than me. He's cute."

Recalling him, and how he appeared as if he himself were the wind, Duende smiled.

"Hmm… Interesting. Can you sense if he is near us now?"

She tuned in the way she always did, feeling for his presence in her body. Nothing made her sense he was near. No unusual smells or sounds either. "No. I don't think so."

"What language does he speak?"

It had never occurred to Duende to wonder what language her friend spoke, since she had always understood. It wasn't Spanish, though. No. Was it German? No, not that either.

"I don't know."

Lázaro seemed confounded by her answer. "But you understand him, right?"

Duende nodded. She couldn't explain the way she understood the little man anymore than Lázaro could, so she changed the subject, told him that she'd gone dancing the other night.

Lázaro looked more perplexed than ever. "Dancing?"

"Yeah."

"Where? When?"

"A few nights ago. I went to a bar," Duende said matter-of-factly.

"A bar?" Lázaro appeared to have trouble holding his flimsy door up.

"My grandmother's spirit woke me up, and she kept telling me to follow the Gypsies."

"Are you sure you weren't dreaming, child?"

"No. She just kept telling me over and over again. So I did it and went to them."

"You did what?" Lázaro pulled himself away from his door-frame and leaned forward. "No grandmother, spirit or not, would urge her grandchild to go out into the street with the Gypsies late at night. Mine certainly wouldn't have encouraged that behavior."

Duende knew that he would never directly criticize her, and that at some level he understood that she had done what she had to do. "I crawled down a rope out of my room. Then I followed them. I just followed the kids until I arrived at a bar."

"Duende. You're making this all up. You have such an amazing imagination." Lázaro threw his hands into the air and sat on a big rock to the left of his shack.

Duende turned toward him, crying. "I'm not making it up! She told me to do it. And—and I wanted to go. I danced," she said defiantly. "A woman taught me."

She crouched in the sand and began playing with the small granules. Duende made them jump into her hands and bounce in place. No effort, just her eyes moving matter into action. This calmed her. "I wanted to go."

"And your parents? Where were they during all this?"

"Asleep."

"This is a hard one to believe, you know."

"Well, it happened." Duende smiled. She pictured herself moving with grace in the bar and the streets. "I liked it. I *really* like dancing."

"This business about the Gypsies and hearing your grand-mother's voice, and your friend here on the sea, does it frighten you?" he asked. "And your dreams. Are they still so vivid and crazy?"

"Yes." Duende thought about how her dreams had changed since her grandmother's death, but wasn't sure whether to tell Lázaro yet.

As if reading her thoughts, Lázaro responded. "Next time you can tell me about them. Now, I'm tired. You must go."

Duende didn't want to leave. She liked sitting with Lázaro, who listened to her stories. "Do you see your grandmother like I do?"

"No. Never have. She's also been gone a long time. I miss her, though." He looked toward the ocean. "That would be nice to see her like you do your grandmother."

Duende wished she could help Lázaro see like she did.

"Now, go home… ," Lázaro began to say, but then remembered something and turned to go inside. "I almost forgot. I have something for you."

He returned with an old wooden flute. "Just breathe into it here," he said, pointing to the lips of the mouthpiece. "Put your feelings into it."

Duende took the flute into her hands, running her fingers along the weathered instrument and its holes. She grinned big, imagining playing for her whistling friend.

Lázaro smiled. "Now, go home."

Grasping the flute firmly in one hand, Duende skipped happily down the beach. With evening approaching, she turned up the first road to her house.

Days later, at home, a warm spring late-afternoon breeze blew through the window. Tears rolled down Mutti's thin face. She pushed a knife into onions that splayed into pungent pieces on the cutting board. Chop, chop.

Duende watched, unnoticed by her mother.

Mutti rubbed the back of her hand across her closed eyes and along her short, dark hair. Then chop, chop. The onions broke into smaller pieces, smaller and smaller, until her mother lifted a whole cupful into the same hand that had wiped the moisture from her face.

Duende wondered what Mutti did all day while she was in school. She knew that her mother shopped, cooked, and cleaned, but was there more to her daily life, something that made her smile?

Her mother now scraped the remaining pieces of onion from the board into the frying pan, which released a blistering sound. Duende stood in the living room like a ghost.

After stirring and waiting for the onions to soften, Mutti bent over the kitchen sink, running water over a colander of mushrooms before dumping them on a cutting board. Chop. Chop. Her body surrendered to the task at hand. Duende had a hard time imagining her life like that.

Mutti now stirred mushrooms into the pan of onions, releasing an aroma of sweet earth through the house. Duende breathed in this smell her mother helped create and then stepped forward. "Mutti," she whispered so as not to scare her.

Mutti jumped when Duende spoke to her, distracted momentarily from her task. "You startled me," she said and quickly returned her attention to the stove.

Duende stepped into the light of the kitchen. "Why don't we go to church?" she said, doing what she could to get her mother's attention.

"Why do you ask? Do you want to go?" Mutti spoke as she often did, answering a question with another question.

"No, but why do so many others, like Latia, go, and we don't?"

"Because we're not Catholic and we don't belong to any other religion either. We don't believe in that."

"What do we believe in?"

"Many people go to church because they want hope. They pray to God, to Jesus."

"What do we do?"

"All the praying they do doesn't change anything. It's up to us to determine our own life. We determine our own fate."

Mutti stirred oil onto pieces of chicken now in the pan. She was always stirring, and while she stirred, it was hard to get direct answers.

"What's fate?" Duende had heard that word before but didn't really understand it.

"It's what happens to you in your life. It's your future."

"Oh." Duende thought she understood, but now found herself trying to figure out what the future was. She had a hard time imagining any kind of future after what she had experienced inside the earth. If there was one, it felt far away.

"Why do you ask all this?"

"Because."

"You ask a lot of unusual questions, Duende. Now, you know I need to focus on my cooking. Go find something to do until dinner is ready."

Duende returned to her room and sat on her bed. She dropped her head to her chest, resigned. She wished she could talk to her mother more, share her dreams and adventures the way she did with Lázaro, especially lately, since her dreams had become stronger and almost frightening.

She used to dream about fantasy worlds, embarking on an adventure of colorful brushstrokes that would keep changing form and shape. Her new dreams, though, were all about Jesus, and they had started with Oma's death. Duende didn't understand why she dreamed of Jesus. Even though she had grown up with religion all around her, neither she nor her family had ever entered a church.

At first the dreams had simply been intriguing, many of them of Jesus on the cross, based on pictures Duende had seen.

Then there had been Jesus in a boat, Jesus on a lake, Jesus flying on the wings of some angel, or maybe it was some kind of bird.

Now her dreams were set inside a church, with beautiful multicolored lights streaming through stained-glass windows. Angels gathered everywhere. Smiling, they flew from the glass, along the ceiling, swooping down like soft-feathered humming-birds through the aisle. Their heads looked like birds' heads, their bodies angels.

Jesus hung above her head, his eyes filled with pain. And then great cathedral-like doors, banging against a stone wall behind Duende, were thrown open. The Gypsies paraded in, with Graciela, the queen, in the front, clapping her hands, counting the way she did when she danced: "One, two, one, two."

"Take Jesus down off the cross," she heard her grandmother say repeatedly, vines surrounding her and trailing behind her spirit. "It's time. Take him down."

Duende remained perplexed and frightened by her dreams. She couldn't understand her grandmother's request, yet—as was her nature—she felt curious. How could she do what her grandmother asked her to do? Why?

The thought frightened her, and she had no one to turn to, especially not her mother. Duende reached for her new flute. Maybe she could make magic happen with it, perhaps even summon her grandmother.

"Just breathe into it here," Lázaro had told her. "Put your feelings into it."

Duende lifted the flute to her mouth and blew. A small screeching sound released itself from the thin piece of wood. She tried again. She moved her fingers up and down the flute, delighted to create different sounds as fluttering images freed themselves from every hole. They danced out of the instrument and filled her room with a life that, inside her imagination, carried her back to the tavern, to the same small spirits dancing, moving through that place with the Gypsies.

Duende continued playing as best she could, less concerned with making perfect music—not that she knew how to anyway—and more interested in choreographing magic in her room. Is this what happened to Lázaro when he played? Did he make the sea skip waves toward him?

She remained in a trance, watching the familiar dancing spirits swirl around the room until her heart expanded to fill the space, and she was no longer an observer. The light-blue and emerald-green spirits changed form and color, tickling her insides. Duende laughed as her body fell back on the bed. All the while, her hands and lips still held the flute, its hollow insides letting out a piercing note that set the spirits into faster and faster motion. There was no stopping them now, for they were all one and the same as long as Duende kept playing.

They danced and danced together inside a magic-making musical symphony. From inside her, these spirits guided Duende into the streets, down the branches and roots of a cypress tree, following the liquid flow of life into the ground. She hadn't had this much fun in a while.

They glided down a saplike river, the flute's now-deeper sounds awakening a chorus of life prodding them on. It seemed everything around them—molecules of dust, miniscule earth beings, and flower seeds that had yet to be—rose from a gentle slumber and danced with them. All to music that somehow Duende managed to keep playing.

Her insides lit up inside this river of life she had become. This is where life began, she sensed. This was the beginning, how she and the entire universe came into being. On a note of sound, laugher, and joy springing forth.

Duende and these spirits glided through space and time. Little voices, all speaking, singing, intoning a different language than she had ever heard, led them down tunnels and openings that broke into other domains. She was a cloud, wind, air, moving through these tiny places where seeds waited to sprout. This felt like forever, a delicious forever that…

"Duende." A voice broke through the sounds. "Duende."

She suddenly shook, scrambled for reality. The sound faded. The note on the flute disappeared. Duende could feel her hands again. They tingled. They felt big. She dropped the instrument onto the bed, which sent a soft sensation to her legs and back. She sat up. Opened her eyes. Her mother was standing by the door.

"Duende." Mutti looked baffled.

The girl's spirit was still making its way back, tighter, into her body. She shook more. Her mother looked concerned and approached her.

Duende forced herself to come back sooner, to utter a word, so as not to scare her mother. "Hi, Mutti," she said.

Her mother didn't seem consoled. "What are you doing?"

"Just playing." Duende tried to sound as normal as possible.

"Playing?"

She nodded.

"You were shaking, Duende."

"Oh… I was just playing my flute."

"Your flute? You don't have a…" Her mother looked at the flute on the bed. She picked it up. "You don't own a flute."

"Well." Duende looked down at her lap. She wasn't sure what to say.

"Where did you get this from?"

"A friend," the girl said, but then wished she hadn't.

"What friend?"

"Actually…" Duende thought quickly of what to say. "I found it."

"So it's not from a friend?" Her mother sat down on the bed. She looked confused and somewhat irritated. "I know how you tend to talk to complete strangers. If you got this from a stranger in the street, then you need to tell me," she said. "I've told you how you shouldn't talk to just anyone. It's not safe."

Duende was more concerned about mentioning Lázaro—since her mother didn't know about him—than making up a story, so she told her she'd found the flute on the street somewhere, in an alley, and brought it home.

Her mother frowned. "You just said it was from a friend," she said. "Which one is it?"

When Duende stuck to her second story, Mutti responded, "You need to be careful. You don't know who's played that before or where it's been." She looked at the instrument in her hand. "As soon as your father comes home, he'll take care of this. In the meantime, you can wash your hands and help set the table."

As Duende walked into the dining room, her mother screamed, "*Scheisse*. Now look what you've made me do."

Finding that Mutti had burnt the chicken, onions, and mushrooms, and that she was now busy trying to save her meal, Duende lowered her head in shame and began setting the table.

Her father walked into the house in a more relaxed manner than usual. "Smells like burnt food in here. I should have eaten something at the bar."

"Your daughter took me away from my cooking, and now look," her mother said.

The silverware shook in Duende's hands as her father demanded to know what had happened. She told him, but was surprised when he merely said, "A flute. It would be good to learn an instrument."

Mutti filled a bowl with potatoes. "It's not that she's playing it that's of concern. It's that she picked it up in the street somewhere and has no idea where it's been before."

Her father frowned. "Duende, you know better than to pick something up from the streets. That's a great way to get sick."

Duende looked down at the table. Mutti walked to the

doorway and leaned down to pick up the flute she had placed there. She handed it to her husband.

"This is where it belongs, Duende," he said, putting it in the garbage. "Don't ever pick up trash from the street and bring it into this house again—let alone put your lips to it. Do you understand?"

Duende nodded. She hadn't moved from her place by the table and didn't dare do so. The girl couldn't begin to understand why playing a flute, or even finding one in the street, caused so much concern.

"Now go to your room as I help your mother get some food together here."

Duende was glad to go to her own space. Once there, she buried her head in the pillow. It would have been like her to have gotten up in the middle of the night to retrieve the instrument when her parents were asleep. But she knew it was a lost cause. Her father would have noticed the flute gone from the trash.

So instead, Duende pictured Lázaro and his disappointment. She had lost the one gift Lázaro had given her. How would she approach him now?

INGRID

INGRID

A sudden wind approached the house. It carried the sound of fluttering birds and startled Ingrid awake. Roger was already up, standing by the open window. "Unbelievable," he said. "Take a look. It's a madhouse."

Rubbing her eyes, Ingrid dragged herself out of bed. With the window almost completely open, vines crawled across the opening. Roger pushed them away so he could see beyond their room.

What are you doing? Don't let them in!

But then Ingrid saw what he was observing. Below them were strangers climbing the walls, high up on ladders, their hands and fingers pressed against the house, wrestling the vines, smelling them. Photographers and journalists, as well as scientists, were scraping the walls for specimens, and in the background Ingrid thought she saw a few priests.

She rushed to the bathroom to clean the night from her eyes, which were glowing as they hadn't in a while. How long had it been since she had had such a good night's sleep? Had she actually slept through the night on just wine and laughter?

"They're going mad out there," she said, putting on a pair

of jeans and a clean shirt. She joined Roger who, camera ready, was waiting for her in the hall.

They ran downstairs, almost tripping over Señor Ramos, who stood at the foot of the steps in clothes that looked like they'd already seen a whole day's work, and out the door into the morning, which greeted them with oppressive heat.

From the steps, Roger measured the light and played with the settings on his camera. Meanwhile, Ingrid walked toward the front of the house, stepping over and through moving vines that coiled around her until she climbed onto a rock from whose vantage point she could watch the chaos.

Eventually she moved closer to the wall, pushing vines back from the house—they seemed to move more easily than she had expected—and for the first time she touched the wall. Simply morning moisture, that's all, she thought as she brought her finger close to her nose and smelled the rust-colored substance. But it wasn't quite water either—deeper, perhaps, richer.

Ingrid closed her eyes and brought the liquid to her lips. She licked her finger, tasted a smooth, sweet, yet bitter sensation.

What are you doing? She opened her eyes to her one finger in the air. The dew may have tasted a bit stronger than water, but it was still dew.

As Ingrid dropped her finger and hand back to her side, Roger, who had moved in behind her, proclaimed, "It's blood, all right."

She turned her head.

"The man over there, that scientist"—Roger pointed to a man stooped over in the field several hundred feet away—"says he tested it. He says there's no doubt that it's blood—unbelievable!"

"Come on, Roger," Ingrid said, more to convince herself than him. She could barely make out the scientist Roger was talking about. "They'll say anything for a good story."

Roger ignored her doubting tone. "I think this blood, you

know, may be the next generation of wine. What do you think?" He grinned with enthusiasm at his discovery. He seemed impervious to the vines that crept across their feet.

"Roger... ," Ingrid repeated, frustrated. She used her hands and feet to push away the vines that had begun to crawl up her legs. "These things don't quit," she cursed.

"Better talk to the man over there. He's worth the interview," he said.

Before Ingrid could respond to Roger's suggestion, he walked off to resume photographing—her cue to consider his advice. She stomped clumsily over vines that felt like everchanging currents shifting below her as she balanced herself against trellises.

Ingrid approached the scientist, who seemed to be collecting specimens. The thin, bespectacled fellow with a goatee narrowing to a fine point looked up at her and soon introduced himself as Siegfried, a German botanist on assignment for a month in Spain.

"My photographer Roger says you've tested this so-called 'blood,'" Ingrid said, nearing.

"*Ja*, that I have. It's blood. Most definitely," he said.

"What kind of blood?"

"Blood, like you and I have. Human blood." Siegfried seemed impatient with the question. "Maybe what we have here is a new breed of plant. Imagine. A plant that has evolved to sub-human status. Human blood in a plant. Quite extraordinary."

"And how do you explain the crazy growth of these vines?" Ingrid asked.

"We have yet to figure this out."

"How can you be so sure about the human blood, then?"

"Of course, this is the most unusual thing I have ever seen," he said, "but tests are tests and blood is blood. Science doesn't—"

As Ingrid hastily took notes, an elated, bewildered

scream—loud enough to produce echoes—tumbled down the field. She and Siegfried turned toward the sound.

The strident call had dissipated, its echoes absorbed into the mountains that surrounded them, by the time the two reached the wall of the house where everyone had gathered.

Ingrid arrived, one of the last ones there, sweating, trying to get beyond Roger's towering figure, which blocked her view of what had happened. Roger stepped back to make room for her. Next to the wall, Señor Ramos cried and a priest held his hand.

It was like a funeral. Somebody had died, Ingrid was sure of it—until she saw for herself the cause of the loud cry.

In front of her, where only moments ago she had stood, touching vines and smelling the moisture on the wall, was a grape, robust, red, growing from the plant. But how had that happened in this jungle of barren vines?

Ingrid's heart pounded quickly, loudly, more than it should have after her short run. *Slow down, calm down.*

Throughout the entire estate, workers had waited for the growth of even one grape. Just one, and yet, according to Señor Ramos, there hadn't been any. Now, they all saw one grape, fully grown within minutes out of nowhere. Nowhere.

Señor Ramos was still crying with joy, as if the first drop of rain had fallen on his land after years of drought. A prayer had been answered from above, and a priest was there to bear witness with him.

Ingrid stared at the grape along with the others. *How could this be? How could this be?* As she grasped the reality that this grape had appeared in the exact spot she had touched minutes before, the memory of the old man she had known as a child and his fate flooded over her. It pressed down upon her shoulders with an immense weight that may have always been there, but now it seemed more oppressive than she could bear. Was all of this connected to what had happened to the two of them?

Ingrid looked down at her feet and the mass of vines below her. *Don't let it happen again. No, not again.*

The priest was making the sign of the cross continuously over the lone grape. It was as if he didn't know what else to do, as if he weren't sure if the one grape was a sign from God or the devil.

"Diós mío," Ingrid heard him mutter.

El dueño repeated after him. *"Diós mío... Es un milagro.* A true miracle."

The other journalists were taking notes and a few photographs, but quietly, inside an ambience of reverence.

Meanwhile, a small bird hovered near the crowd and then flew off on the tip of a sudden breeze. The heat of the early morning beat down on the group. Nobody dared move lest the grape disappear as soon as they took their eyes off of it.

This couldn't be true, Ingrid told herself, determined to avoid her possible role in the grape's sudden growth. Maybe someone dear to Señor Ramos had done it—possibly the priest—as a way to give him hope. She was willing to believe anything to deny what she was feeling, to clear the weight that grew heavier with each heartbeat.

Ingrid held her hand to her chest, hoping to slow down its anxious rhythm. With her eyes closed, the piercing sound that had tried to push through her wall yesterday came back to her, suddenly transporting her to another place and time.

Go away, go away, she thought while descending further into memories and a place inside where the weight intensified. *Go away. Go—*

A voice broke her descent, pulled her out of the space she was in.

"El señor needs a few moments here," she heard as she opened her eyes and saw the priest pointing toward Señor Ramos and his family. They were weeping and embracing each other.

No one seemed to notice her, for their attention was on the family. Ingrid's heart slowed down with relief.

She looked up at Roger, who stared ahead of him, his brow tense with thought. He appeared oblivious of her condition as they cleared the space along with the others.

The morning followed them inside, except for the oppressive heat and supernatural vines. Ingrid and Roger sat in front of the empty fireplace. She looked down at her nails and found one with an uneven edge to bite. He seemed to remain in a state of awe.

After all, these early hours had moved so quickly. She and Roger had awakened to find a swarm of journalists and scientists outside their window. Then there was the scientist, Herr Siegfried, who claimed the dew was actually blood, and human blood at that. Now everyone was mesmerized by the sight of a grape that had come from the vine Ingrid had touched.

Ingrid took a deep breath. *Thank you. Thank you,* she said silently to some God that may have been listening. She was glad no one knew, but couldn't help but wonder if she still had powers that she hoped she had lost.

That evening, before the sun had fully fallen from the sky, Ingrid stepped outside, alone. Señor Ramos was locked in a room in the house, praying, pleading for more grapes, begging for an end to the disaster, and thanking some mighty force for that one grape.

Ingrid had never seen someone so reverential. It was all for just one grape she wasn't even sure was real.

We must have all missed it, Ingrid kept telling herself as she stepped outside. There's no way it grew so quickly. Or someone had to have placed it there, and Señor Ramos and his priest friend were buying into the whole "miracle" idea for the price of hope.

Ingrid had already convinced herself that there was some explanation for it all, one unrelated to her or any power she may have had. Instead, she strolled through the rows of vines, their arms wrapped around each other from the early morning twisted madness that had slowed to a halt by late afternoon. Stillness now gripped the entire field as the sun arched its way toward the surrounding mountains.

The girl in Ingrid's dreams had stood in a field like this one, but the earth had been moving then, the vines pulling both child and adult into the ground. Now an unusual quietude permeated the vineyard, and despite the slight eeriness of the moment, Ingrid found herself hearing that voice again, that ancient song.

It slid, vibrated, rose within her as if it was her own voice. It belonged to the earth, it seemed, and it was only now, with no distractions, her worries having temporarily ridden away on a wave of deep breaths, that she could hear and feel this place within her.

Ingrid treasured this unfamiliar sensation—an eternal exhale she wished would last forever. She let go of wondering about the single grape and walked farther from it, toward the sun that shone its orange hue on her. The vines crackled below her feet as she moved with an unlikely ease above them.

She didn't bother to wonder where Roger was. The voice continued to sing within her. Did the man still sing like he used to? If she heard him now, would he awaken in her that longing she once knew so well? Would her old friend appear inside this longing, despite her being in the mountains, away from the sea where he had resided?

As Ingrid lingered in this space of song and stillness, inside moments of the past weaving with a forgotten grace into the present, the wind suddenly picked up. It gathered speed, whistling at a familiar high pitch that promptly made Ingrid's heartbeat accelerate before it swept her feet up from behind and sent her to the ground.

By the time Ingrid could make sense of what had happened, the wind had abruptly stopped. She lay on the ground, trembling, scared to look up and discover what had happened, or what was before her. But she knew. She knew she had a visitor she wasn't ready for.

Slowly she raised her head. He was stomping his foot on the ground. Her past was catching up with her.

A small man with a furry, cone-shaped head and pointy ears stood before her. He appeared frighteningly angry as Ingrid tried unsuccessfully to lift herself from the ground. Why was it so hard to do so?

Although the man's eyes were small, no bigger than pebbles, and his stature short, his gaze burned. Burgundy dots covered his thin and transparent skin, and his heart, thoroughly visible to her, thumped a loud drumbeat.

This man appeared familiar to Ingrid in some ways, but not in others. She sensed his origins, but didn't recognize him.

He seemed to believe otherwise. "You know me, but you've forgotten," he said and spit on the ground.

Ingrid struggled to listen to words that broke into pieces by the dense wind that had carried him.

"You listened once, but now look at this place. Just look."

She looked around her while still on the ground, stunned. Ingrid was determined to believe that all of this—all of the vines growing out of control, and the one grape growing from nowhere—had nothing to do with her. And why would it?

But the little man continued to speak. "Don't discount the magic," he said while Ingrid pulled herself up from the ground, bit by bit.

The idea of magic frightened her, she wanted to tell him. Plus, he didn't know what it was like being human and being able to make magic happen. What did he know?

As Ingrid gained strength and became taller, the man held her gaze, still as angry as when he had first arrived. But then, his body, as short as it was, began disappearing into the ground effortlessly. No wind, just gone.

Ingrid struggled to move. She was certain she had never seen this man before, even though he had claimed she knew him. She dropped her hand to her side and sighed fully, letting go of the moment.

A salty smell tickled her nose. The old song returned to her, soft, subtle, as if it carried the sea to this place high up in the mountains. With it came the memory of a little man she had known; a man like this one, but one who had been content.

Ingrid gathered her senses below the sun that wandered lower in the sky. She reentered the house, went softly up the stairs, and stepped into her empty room. Where had Roger gone? She felt too dazed to care as she dropped onto her bed and quickly fell asleep.

Ingrid dreamed of vines again, but without fields. She was in a magnificent, high-reaching Spanish church, far from the mountains and Señor Ramos's vineyard.

At first she felt the same calm as she just had in the fields. Alone, Ingrid faced the altar and all around her light filtered into the church through the long and colorful figure-laden windows.

But suddenly, the calm was interrupted by a loud crack as the cement and stone below her feet broke into smaller pieces. The earth split into long fissures, her feet desperately seeking solid ground. The man with the piercing eyes stood there, watching, and shouting, "Remember me. Remember me."

He then sunk into the fissures, and rising from where he had dropped were tiny shoots of green that spread like fire throughout the church. This time these vines produced grapes, and their tentacles stretched and grew with incendiary speed, upward, out, along the walls, the pews, the pulpit, the windows, across everything they could grab onto.

As the earth fractured, vines crawled up Ingrid's body, covering her skin. She tried to break free, but the more she moved, the tighter they held, until she found herself slipping down into sand. She was becoming one with the vine that enveloped her.

"Ayúdame. Ayú—" she screamed before realizing someone was shaking her and calling her name.

"Ingrid. Ingrid," She could hear Roger calling her now. His arms were suddenly around her, holding her. "You had a nightmare."

Ingrid held onto Roger, afraid to let him go for fear of falling back into the dark, tumultuous earth of her terrifying dreams. For the first time, she was glad he was there. He felt warm and comforting.

The moment didn't last, though, as Ingrid slowly awoke. She pulled back from Roger's arms. Sitting up in bed, she wiped away her tears.

"I'm sorry," Roger said. "Do you want to tell me about it?"

Ingrid looked away, embarrassed. "These vines… they're following me," she told him incoherently. "On the train, before I met you, I dreamed of these vines and now, again, but in a church… Last time, I was in a field like this one, and the earth, it broke, and a little girl… and I fell. The vines, they strangle me in my dreams. And I fall into the earth. There's nothing to hold on to. Nothing. And then I wake up."

Roger listened without consoling Ingrid as she wished he would. She felt like a fool and regretted sharing her dream with him. It wasn't real anyway—just a dream. She had been fine just minutes before falling asleep, she told herself.

Ingrid turned away, toward the window. She recalled the church in her dreams. It was familiar, from long ago in Málaga.

It's just a dream. And the grape earlier today was just a grape, and the little man was just a little man. No more. No less.

Ingrid moved awkwardly in her bed. The feeling of the church lingered in her. She wanted to get up and shake the nightmare off.

Roger took the cue and stood up. "They're calling us

for dinner," he said. "That's why I came here… and then I found you."

Ingrid forced herself up and gave Roger a wan smile.

"I'll let you get dressed then," he said and went downstairs.

Ingrid sighed deeply as if she had just survived a battle. She looked at herself in the bathroom mirror. Her face was pale again, her eyes hollow and drawn.

You're losing control.

She threw water on her face, determined to get herself together, and joined the others downstairs.

Dinner that night was a giant celebration for Señor Ramos and his family. Although it was just the immediate family, in addition to Roger and Ingrid, they drank as if they had a roomful of guests. El dueño displayed a renewed confidence that his vineyard would yield an entire new crop of grapes, and shared his exuberance with innumerable bottles of wine.

Ingrid drank and ate slowly, feeding an empty vessel. She didn't need the wine to soften the edges of her perceived reality.

She felt invisible, yet by laughing and speaking on cue, she doubted anyone noticed. Ingrid had spent years perfecting her public face.

Later, after dinner, back in her room, she kept her anxiety hidden and waited for Roger to fall asleep.

Ingrid lay in bed, facing the wall, listening to Roger shuffling, pushing back the covers, fluffing his pillow, exhaling, and then finally, gently snoring.

Ingrid, however, remained immobile, too frightened to close her eyes and relive her dreams. Her earlier ease seemed out of reach, although images of the familiar church and the man remained with her. It was, she realized, going to be a long night.

DUENDE

DUENDE

Teri-Amo cracked a big smile, revealing the wide space between her bottom front teeth. Sometimes she could fit the corner of her pinky in to clear away food. Sunflower seeds were the worst with their sharp edges, but she continued to eat them. Also known as Teresa de Amor, she chewed the seeds and shells as finely as she could, but a few lucky pieces always escaped, riding her saliva into narrow niches between her teeth.

"Patri!" she practically screamed her client's name as she watched the scene inside a clear, white ball before her, its patches of purple highlights swirling through the white. "Patri, you got a good life," Teri-Amo said, laughing. Her client leaned forward on the other side of the table, hoping to catch a glimpse of what the fortune-teller saw.

"What? What is it?" Patri moved her head around the crystal ball, staring hopefully into the eyes of this big woman she visited on a weekly basis. "Amo, tell me."

What Teri-Amo saw was something she hadn't seen in fifteen years of reading crystals, palms, and faces: a man and a woman embraced each other, sighing and groaning in a way that made her feel as though she were about to explode into a world of pure sensory overload. She had almost let herself feel these sensations in front of a client once, let herself sink into her own reality and ignore their needs. But now wasn't the right time for that. Clearly Patri was becoming anxious.

"Oh, Patri, I wish you could see these images with your own eyes," Amo said. *"This time I wish you could see."*

The two figures in the ball were making love like beauty and the beast—only this time the characters were reversed, but Amo didn't dare tell her client that.

Patri had been coming to Amo for guidance on her love life, whether she'd ever have one, whether any man would consider her worthwhile or see beyond her face, which was more like a smashed egg growing wild turkey feathers than the face Patri wished she had. Teri-Amo was the love queen, the one who gave people hope when there was none. This time, finally the news was good, and Amo was getting signs that the fairy-tale story could actually come true.

"Two years… two years and three months… six days, during siesta hours. Mark it on your calendar."

Patri rummaged in her torn brown pocketbook for a piece of paper and a pen. She stared at Amo and waited for her to repeat the figures, hope coursing through her face.

Amo sighed and repeated, "Two years… three months…"

Patri wrote, then scratched out, then wrote until she got it right. If this was the day she would meet her Romeo, it was important to be accurate.

Teri-Amo tried her best to describe the scene. It almost upset her to do so, took the juice out of the experience she was having. Patri's eyes were big now, growing brighter with each word, while the fortune-teller's body heated up to the sight in front of her. Teri-Amo described each scene. She couldn't believe the orgasm was lasting this long.

"God will prepare you now with the strength and fortitude you'll need to handle this one," said Teri-Amo as Patri sat like a stone. "A lot more sit-ups," she added, knowing that her client spent most of her time knitting and taking care of her aging mother. And as for the other kinds of exercise, she was still a virgin with flabby thighs. For a fifty-three-year-old woman, she was going to need a lot more physical preparation for the young man Teri-Amo was watching her entwined with.

Amo tried looking away from the crystal, expecting the images to stop. But they were still making love. Was it possible? Maybe she needed to get her crystal checked out, tuned like a piano. She felt a pang of jealousy, hoping she had inadvertently seen her own future, not Patri's. She wished it were true. She was a selfish Gypsy and she knew it.

Patri jumped up from her seat and slapped several hundred pesetas on Teri-Amo's table—a bit extra for the good news—and walked through the narrow red curtain to the street.

Amo knew that her client couldn't wait to tell her mother, who was constantly asking her why she wasn't married, why she'd never made her any grandchildren like her other daughters had. Furthermore, she knew she'd be back for more, that Patri would begin to worry—would her Romeo's plans change or, maybe, possibly, would he come any sooner? Amo would look into her crystal, see the images change, and tell her only the part that Patri wanted to hear. That's why they all came to her—for a bit of hope. People were always willing to pay for a bit of hope, even if that's all they got.

Her next client was due in half an hour. And she was usually late—a pretty girl who could attract all the men, yet still came for that special Romeo inside Amo's crystal ball.

They all paid for love.

Amo's real work was different, though. She was a protector of the public. She could foresee tragedies in her ball—an accident about to happen, a child falling from a second-story window. And when that happened, she'd find out who it was, warn the right people to take precautions. It was her God-given job to predict, warn, or prevent harm from occurring.

Most of the time, the future victims didn't even know that she was the one giving the news. Since she was the most popular love psychic in Málaga, enough of her clients knew somebody who knew somebody who knew somebody.

Lately she had seen images she couldn't interpret. They were of a little girl and, at times, of vines. The scenes seemed unrelated, yet occurred at the same time.

Teri-Amo had no accidents here to work with, nor action or purpose. Just a girl with brown hair, and eyes the Gypsy couldn't make out. But it felt important because the simple images kept reappearing, like an unsolved puzzle.

Everyday Teri-Amo pleaded for more information; and she prayed every night for a breakthrough. But the crystal ball wouldn't reveal anything else. It wasn't that easy, not even for someone as skilled as she was.

The curtain parted, and her next client came in looking more tired than usual. It had been a long day for Amo, and she could sympathize. After her last exhausting session, she would rather have taken a nap than help another client.

"Buen día, Latia," she said to the young client who sat down and greeted her. There was no need to ask why she was here. For months she had come, impatient to be told that a lover was in her future.

Teri-Amo cleared the last scene from the ball and quietly muttered a few words. She looked up at her client, at her long, beautiful hair and those dark-brown eyes deep set behind her thick eyelashes. Why, why did this young one need to come to her?

᪥

The night air received the smoke that rose and fell with the wind, but inside El Carbonero, the smoke rose but never fell. Instead, it formed clouds below the ceiling, hovering above the music, embracing dancing bodies.

Duende was back inside the bar again, carrying with her another place and time, yet searching for that song, that dance that had made her feel so free, here in this place.

As little Duende again, and not the giant creature she had become inside the earth, she looked at the men around her. The tavern filled with smoke as it had the first time she'd been here, but tonight an unusual stillness crawled along the shadows of the bar.

Slowly and deliberately, several women moved their hips to the sound of an old man playing guitar in a dark corner. The light from a streetlamp shone through a solitary window and rested on his thin, curved fingers plucking the strings with the fullness of lost love, searching for sounds. If it weren't for the soft movement of the dancers, the meticulous listening of their feet, it would have appeared as if they, along with everyone else, were oblivious to the old man's music.

Graciela was nowhere in sight, nor was Paquito. Duende could still hear remnants of his voice in the room, but that was all. It was her second night out and no one was there to introduce her this time, no one to teach her how to dance. Just the faces of strangers making quiet sounds around her.

A bartender leaned over the counter and called out, "*Niña.* Who you looking for? Lost your parents?"

Duende froze. She didn't want to get in trouble, didn't expect someone to ask her about her parents. This man calling her niña hadn't been there the night she charmed the crowd with her little hands, her brown pants, and flat shoes, trying so hard to match Graciela's elegant movements. Duende hadn't figured that this place would look so different.

"What's your name?" the bartender asked again and seemed surprised when she simply said, "Duende."

"Where's your family?" His gentle mahogany eyes rested on her as an older brother's would.

Duende shrugged. She wasn't about to tell him that she had

escaped through her bedroom window without her parents' permission.

"This is no place for you to be alone."

Two men reached over her for their drinks, suffocating Duende with their drunken breath. "Take the girl home," one of them said, slurring his words.

The bartender wiped his hands on the towel around his waist and called for another worker to take his place behind the bar.

"Let's go," he told Duende. "I'll take you home."

She stalled. Her feet gripped the floor. Duende was certain she could expand beyond this place if she needed to, but she didn't dare try. Instead, the girl pictured the bartender walking her home, waking her parents up at two in the morning to tell them that their daughter had been in a bar. Her father's anger would destroy her. She would lose any hope of freedom.

"Come on." The bartender grabbed her hand and tried walking her out. Duende fought his hands and screamed as her eyes caught sight of wineglasses on the shelf behind the bar. She stared at them long enough to make one of the glasses break before falling to the ground.

Everyone turned in the direction of the shattering glass. Duende stopped wrestling the bartender, who looked toward the bar and then at the door. When he finally managed to get her halfway to the door, someone shouted out from a dark corner opposite the entrance: "Wait. What are you doing to my little girl?"

A large Gypsy woman lifted herself from her chair and marched with a slight limp into the light fluttering from bulbs above the bar. Her size was menacing, but her voice was filled with concern as she called the girl to her.

Duende looked at her, both alarmed and relieved by her presence.

"Esteban, leave Duende now. She's with me," the woman told the bartender, who released his grip.

Duende cautiously approached the big woman, watching the way her forehead stretched wide like a big lampshade above penetrating, knowledgeable eyes.

"Duende," she said.

The girl shook at the sound of her own name.

The woman sat down and pointed to the seat across from her. "Sit."

Duende obeyed as she scanned the room. The red candle on the table flickered with her movement and then calmed. The bartender began talking with a couple that approached the bar, acting as if nothing unusual had happened.

"Duende."

The girl turned her gaze back to this woman who pretended to know her. The darkness veiled most of the stranger's face as she laughed.

"Do I scare you?" the woman asked.

Silence.

"Don't be scared." There was little consolation in her voice. The Gypsy softened her demeanor. "Duende, I'm here to talk to you."

Duende's brow creased with confusion. Right now she wished she could see or hear her grandmother, get some sense of what to do with this big woman.

"I'm a fortune-teller," said the Gypsy. "I know who you are."

Duende had heard about women like this. "Witches," her father had called them. "Just plain old witches stealing money from the poor."

Sometimes fortune-tellers would read fortunes behind windows for everyone to see. They'd advertise themselves with musty old Bibles standing upright in the window, their pages bleached by the sun; colored cloth and crystal stones hanging from the ceiling, turning in the light; surrounded by multiple crosses, pictures of the Virgin Mary and other small artifacts. Duende had seen the way fortune-tellers stared down at someone's palm as if reading the lines of the earth, although she had never watched for too long, careful not to be cast into a dried-out fish by their spells.

"I have seen you in my crystal," the Gypsy said. "I see into the future, my dear. I have seen you…you have something to tell me."

Duende, feeling completely helpless, placed her hands below her hips on the hard wooden chair. This woman was different from Lázaro. She wasn't mild like him, nor old—yet Duende sensed that she was wiser than he was.

"You have very strong dreams, don't you, dear?" The Gypsy rested her head on her hands while leaning forward into the silence.

Duende could see the woman's hands more clearly now. Rings on all her fingers but one—her pinky, which looked crushed, as if by accident. The nail bled its edges into her skin.

"Tell me about your dreams."

The weight of Duende's body kept her hands from shaking as she looked down at her lap and began to tell her dreams. She told the Gypsy about Jesus, recounted the scenes in the church, in the streets. As she did this, she felt alone inside a darkness that had thrown itself onto the table, separating her from the stranger who was listening so intently to her every word.

"Do you know what dreams are for, Duende?" the woman said finally.

The girl shrugged. She didn't want to know.

"To follow, Duende… to follow."

Duende suddenly felt warm. Follow? How was she going to follow dreams like these?

"I'm here to help you follow them."

Duende took a minute to catch her breath; her insides felt

hollow, emptied. She pined for the comfort of her grandmother's spirit.

"Your dreams are Gypsy dreams, dreams that go back centuries," the woman continued. "Gypsy dreams. You don't know what that means, do you, my poor girl?" She chuckled.

Duende noticed the crack between the woman's teeth for the first time. It added, she thought, a frightening intensity to the Gypsy's laugh.

"Now, go home! We will meet again. I suspect that you know the way without Esteban's help." The woman looked up at the door, away from Duende for the first time since she had laid her eyes upon the girl.

Duende got up quickly. The words "we will meet again" followed her. As she took her last step toward the door, she heard the Gypsy's voice again. The woman had limped forward from the darkness.

"Teri-Amo," she said, raising her eyebrows and pointing to herself. "You ask for Teri-Amo next time."

Duende slipped out of the bar knowing that, although she never wanted to return, she hoped that she could dance with Graciela again. The Gypsy's power held her in a spell that no one else could see.

Despite the soft spring wind that blew through the street, Duende shivered, carrying Teri-Amo's words home with her, close to her heart.

INGRID

INGRID

Ingrid's heart beat heavy to the sound of Roger's snoring. She lay in bed gripped by a fear that her nightmares might come true should she fall asleep. The vines had stopped moving, as had the wind and the whistling sound through the walls, but it was only a matter of time before they would visit her in her sleep or beyond.

Knowing this, Ingrid left Roger to his nightly sounds and tiptoed downstairs, out the door. The moon was full, a silver coin glowing through the branches of the trees that marked the entrance to the house. She walked over sleeping vines under Orion the Hunter and countless other stars making holes in the azurite sky.

The night was still, deathly still, as Ingrid searched for that single grape, that so-called miracle. Perhaps, if she could prove it wasn't real, her recent fears and nightmares would quiet themselves.

But within minutes, Ingrid found the purple fruit and reached out for it, feeling its thin, delicate skin. She held its soft surface in her hands, careful not to dislodge it from the vine. It felt so real. So real. But could it be? Could this really have been a miracle? How? And what was her place in all of this?

Abandoning the grape, she began to feel her way along the vine, as if she were a blind woman following a thin, eternal thread. She followed each fibrous vine with her touch, her hands searching their way into the night, farther away from the wall, out toward the field. Dancing, weaving herself in between rows and rows of vines, she surrendered her body to a spirit beyond her own until she found herself kneeling close to the earth.

What was happening to her? she wondered, tears streaming down her cheeks.

Ingrid wanted to make sense of so much, but all she could do was kneel and touch the ground, the vines crumpling below her.

With the gentleness of a lover, she touched a vine, stroked its back, her eyes closed. It was dry, thirsty. A woven basket of tangled tapestry. Her touch slid onto other vines, arching over them, back and forth, caressing a deep sorrow within her. A sorrow that had followed her into the night. A sorrow of a lifetime.

Ingrid crawled along the ground, crying, following this thread, until she got scared—scared the earth would cave in below her, that the vines would envelope her as they had done in her dreams.

"Don't you remember?" she suddenly heard a voice say, almost laughing. "Don't you remember?"

Ingrid stopped breathing for as long as it took to listen, to really listen as the earth moved below her, ever so slightly. Something was different. It was the voice, which seemed to be coming from the ground itself. The gentle movement was the earth speaking.

"Don't you remember what I told you, what I showed you?" she heard again.

Ingrid tried to place the sound, to follow its resonance deep into the ground. She had forgotten, had chosen to forget, but she could feel, for the first time, a place inside herself slowly opening to the person she truly was.

"Remember," she heard the voice say as it faded away. "Remember."

The earth lay solid and still below Ingrid, holding her as she relaxed, her heartbeat slowing down. She settled into herself and felt an intense calm that blanketed the fields and stretched across the sky and mountains.

Ingrid finally lay on the ground, exhausted, as she heard a different voice, that of a woman, whispering, "Sleep, child. Sleep." Inside a cradle of vines, she responded like an obedient child listening to a lullaby, and fell asleep.

✺

"Get up," someone said, interrupting Ingrid's dreams.

"Shut up," she replied. *Let me sleep.*

"Get up." The voice was louder this time. Ingrid tried to quiet the sound by hitting the air with her limp hand. But it wouldn't relent. "Get up!" an older woman yelled through Ingrid's resistance.

Ingrid heard cars in the distance—the sound of tires rolling over vines and gravel along the driveway. Copious, irritating tires treading on early morning dew. *Go away.*

But the sounds came closer.

"Get up," the voice repeated. "Get moving."

Something felt familiar about the voice. Wasn't it the same as the voice Ingrid had heard last night? The same voice she'd heard long ago?

She stretched her stiff body along the hard surface of her bed—or what seemed like her bed—and then felt it. Something crawled below her, around her, moving incessantly.

Was she dreaming? Where was she? "Get off of me," Ingrid tried telling this strange, moving mass. The voice urging her to get up was relentless.

Slowly, Ingrid awoke. She began to remember. Yes, she was

outside. Last night she had been among the vines. This morning they were crawling…

She bolted upright and removed the branches from around her. "Out of my way," she told it, opening her eyes fully.

The memories of last night under the midnight sky came flooding through her body, but Ingrid had little time to reflect on them. The increased volume of voices told her people were approaching.

She rose to her feet carefully so no one could see her and tripped over thick vegetation. As Ingrid scrambled for balance, her arms brushed against something soft that hadn't been there before. At first she thought nothing of the sensation. But within seconds, as Ingrid staggered forward, her eyes squinting in disbelief, she saw clearly what she had felt. Surrounding her, on every vine, in all directions, were grapes. Grapes everywhere.

What the hell had happened? What the hell *was* happening? This was madness.

Ingrid moved faster and faster toward the house, panic following her every step as grape after grape revealed itself to her. There was no dodging them, yet the voices in the parking lot grew louder. She didn't want anyone to see her, but they were coming her way.

Ingrid approached a side door to Señor Ramos's house. She reached for the handle and wrestled with the latch. "Please open," she said in a whisper. "Please…"

The door released its grip, and she stepped inside just as a group of journalists arrived at the spot where she had spent the night. They called out to one another, ecstatically, to look, to document yet another miracle. Click. Click. Camera shutters filled the gaps between awed exclamations.

Inside, the house was surprisingly quiet, and although Ingrid was relieved not to encounter anyone, she wondered where the extended Ramos family had gone. Too stunned to figure it out, she hurried up the stairs and found Roger, who, camera in hand, was running down the stairs. He grabbed her.

"Did you see what's happened?" he said and then noticed Ingrid's disheveled state. "Oh, yes. You must have seen it, the grapes growing everywhere. Right? You—"

Ingrid cleared her throat. "Listen—"

"Wait, why are you coming up the stairs?" Roger said while still holding onto her. He seemed perplexed, yet too impatient to wait for an answer. "We've got to get out there. Señor Ramos is already there."

"Listen, Roger…" Ingrid couldn't get herself to move. "I'll come outside with you, but then I need to go. I need to leave. Promise you'll get me out of here."

Roger let go of Ingrid's arm. "What? Not now. This is what we came for. We can't leave now."

"I have to go," she said. "I have to get out of here."

"Why?"

"I just do." She gazed at him pleadingly. "Will you come with me?"

Though still confused, Roger acquiesced. "All right. But let's get downstairs then. I have to see this first."

Ingrid sighed deeply as she turned to return down the stairs.

Roger, acting like an excited schoolboy, skipped down the stairs behind her, his camera propped up in front of his chest.

Although relieved to have Roger on board, Ingrid would have preferred to hide in her room, out of sight, left alone indefinitely. Instead, she focused on catching her breath and calming herself before walking outside to the immense miracle of newly grown grapes.

DUENDE

DUENDE

From outside Lázaro's home, Duende screamed, "I had a dream!"

Behind her, the sea dropped a wave and then another as she waited, eager to be comforted by his presence. She carried the heaviness of her encounter with the Gypsy in the bar, and the fullness of dreams that had intensified since meeting the big woman.

After several waves crashed to the shore, Lázaro appeared. He smiled upon opening his door.

"I had a dream with *you* in it," she declared elatedly.

Lázaro twisted his mouth, as though he were chewing on Duende's words.

"You were walking with everyone in the street. You were dressed as a priest," she said. "You were crying and holding your hands up toward the sky. The Gypsies were carrying Jesus on his cross."

A shimmer of light bounced off the middle hinge of the door as Lázaro's eyes reflected the sea behind Duende. "What else?" he asked her.

"Jesus fell to the ground. Fell. No one could hold him up. People were naked, crawling, scared, running and—and you were crying out for help so I came flying down to you. I felt sorry for you. We tore the nails out from the cross. Let Jesus go, just like that. It was fun. That part was fun. You were happy pulling the nails out. We counted them."

"How can you dream such things?" Lázaro demanded, and she saw the smile was gone.

"Oh." Duende felt suddenly ashamed, although she couldn't understand why. She dug her feet deeper into the sand.

Lázaro continued to hold the doorframe with his body. "Jesus is sacred. *Sacred*," he said. "Listen, Duende, I never told you, but I was a priest once. For twenty years. I prayed to that man you dreamed about. Every day. Every day I dedicated my life to Jesus and the church. Now, look at the sea, child."

She turned toward the vast body of water. The waves crashed low.

"Now, you wouldn't change the sea by taking away the water, would you?" he said. "The sea is sacred because of its water, just like Jesus is sacred when he's in the church, on the cross for you and me to see. When he's there, he reminds us of how he died to save us from our—" Lázaro stopped short. "It *has* been awhile since I've been in the church."

Duende looked back at Lázaro. His words about Jesus seemed foreign to her. "That's silly. Why couldn't he just be Jesus?"

Lázaro paused as sadness crept along his face. "Maybe he was just too good for this world." He let the door close behind him before stepping forward and kneeling closer to Duende. "You know," he said, looking toward the sea, "when I think about it, Jesus had a dream for this world. He really believed we could have heaven on this earth. Imagine that."

Lázaro's eyes moistened. He seemed to be elsewhere as Duende watched, carefully, reminded for a moment of that still place inside the earth.

"You know, he really didn't want to be on that cross," Lázaro said, nodding. "Why in the world would anybody want to suffer like that anyway?"

"So why was he on the cross then?" Duende asked.

"People put him there. They didn't want to hear what he had to say."

Duende crunched her forehead. "What did he say?"

Lázaro remained in an altered space. "He stood for living a different way on this earth. That was about two thousand years ago, you know, although I wonder if that time will ever come."

Duende couldn't imagine so many years ago and she was confused by Lázaro's last words. "What time?" she asked, breaking Lázaro from his spell.

He looked toward Duende. "The time for Jesus's dream to come true, I suppose."

"Well, you had fun taking the nails off the cross in *my dream.* So maybe my dream will come true!"

"That would be nice, Duende," Lázaro said. "Unfortunately, dreams are not the same as waking life, like you and me are living right now."

"I wish they were."

"I know. By the way," Lázaro said, "did you play the flute I gave you?"

Duende rubbed her feet in the sand again.

"What's the matter?"

"I got in trouble. My parents threw the flute away," Duende told him. "They wanted to know where I got it from... but—"

"You didn't say it was from me, did you?" he said. "They don't know you come here, right?"

"No." Duende lifted her head.

"I understand. They're being parents."

Duende was surprised by how well Lázaro took what had happened to his flute. "But your flute..."

"It's okay. I just thought you'd like it. I'm sorry you got in trouble."

Duende told Lázaro how spirits had danced out of his flute and how she journeyed on its sound when she played it, and how she wished she still had the instrument.

He seemed pleased by her words. "Now, it's time to go home before your parents get worried about you. And next time you come here, you can tell me about a different dream."

As Duende walked away, she saw Lázaro watching her through the dirt-speckled window. He had tried to listen to her, she knew this, but her words had only made him sad.

Duende didn't understand why, because all she wanted was for somebody to really hear her—someone other than the frightening big Gypsy to tell her that her dreams were real and had a place in this world.

Duende's words stayed with Lázaro far longer than she may have imagined. He hadn't seen the little girl in more than a month—since she had last shown up with dreams about Jesus, and he had missed her, missed her knock on his door. And now, more than ever, he was concerned about her, wondered if she would try to bring her dreams of Jesus into reality.

Lázaro hadn't been able to sleep the previous night. The land had been calm, the summer air teasing him as it always had and melting into a moisture that had made his skin turn damp, making his room no place to sleep. So he had carried his blankets onto the sand, close to the water, to allow it to lull him to sleep. The stars, soft drops in the sky, had helped clear his mind and offered several hours of rest, until this morning, at seven, when the morning light woke him.

Now, a cool wind washed the long waves onto the shore where he lay. He sensed the early morning sun gently wringing out his sleep as he began to dry from the dampness.

Maybe he had reprimanded Duende too harshly for her dreams during their last visit, he thought. Had he, perhaps, sounded too much like a parent, and scared her away? But Duende didn't seem to scare so easily.

Lázaro returned to his shack for coffee and then strolled into town to seek advice from a friend he hadn't seen in years.

The stillness of the early morning shrouded the streets. But Lázaro's friend, if he hadn't changed, would be up already, chanting his morning ritual between the rectory and the empty aisles of the church, which, the last time Lázaro had been there, had been filled with small potted plants hanging from the ends of the pews.

Father Jorge Ignacio Rodriguez sat at his desk, hunched over his books the way his father used to do. He wasn't the poet his father had been—the legendary Azúcar, whose poetry converted good Catholic girls into runaway nymphs. But he carried his father's grace and passion for words and, with this gift, won back some of those nymphs to Catholicism.

Lázaro surprised his concentrating friend with a knock on the door, which was already half-open to let in the blue morning. His white collar was flipped inward to hide dirt, and several holes were missing their corresponding buttons. He slouched, playing the humble visitor looking for a few scraps of bread in his friend's home.

"Lázaro, if it's not you," Father Jorge cried. It must have been at least a dozen years since Lázaro had seen him.

"Yes, it *is* me."

The two embraced and then stepped back to look at each other in silence. They each waited to see who would speak first about who had changed and who had not in so many years. But neither said anything. Instead, Father Jorge pulled up a brown soft-cushioned chair that weighed more than his fragile hands seemed to be able to handle and gestured for Lázaro to sit. Lázaro eased into it with his eyes on the Father. *He sure has aged,* he thought, yet his smile was as young and warm as it always had been.

"After all this time and we say nothing," Father Jorge said finally. "We always did well together in silence, didn't we?"

"That's true."

"So where have you been, my brother? Still down by the sea?"

"Yes, still there, watching the sun rise and set."

Father Jorge smiled, reluctantly, as if embarrassed that Lázaro was still living in the shack that sat at the mercy of the river that occasionally flooded down from the San Antón Mountains into the sea. "Do you miss it? Priesthood, I mean," he asked.

Lázaro took a minute to think about it, and then shook his head. "No. Well, I miss the people. But, no."

"What I wonder, you see, is, well, if I suddenly took off and lived alone by the sea, I suppose I would miss the rituals. Like my daily prayer or just being in a sanctuary of sorts. I guess I wonder, do you still pray?"

Lázaro nodded reluctantly, as a schoolboy would when he's not certain which answer is correct. Wasn't the kind of silence he lived every day a kind of prayer?

The priest had probably never seen his friend so humble. In all their years together, sharing their secrets and lives as neighboring priests, wasn't it Lázaro who had spoken his mind more than others?

"I'm sure I seem changed, but I am not. I guess I've just stopped polishing my soul, so to speak." Lázaro no longer hesitated.

"Polishing your soul," Father Jorge tried the words on. "I wonder," he said, "whether I have been… polishing my soul or, rather, carving it into little figurines that will keep me company in my loneliest hours."

It had always been like this when they were together, the sharing of thoughts. But today Lázaro wanted to get on with his visit, speak his mind before the hours chased his thoughts away.

"What would you say," he asked in a single breath as the Father leaned toward him, "if you knew a little girl who was having dreams about taking the nails off the cross and letting Jesus down?"

"Jesus!" he said. "How odd. It sounds a bit like a line my father would have written in one of his poems... that is, if he had thought of it."

Lázaro shifted uncomfortably in his seat.

"Well, people have all sorts of dreams," Father Jorge added. "I guess taking the figure of Jesus off the cross wouldn't be any stranger than most."

"But what if this girl is having these dreams all the time, if she can't escape them?"

"It's odd. I agree," the priest said. "After all, our Jesus is not alive up there. I mean the one made of plaster and wood."

"But what if, in her dreams, he seems as alive as you and I, and still suffering. And—"

"But where are you getting all this from, my dear Lázaro?" Father Jorge now looked at his friend as if too much time living in a shack had gotten to him.

Lázaro sat still with his head down, pondering what to say. "I'm just asking about a friend."

"A friend? Maybe she needs help."

Lázaro felt anger rising like boiling water within him. He felt insulted, as if Duende's dreams were his very own.

"I don't mean to disrespect you, friend," Father Jorge assured him. "I just don't know what... to say."

Lázaro lifted his head and looked carefully at his friend. "I guess I am telling you this because... I wonder... how do we know what is right? Some people, like your father, use words to speak the truth. You share your truth with your actions based on your Christian beliefs. Yet, this girl may be guided to act on her dreams.

"What I wonder is, what happens if the little girl not only

dreams of taking Jesus off the cross, but does it?" Lázaro continued. "Is that wrong? When is it wrong to cross over from the symbolic to the literal, from dream to reality? It would be like acting on our inspiration and imagination. It would be like recognizing the power of the symbolic and changing it in order to change our reality."

Father Jorge stood up abruptly. "But what are you saying, my friend?" he said condescendingly. "Why would a little girl want to act on dreams like that? She wouldn't even have the strength to do so! This is silliness."

"That is what I thought at first," said Lázaro, "that there would be no point to it all, and that no one would want to do that. But then I thought about it. Don't we priests give credence to the symbolic? We pray to these plastered, wooden Jesus figures up there, the way we drink from a cup that contains Jesus's blood, the way we carry rosaries and break bread. So why wouldn't someone take seriously the symbols that we ritualize into reality? Don't they mean something? Doesn't the representation of Christ's suffering mean something? Doesn't it stand for a way we live today, the way we go about our everyday lives?"

Lázaro hadn't felt this much passion in a long time. The solitude of the past ten years—and the years before that, during which blind observance to codes and laws and rituals never led him to the promised land—had built up to this moment with a friend, once dear but from whom he now felt estranged. He could have been a child again, arguing the laws of the universe with his father, thinking outside the box, while his father tried to lead him inside to safe and certain places.

Father Jorge was standing by the window, now apparently absorbed in watching the way the branches of the chestnut tree moved outward and up at the same time.

"My father, on his deathbed, held my hand, looked me fiercely in the eyes, and said, 'If you think for one moment that there's a difference between the words I write and the sermons you give, then you are making a distinction between the way you feel in your heart and the way you act in the world,'" he told Lázaro. "I repeated his words often in my mind after that day, without understanding them… but maybe what he meant by it is that no matter whether we write a poem, have an idea, or act out our dreams, it is an attempt to be at one with God, and no one way is better than another."

Lázaro contemplated these words. A current of excitement ran through him. He abruptly stood up and walked toward Father Jorge, took his hands in his own, and bowed his head slightly. "Thank you."

Father Jorge appeared dumbfounded.

Without saying another word, Lázaro walked out into a sudden downpour.

INGRID

INGRID

Ingrid and Roger walked outside to the miracle of newly sprouted grapes. She shifted her awed gaze from the rows and rows of robust fruit to the journalists who were swarming where she had been last night. Señor Ramos, who was among the journalists, quickly approached Roger and Ingrid, wiping his hands free of earth.

"¡Buenos días! ¡Un buen día definitívamente!" He embraced them with a smile that stretched the width of his face. "It's definitely a good day. Our Lord has blessed us with good fortune."

Despite his joy, Señor Ramos seemed surprised they hadn't made it outside until now. "Señorita Ingrid," he said. "Did you see what happened?"

Ingrid told him she had seen the grapes, but wasn't feeling well. As she spoke, Roger joined the journalists for a few photographs.

"I am so sorry," he responded. "You must rest then."

"I know, but not now." Ingrid looked around her in the full light. The magnitude of Señor Ramos's joy resided in hundreds, maybe thousands, of grapes that hung in full bloom from vines.

Did he wonder how they'd gotten there? Had he seen her lying out there this morning or last night?

"Cómo pasó?" Ingrid asked, afraid to hear his thoughts. Her feet grew restless as she stood there.

"*Diós*, my dear," Señor Ramos said. "God brought this. This is the only way. How else? I have *never* seen a grape grow like this overnight. And this many." He pointed all around him. "Only God can do this."

Ingrid looked down at the ground, shuffling her feet. "Señor…"

"*Sí*, señorita?" El dueño turned his gaze from the grapes.

"We need to talk to our editor, but we can't get reception from here," she said. "We'd like to drive to a better location."

Ingrid was glad Roger wasn't standing next to her and didn't understand the language, because she was sure he would have told Señor Ramos that they had fine reception and had already called Franz on her cell phone several times since their arrival.

"Oh, would you like a lift to town?"

"Well, I don't want to trouble you. Maybe we could borrow your car or—"

"Ah, I know," said Señor Ramos as Roger, smiling with delight from having photographed the blossoming grapevines, returned to where the two were standing. "Come with me." El dueño led the two of them to a small rusted shed without a door. "Just the thing for you, although you aren't feeling well and the Englishman will need to be very careful."

El dueño stepped inside the tiny makeshift building. He came out with a *moto*—a small moped that seemed to barely fit Ingrid, let alone Roger. Señor Ramos nodded with pride. "Just a little kick and it starts fine."

Roger and Ingrid looked at each other, trying to hold back their laughter. The fact that she found humor in their situation came as relief to her.

"Thank you, Señor Ramos, this should work," she said. "It might help me to get out of here for a bit."

Roger added, "Graaacias. Muuchoos Graaacias." Ingrid

sensed they were sharing the same thought: *How the hell are we both going to fit on this thing?*

Determined to make it work, they wrestled their way onto the scooter. She clung to Roger, and he to the moped that they drove out of the driveway stop-and-go style, leaving Señor Ramos to his new growth of grapes.

They climbed into the surrounding mountains, riding frightening hairpin curves. "Did you see those grapes? It's amazing!" Roger yelled, as Ingrid pressed her arms tightly around his waist, desperately holding on.

She had no interest in responding. She was more content with the calm she began to feel straddled on the back of the moped, barely seated and wrestling the wind.

The little moto struggled like an asthmatic up the hills, puffing out exhaust and gulping the air. They were crawling now, up and up, hoping their new friend would make it to the top.

Finally, tired of clinging onto Roger and the thin seat below her, Ingrid began looking for a place to stop. Her companion seemed content to ride ceaselessly, pressing onward and upward, his curly hair blowing in her face.

"Roger!" she screamed over the exhausted scooter.

"Yes, my dear." Roger responded as if their ride on this locomotive of Lilliputian proportions were pure romantic fiction.

"Let's back up. We just passed a place—an overlook. We can see the sea from there."

A few minutes later, as the two stood silently admiring the expanse, Ingrid recalled an Arab man who used to live in a place like this, here in the hills of Málaga.

"My parents and I met him once when we were walking alongside one of these roads here in the mountains. We had climbed halfway to the top to look out toward the sea," she said. "The man actually drove us the rest of the way in his jeep and promised if we went with him, we'd be able to see Africa from his home.

"I remember him vividly now, pointing past the green-blue waters that lay at the end of his fingertip. 'Do you see it? Do you see sweet Africa?' he had said. 'I looked and looked, but I couldn't see Africa no matter how hard I tried."

Now Ingrid was like the Arab, pointing in the direction of the sea, asking Roger if he could see Africa—perhaps with the help of his camera. The brilliant waters glistened in the sun.

Roger took out his camera from its bag, screwed his largest lens onto it, and looked. "There's no Africa," he said. "It's one big lie, I think. There's no Africa at all."

"Just because you can't see it, doesn't mean it's not there," Ingrid retorted.

"That's rather interesting coming from someone who doesn't even believe those grapes are real or that the vines are bleeding human blood," he said, grinning at her fondly.

"Not now... *please*." Ingrid sighed. "Don't tease me."

"Okay," Roger agreed. "So did you ever see Africa from here, on that day you came with the Arab?"

Ingrid looked at Roger, guiltily.

"So you didn't either, did you?"

"No," she admitted, remembering wanting so much to see Africa, to see beyond the horizon to some mysterious, far-away land.

"Well, then. When do you expect to see this Africa that doesn't exist?" Roger asked.

"Perhaps tomorrow."

The two sat down against a gigantic rock overlooking a thin strip of sea. Above them black clouds moved in, threatening rain. Roger leaned back, his head resting in his hands, and said, "Looks like rain."

"It will be a relief from the heat." Ingrid leaned back as well, relaxing for the first time in a while. "I wouldn't mind a few drops—that is, once we get back and off that two-wheeled thing over there. And Roger, I—I don't want to go back yet."

"That's fine with me," he said. "I took enough photos and can take more after we return. I expect that Señor Ramos is praying for the rain to hold off until later today."

Ingrid sat up, looking at Roger dubiously. It seemed as if everyone thought the solution to all problems was prayer. She wondered if Roger really believed in miracles.

"Señor Ramos seems really good at it, you know," Roger said, lifting his head up from the rock. "Look at what he's done so far! Pretty good stuff, if you ask me."

"You *actually* believe his prayers made the grapes come back?"

"Ingrid, I don't know what to believe anymore," he admitted. "But what the hell. Prayer is just as good as anything at this point. Plus, how are you going to explain what happened when you write about it? It's all fantastical if you ask me. But I like it. I mean, it's much more interesting than anything I've seen in this bloody life of mine."

"Fantastical?"

"Oh, it's one of those made-up words, as far as I know. But I quite like it. Like fantastic, you know, but bigger. You know, it is *quite* nice here… but why the rush to get out of Señor Ramos's place?"

Ingrid ignored his question. "You really think Señor Ramos and his prayers have had an impact?"

"Like I said, it works for me."

"That's too easy," she countered.

"Well then, what do you propose?"

"I don't know." Ingrid wished she could offer a rational explanation that would cast out her own recent, irrational experiences.

"So why did you need to get away from the vineyard?" Roger asked for the second time.

His words made her heart beat faster. She wished she could ignore them.

"Roger," Ingrid started up.

"Yeah?" He stared at her intensely.

She looked away from him, out to sea.

"This morning… about the grapes that showed up," Ingrid stuttered as she gazed into the distance. "I slept out there last night."

Roger looked at her incredulously. "You slept out among the grapes?"

"Among the vines," Ingrid corrected him. "There were no grapes then."

Roger appeared perplexed, deep in thought. "So that's why you were walking up the steps? And I thought you were in our room last night. But no, you were out there until this morning, when the journalists came, and no grapes until—"

"I—I went out because I couldn't sleep. The vines weren't moving and—and well, I just fell asleep."

"And the grapes? When did they appear?" Roger looked a bit taller in his excitement as he seemed to ponder what had actually happened last night and this morning. "And you… you saw… you…"

"You're going to think I'm crazy."

"You? Crazy? Miss Rational?" Roger laughed.

She felt insulted. "Forget it."

"Come on. You *have* to tell me more."

"Why?"

"Because if you don't, you *will* go crazy."

He was, she knew, right. She had to tell someone, and he seemed to be willing to listen.

"Well," Ingrid said. "I touched that one grape, and then— I don't know why—I walked back and forth through the vines until I was so tired that I simply lay down and slept, and when I woke the grapes were everywhere. I was as surprised as all the journalists were."

"Amazing." Roger leaned toward Ingrid, who drew away.

"You know what I think? I bet that all those places where the grapes grew were where you touched the vines. Think about it. Even that first grape... you touched that same vine right before it grew."

"Roger, now you're the crazy one!" she said and found she felt better for saying that. Because he had articulated her greatest fear, the fear that had threatened to destroy her when Franz had sent her here.

"Fine. Then I'm crazy. But it fits. You made it happen. You did something magical."

"Stop!" Ingrid cried. "Just stop." Tears welled up inside her throat. "You might love the idea of making magic happen, but you don't know what..."

"What?"

Deep breath. Deep breath. Don't let him see you like this. Don't go there.

"Forget it," she said, avoiding his eyes.

"This really scares you, doesn't it?" he said softly. "It *really* scares you. Your nightmares—"

"Enough!" Ingrid told him, turning her face away from Roger, who stopped speaking.

An awkward silence overcame them as they sat looking out at the horizon, waiting for a cue as to what to do next.

In the stillness, Ingrid let herself cry, gently. Her body began to relax even more than earlier. She could feel that door inside of her opening a bit more. There was no turning back from what was happening, or from her past.

Roger reached for his camera bag and took out a cigarette and matches.

"Since when do you smoke?" Ingrid said, glad to change the subject. He looked good, actually sexy, as he gently blew circles of smoke into the air.

"I don't smoke. Well, not regularly, that is. Just when the mood is right, like now."

"Why now?"

"It clears the air, takes all the clutter and crap out of here."

Ingrid felt like that clutter and crap he was trying to clear away, and was surprised to hear herself say, "I'm sorry." It had been a long time since she'd told anyone that.

"Sorry about what?" Roger said between puffs.

"For the crap."

"It's not your fault. This stuff is just happening, and it's hard to make sense of it. Anyway, it's happening to you, not me."

Ingrid smiled, glad to hear she wasn't to blame, although it was hard to feel truly blameless.

"Can I try one?" She pointed to the cigarette in Roger's mouth.

Roger looked at Ingrid dubiously and then took out another cigarette and lit it for her.

"I know you're not much for prayer," he said, "but just try it. Each time you take a puff, send out a prayer, like this."

It was the first time Ingrid had ever heard anyone talk about smoking as a good thing. But she did as he said and found that she felt increasingly relaxed, watching ships and large barges float across the open water until they were small in the distance.

It was then, as Roger began photographing the sea, that something truly miraculous happened. "I see it," he suddenly cried. "I see Africa. It's there. Look in the viewfinder."

Ingrid did. "We can see it," she said, smiling. "We can see Africa. Years later, the Arab was right."

And there it was—a narrow strip of land in the distance with forms that looked like trees. Miracles could happen after all.

As Ingrid peered through the camera, gentle drops of rain fell on her hand. Roger snatched the camera from her and placed it quickly in a plastic bag, then in his camera bag. A moment later, as the clouds opened up and the rain came tumbling down, the two raced for cover under a small piñon tree where they sat leaning against each other, curled over Roger's camera bag.

"Quite romantic," he said.

His words were no doubt intended to be lighthearted but managed instead to create an awkward space between them. Neither knew what to say so they sat in silence, watching the rain fall and waiting for the cooling storm to clear.

✧

It rained for days, as though it would never end, after their moped adventure. Roger and Ingrid had returned to the vineyard, drenched and cold, and they remained there, photographing and writing their article.

Señor Ramos harvested the grapes that had sprung up overnight, leaving a few to remind him of his blessing. Meanwhile, Ingrid didn't dare touch the vines again, for fear of what would occur. And while everyone waited for more grapes, they never sprouted.

Ingrid continued to dream of vines, although the images were less intense and intimidating. She seemed to be getting used to them, and the more she stayed away from Señor Ramos's field, the less vivid her dreams became. She preferred it that way—preferred not touching any more vegetation, enjoying a respite from her gnawing anxiety.

Señor Ramos, on the other hand, grew more anxious, hoping and praying for additional grapes to appear. He couldn't understand why some had shown their faces and others had not. Every morning he, along with a few journalists, waited for more, but to no avail.

Ingrid felt for the man and his situation, but was determined to focus on her job. She interviewed him and spoke with other workers and visitors, while Roger accompanied her with his camera.

It was Roger's presence and awareness of what was

happening to Ingrid that helped her relax. With him, perhaps she could open up, share her concerns about returning to Spain.

Roger had also become more supportive and pried less, which made her more receptive than she might have been when, toward the end of their stay with Señor Ramos, he spoke with Ingrid about visiting central Málaga and her old neighborhood, El Palo. Earlier, Ingrid would have resisted this idea, but she'd come to see that she couldn't turn her back to the nightmares and fears—she couldn't return to Germany with the angst that had now shown its face. She needed to heal, or at least try, and Roger was there to help.

After several days of waiting for grapes that never appeared, Señor Ramos drove the two to a small town where they planned to catch a bus to Málaga. But having missed the one they had expected to take, they found themselves waiting at a bus stop near a graveyard bordered by a long white wall and, beyond it, colored flowers marking the graves of people named Concepción Navárez, Ángel Paz, Rosario García. With the flowers was a message: *You are not forgotten.*

"What a nice place to be buried," said Roger. "And look at the view."

Beyond the palm trees and roses that surrounded the cemetery, mountains and the small town of Paz lay like bright chalk marks in the crib of a valley.

"Don't you think it's a bit soon to think about where you are going to be buried?" Ingrid asked, although she suddenly wondered what would happen to her when she died. The view here wouldn't really matter, she sensed, because she'd go somewhere else, maybe to that place she had been told was her spirit's home a long time ago. The idea of returning there didn't seem so bad, but Ingrid felt far from ready.

"Well, you never know, right?" Roger said.

"Yeah," she told him, realizing how she really hadn't felt at home here, on the earth, or truly alive inside this shell of her body for a long time.

"You know," Roger continued, "If I died right now, I'd like to be remembered as a man who wasn't afraid to live, who wasn't afraid to step outside of his comfort zone and proclaim, 'To hell with it all!'" He threw his hands into the air. "What about you?"

Ingrid found herself admiring his fullness in a way she hadn't before. "I have no idea," she said. "All I know is that I don't want to be remembered in this form."

"Why? What's so wrong with it?"

"It's okay," Ingrid said. "It's just that... I'm so not finished."

"Well, perhaps. But we can't know, can we?"

She nodded, ready to change the subject. "Let's walk to town and make some better use of our time."

"Good idea."

The two sauntered down a steep path that led to a street. The hooves of a mule tapped against the cement as a man pulled his animal past them. They followed him, walking by a group of kids who ran after a dog chasing a soccer ball. They didn't seem to mind the rain, and a select few children appeared to especially enjoy it while they played in a small foundation, getting wet from head to toe.

Roger and Ingrid arrived at a plaza, where they entered a local bar to find that the only other customers were three old men, sitting at a table, smoking cigarettes and looking intently at an afternoon soap opera.

The two ordered a couple of *claras* and *tortilla*. The old men and their eyes remained glued to the TV screen until the commercials arrived. Then their silence gave way to gentle arguments about the outcome of the next scene.

When one of the elders asked Ingrid if she and Roger were tourists, she explained that they had been staying at the vineyard with the bleeding vines.

That caught the men's attention. They frowned. "Sí," the

one with the crooked smile said. "We know all about it. The poor man. It's hard enough."

"Did you ever work in the fields?" Ingrid asked.

Another man, his brow heavy with age, raised his hand and pointed out the window toward the mountains. "*Sí*, señorita. Over there, I worked all my life, worked so hard to make enough to buy my family a bit of land, so we could grow our own fruit. Never happened, though. Never ever happened."

The two other men remained quiet, watching Roger lift his camera to take a picture. They smiled, awkwardly.

Their attention vacillated between TV entertainment and Ingrid's words. "El dueño, Señor Ramos, says all the tourists are buying up the land now," she said.

"It's true," the same man who had spoken earlier nodded. "Not much left for growing. Nobody cares anymore. And now poor Señor Ramos. No one can understand it. When you spend your life on the land, it's a part of you, you know. And then you watch these rich people coming in like this with no appreciation for what they're buying. They don't care. It kills us."

The old man squinted, covering his face every time Roger aimed a flash at him. Ingrid shot a look at Roger, hoping he would stop.

"When did the outsiders start buying the land, I mean the old vineyards and all?" Ingrid asked.

The old man shrugged. "Oh, *hija*, it's been years. Ten. Twenty. Señor Ramos belongs to one of the last families left."

The commercials ended and the men focused their attention back on the screen. They became instantly enveloped in their telenovela: A young Latina was chastising an older man who had cheated on her, while he ignored her, telling her to shut up.

This was their life now, Ingrid surmised, as she and Roger turned back to the bar and ordered another drink. Was her life any better?

After Roger and Ingrid left the place, they meandered

through several streets toward the edge of town. They reached the bus stop, where they stood protected from the rain under a building that had a slight outcrop. When their bus came rolling in over puddles of water on the cobblestone street, they were glad to get on and sit down. Ingrid found a place in the back and Roger sat next to her.

The bus driver waited a few minutes, but no one else arrived. Slowly, he put the bus in gear and drove down the mountain, toward the majestic, blue-green sea and the lowlands of Málaga.

DUENDE

DUENDE

In Málaga's center, where the church bells tolled, Latia stood cradled in a doorway. The wall shed chips of thin white paint on either side of her. Dressed in an equally thin silk blouse wrapped tightly around her breasts and waist, Latia avoided leaning too heavily against the façade. It was four in the afternoon and she was early for an appointment with the fortune-teller.

One hand of the clock on the church across the street permanently pointed to the number 12. Every hour, as the hands met at high noon, the bell chimed twelve o'clock. A deep, rich sound of metal striking against metal counted time belonging to a world secure in its age-old traditions.

One minute past twelve, the clock read now as Latia closed her eyes to the sound of bells and the noise of children bursting out of school and running through the streets. They always lined up at the kiosk, eager to buy pieces of gum wrapped in comic strips or Popsicles with cryptic messages written on their sticks. One of them, Duende, ran to Latia, throwing her schoolbag on the steps and giving her next-door neighbor a big hug.

"Hola!" Duende screamed, surprising Latia from her still place. It had been several months since the two had seen each other, the little girl who had never had an older sister, and the budding woman who wished she had a younger one.

"Look what I just learned," Duende said, raising her hands and inviting Latia's to meet them.

Latia lifted her hands and laughed.

"Uno, dos, tres…" Their hands met three times, then crossed to find their opposites.

"Is *this* what you learn in school?" Latia asked.

"Yes." Duende quickly jumped up, leaving Latia's hands in midair. "And this too," she said, playing hopscotch on make-believe squares of the sidewalk.

Latia rested her head on her hands and watched. "I wish I went to a school like yours."

Duende continued to jump on one leg, hopping forward, picking up a small stone and then turning back to hop the other way. "You don't go to school, Latia."

"Well, when I went it wasn't that much fun. We had to be careful about every little thing we did. The nuns were strict, you know… and especially back when Franco was alive."

"Sometimes kids imitate Franco." Duende lifted one foot into the air with her leg straight, and then stomped it onto the ground as her opposite arm held a straight horizontal line in front of her chest. She walked forward.

Latia laughed again. "So what do the teachers say when the kids act like that?"

Duende sat down next to Latia. "Nothing."

"You sure are lucky you were born when you were." Latia looked up at the clock on the church, which read 12:14p.m. "Now, I have to go, Duende."

Duende jumped up, prepared to follow her friend, who said, "What am I supposed to do, take you with me?"

The girl faced Latia with a big grin.

After a moment's hesitation, Latia agreed to take Duende

with her. "As long as it's okay with the woman I'm seeing. And you have to stay real quiet."

Latia took Duende by the hand and led her through a red curtain that marked an entrance. Once inside, Latia asked a big woman surrounded by candles if her friend could sit in. The woman nodded.

Before Duende could see who Latia was speaking with, she smelled a familiar scent of sweet lavender. Her mouth opened wide as she approached the same big woman who had called herself Teri-Amo—the one who had worn that scent at the bar—who now watched her through candles and a white ball with purple hues. Before Duende could say anything or run out the door, Teri-Amo spoke.

"Didn't I tell you we would meet again?"

Latia turned around in surprise.

"We met each other about a month ago, isn't that right, Duende?" The love psychic responded, noting Latia's look of confusion.

Latia looked back and forth, from Teri-Amo to Duende, surprised, and then put her hand on the girl's shoulder. "You can leave if you want to. All she is doing is telling me about my love life... if I will have one."

Duende remained still, unprepared for this second encounter, yet fascinated to hear what the big woman had to say about Latia.

"May all the spirits guide me, light up my crystal with images of Latia... Latia... Latia..."

The Gypsy moved her hands around the crystal as if it were the earth and she was trying to pinpoint a goldmine. She continued to repeat Latia's name until her eyes grew bigger, gazing into images that revealed themselves to her.

"Latia... you will have to wait, my poor thing," she said. "It's not time. It's not time." It seemed that Teri-Amo repeated the same news she had read during their last visit.

Latia raised her hands in the air. "I'm tired of waiting and so is my family. My mom keeps saying stuff like, 'Why not José Luis?' after every date I reject." Latia screwed her mouth up and shook her head as if she were now her mother. "'He is not *that* much shorter than you,' she tells me. But she didn't spend four hours with him trying to put his arm around her. Old urine is what he smelled like.

"And my mother doesn't have to sit across from men who speak all about themselves and only remember to ask me what I think or feel when they're about to beg for a second date," Latia went on bitterly.

Teri-Amo listened, her face expressionless. "Sorry, my dear." She shrugged. "I only read what I see. If I could say more, I would."

Duende felt bad for Latia, but when the Gypsy turned to her and asked if she would like to have her fortune told, she sat up in her chair, curious with slight hesitation.

"Don't you think Duende is a bit young for a boy?" Latia broke in with a teasing laugh.

Teri-Amo nodded. "We will look at something else then."

"Other than love, what is there?"

"Dreams."

The big woman placed her hands on the crystal again and repeated the same ritual she had performed earlier. Duende's heart pumped a warning pulse throughout her body. This time Amo raised her eyebrows as she received new images.

"Your dreams, Duende," she said in a low voice. "They will become reality sooner than you think."

It was all Duende could do to keep from demanding to know what it was and when it would happen, but she seemed caught in a spell that couldn't be broken.

"When is your birthday, my dear?" Amo asked. "Somewhere when winter meets fall?"

"November. The day Franco died." Duende's voice cracked

as she told the Gypsy the date the way she had been told to tell it.

Duende had no need to reveal the exact day. This everyone knew all too well.

"That's the day I began sewing the seams of my red curtain, readying it for display like a bullfighter's cape," Teri-Amo said, her eyes lighting up. "I could proudly display my services to Málaga after twenty-some years of working underground, hiding from the Civil Guards."

Duende listened as she'd learned to listen to adults telling their stories, while Latia looked back and forth between the psychic and her friend.

"You know… ," Amo said, appearing to expand her big body into the room as she spoke. "Back in Franco's time, I had to check my crystal before accepting clients. If the ball told me my clients weren't safe, I'd disappear for some time and only come back once my name had been erased from the lips of those seeking me. Ah, yeah. That was a good day, the day you were born. A good day."

"I don't know what this has to do with anything," Latia said impatiently.

"After your birthday, soon after this glorious day that we all remember so well, your dreams will come true," Teri-Amo said, ignoring Latia.

Any bit of Duende that had relaxed earlier tightened as her body shivered.

Latia tried to stand between the big woman and Duende.

Amo showed little concern. "*How?* you ask." Amo cupped the crystal ball in her hands and stared into it intently. "You, Duende, do not know your power."

Again, Duende shivered. The Gypsy's words took her back to her journey inside the earth. That was more power than she was ready for.

"Until your birthday, you will continue to have dreams about Jesus," Amo said.

"Jesus!" Latia said. "Why are you dreaming about him? This is silly. Duende's family doesn't even go to church. As far as I know, they don't practice anything."

"Latia, you want to meet a man who will sweep you off your feet, but the time isn't right," Teri-Amo said. "As for Duende, well, I can't say what it is she wants. But she *does* dream of Jesus even if she doesn't want to. Either way, there's no sense in fighting what is given to us when it is given. To be grateful and use our gifts well is all we can do."

Latia appeared to have had enough. "Amo," she said, "We must go. This is all too much."

Throwing money on the small table, she grabbed Duende's hand and pulled her out the door. The girl followed in a trance, carried forward by something other than herself.

"Until next time," Teri-Amo whispered. "I trust we will see each other soon."

⁓

Latia walked Duende home, holding her by the hand without letting go. They moved quickly past children playing hopscotch on the sidewalk and chasing each other around corners. The side streets were full of little eyes peering out to see if anyone had found them in their hide-and-seek game. Duende wanted to join them; instead Latia was rushing her home because of the fortune-teller's words.

"Now tell me what happened, from the beginning." Latia squeezed Duende's hand so firmly that it hurt. "How do you know Teri-Amo, and *for Christ's sake*, what's all this about Jesus?"

Latia fired questions at Duende without waiting for responses, but Duende scarcely heard her. She was elsewhere, held by the irrevocable grip of Teri-Amo's words. *When is your*

150

birthday, my dear? November... Franco... That was a good day. Your dreams, Duende... a gift... You, Duende, do not know your power.

The word "power" stuck with Duende now. She knew what having power felt like, especially since she'd traveled with her friend to the earth's center and discovered what she was capable of. Taking Jesus off the cross wouldn't be so hard to do, she knew now. But why do it? Lázaro would be upset with her and so many more, and this would be real, as real as Latia's voice that droned on, yet finally got her attention.

"And where did you meet the Gypsy? Where did you go?" Latia asked.

The questions transported Duende to the bar and those last seconds when she walked toward the door and heard Teri-Amo's assurance that they'd meet again.

But then, as if drawing back one curtain after the next, Duende saw an image of Graciela in full color and splendor, twisting her hands in the air, her body pulsating with rhythm.

"I learned how to dance, Latia," Duende said, staying completely in her own world.

"What does *that* have to do with the Gypsy, Duende?" Latia seemed impatient.

"That's where I met her."

"You met her *where?*"

"Where I met Graciela dancing."

Latia looked intently at Duende as they began to cross a street. "And where did you meet this Graciela?"

"At the bar."

"The bar?" Latia stopped smack in the middle of a street, bringing a car to a bouncing halt. "What were you doing in a bar?"

Latia seemed increasingly impatient, as did the young man behind the Window of the red SEAT. "Señorita," he said, stretching his head out of his window.

Duende smiled at the man as Latia looked back and forth between them.

"Señor... a minute please," Latia said, without waiting for a response from him as she faced Duende.

"Maybe I can help," the man interjected. He stepped out of his car, closed the door, and leaned against it.

Latia stared back at him coldly.

"Now, how could such a sweet-looking girl like this have upset you, señorita?" he said.

Duende grinned some more.

Latia reached the end of her patience. "Señor!" She seemed oblivious to the fact that she was the one preventing him from moving.

"If you are going to hold me up, you might as well let me help you." The stranger approached them, much to Duende's delight. She liked the way he spoke, even though he was now focused on Latia.

"Señor..."

"Constantino."

"Constantino then. Do you have children? No? Well, me neither. But my little friend here claims that she goes out dancing in bars at night. Now I don't know about you, but, if she were my child..."

Duende noticed the way the man was looking Latia up and down and found herself wishing he would turn his attention to her.

"You find it appropriate for an eight-year-old to go out on her own dancing in a bar at night?" Latia was saying.

Duende wondered why Latia was being so mean to this Constantino, why she barely let him get a word in edgewise. If anything, she herself felt an impulse to please him.

Ignoring Latia's probing questions, she began moving her feet and hands to the memory of Graciela's voice. Constantino took his eyes off Latia and watched. Latia turned to see the spectacle as well, seemingly impressed.

Suddenly, Constantino raised his strong arms and hands and began clapping to the rhythm of Duende's feet. As the girl became lost in her movement, Constantino followed, his hands moving behind his back and his feet, trying to match her inconsistent moves. Duende could hear Graciela's counting as they danced in the middle of the street. *Uno, dos, tres...*

Her movement and the counting in her head stopped when Constantino suddenly broke into laughter. "What luck I have to be here with two beautiful girls. And I'm still the only car on the street," he said before turning to Latia and asking her if she danced.

"Certainly, but not here," she told him. "Not now."

"When and where will you dance, if not here and now?"

Latia smiled. "Tomorrow."

Duende couldn't understand why Latia was being so difficult.

Constantino didn't seem to mind. "And *when* tomorrow would you like to dance?" he said, grinning.

"I will meet you tomorrow then at ten, at El Carretero on Calle Valparaíso, and we will see who knows how to dance."

"At ten then," he said, returning to his car, "at El Carretero on Calle Valparaíso. I will be wearing my best dancing shoes for the lovely lady."

Constantino slipped into The driver's seat of his SEAT. He kissed something hanging above his dashboard and waited for Latia and Duende to finally cross the street.

They did. Latia barely looked back. Duende turned to see Constantino send them a kiss good-bye before making a right at the corner and driving away.

Latia seemed happier. She held Duende's hand in a gentle grip as the two almost skipped back home.

"You like him," said Duende, looking up at her friend. "I'm glad, Latia, because he's nice."

"You like him, too, huh?" Latia brushed her hand through Duende's hair. "You know what my parents will say?" She tilted her head from one shoulder to the other. "'What kind of woman would meet a man in the middle of the street and agree to go dancing with him?' That's what they'll say."

"Are you going to tell them?" Duende asked.

"Not that I met him in the middle of the street."

"Like me in the bar."

"That's different. You're a little kid. I don't know what kind of trouble you've gotten yourself into. Talking to Teri-Amo in a bar... dancing in a bar. But maybe all of Amo's talk doesn't amount to anything."

Duende felt relief at the idea. She looked up at Latia for more reassurance.

"Think about it," Latia said. "What if Constantino is my Romeo—the one I've been waiting for, you know—then maybe the Gypsy has got it all wrong. Maybe she's not the extraordinary love psychic she says she is, and maybe, just maybe, what she said to you doesn't matter either. You know, Duende, she's wrong—at least this time."

INGRID

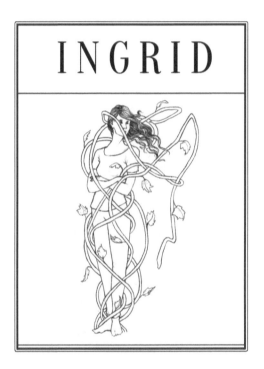

INGRID

"You know, I'm wondering if I should include the material from the old men in my story," Ingrid said to Roger as they rode down to Málaga on the bus.

Roger nodded as he looked out the window. "I feel like their story gives a larger perspective. Here you have Señor Ramos with vines growing out of control, while not producing grapes—or not in any normal way—and then these men who can't even live like they want to or used to, and their old ways of tending to the earth disappearing."

Ingrid looked at Roger. "Their story was so sad. I'm sorry you couldn't understand it."

He turned toward her and smiled. "I understand Spanish well enough. Just don't speak it very well. A real shame if you ask me."

"So you understood the old men and the dinner conversations at Señor Ramos's house," said Ingrid. "You had me fooled."

"You never asked me."

"True." Ingrid nodded. "Well… I'm still wondering how to tie the vines to what the old men were saying."

"Well, look at it this way," Roger said thoughtfully. "You've got less and less land, more and more rich people buying property for a nice little vista, but few caring enough about the earth anymore. And then here's Señor Ramos, who has been tending to his 150-year-old vineyard, and he gets hit by this disaster. Where's the justice in that? You're right. It's a sad story if you ask me."

"You always seem so optimistic, Roger. I'm surprised you said that something was sad," Ingrid said, and then, because he looked hurt, she wished she had kept her mouth shut. After all, he had been nothing but caring and thoughtful these few days. Certainly he didn't deserve her nastiness.

"Don't you find it strange that Señor Ramos's place is the only one affected by overgrown barren vines?" Roger spoke as if Ingrid hadn't said what she had. "I just can't make it out."

"I know. It makes no sense. Nobody seems to have any real answer. Nobody. The only explanation given is that God did it."

"Imagine, how *do* you explain something so unusual, so not of this world?"

"There's got to be some rational explanation," Ingrid said, only to realize that she, at least, was not sure that that was true.

The two looked out the window again, back toward the mountain's peak where the clouds released tears to further moisten the soft earth.

"I know it's raining and overcast, but don't you think it's beautiful here?" Roger said, changing the subject.

Olive groves, with their light-green, heavy-laden branches; piñon trees; and small vineyards covered the hillsides where cascades of water ran down narrow ravines. The bus inched forward down the hill, its fumes a contrast to the landscape.

"Look at the poppies!" Roger suddenly exclaimed. He turned toward Ingrid. "They look like thousands of butterflies fluttering in the wind."

A light smile inched across Ingrid's face as she looked toward the field of red that surrounded them. As a child, she used to brush her face against poppies like these until their color emptied onto her lips. She could still taste their dry, mealy texture in her imagination.

These flowers and the hills that stretched the length of the sea, the curves of their silhouette covered in groves and piñon trees, were indeed lovely, Ingrid thought. And it was all so familiar.

The old men had also made her feel a familiar sense of home. They seemed to know what it felt like to love a place deeply, to belong to the land as if they were the land. That place of home—which, for Ingrid, had been woven with darkness and fright—had also been there in her childhood in Spain.

"Those old men, they've lived on the land their entire life," Roger said. "Don't you think it's wrong that these men who actually know what it's like to feel home, to feel connected to a place, have it all taken away from them by people like you and me, by northerners who are tired of the rat race on concrete streets, people like us who desperately want a place to call home, but instead just bring our homelessness with us? A bit ironic if you ask me. Sometimes you've got to wonder what we're all looking for."

Roger's response made Ingrid think more deeply than she had been accustomed to thinking lately. Was she looking for anything, or just going from day to day, a stranger wherever she went?

As the hills disappeared behind them, she recalled the sea breaking onto the gray sands of her younger years. Would it all be there when she arrived? Would it be the same? Would she recognize her old home?

Ingrid brushed her finger along the moisture that entered through the crack below her window and brought it to her face. The wetness cooled her and followed them to the bottom of the mountain, past white-washed towns where children played soccer in the rain.

When the bus drove onto a highway carrying a mist of the

sea on its back, Ingrid knew they were near. The smell of the sea permeated the bus. She breathed it in slowly, fully, until the bus pulled off the highway.

Ingrid's heart began to race. They were driving down a ramp that led into El Palo, her old Málaga neighborhood.

"Oh, my God," she said when the bus drove past familiar streets leading to the sea. "This is it! This is my old neighborhood. We should get off here."

Roger sat up taller in his seat. Ingrid's fear and uncertainty mixed with a tinge of excitement as she led him off at the next stop and followed Calle Rosario down a narrow pedestrian street.

The sound of the waves echoed against humble walls of homes that marked the edges of their walk. Ahead of them, rain fell inside empty alleyways, and they soon found themselves on what was for Ingrid an unfamiliar boardwalk that ran along the sand.

In the late afternoon, the waters crashing onto the beach, as warm as the first drops of a summer rainstorm, were so evocative of her childhood that she couldn't resist wading in the sea. Ingrid lifted her pants above her knees and drew in deeper. She had missed this liquid body, this consoling place.

Roger followed Ingrid into the water. "This is beautiful. What a place to grow up," he said.

Ingrid took a step back as the sea brushed against her clothes and Roger reached out to her. "Did a big fish bite you?" he asked laughing, and she suddenly felt embarrassed at having let him see the child in her.

The crash of the waves grew louder, filling in the awkward silence between them. Ingrid looked toward the water, avoiding Roger's eyes.

Ingrid waited for the next wave in the far distance to curl forward and arrive on the shore. Her heart rode that wave, trying to hide inside its speckled folds, although she knew it would eventually have to open onto land and come home.

≪⑥

The next morning, Ingrid lay in bed listening to the waves playing their timeless rhythm below clouds of rain. Through the large window that opened onto the balcony of the pensión she and Roger had checked into late yesterday afternoon, she could see the hazy horizon of her childhood sea.

The sound of the waves had awakened her, but the memory of the vines that covered everything, even the sea itself, remained with her.

Their shadowy outlines crawled below her eyelids, and all Ingrid had to do was close her eyes to feel them. They were moving, breathing, growing, as if the gentle hand of time had leapt forward and one hundred years of plant life had passed before her in seconds.

With the vines came the voice again—the one Ingrid had heard that morning in Señor Ramos's field, the voice of the older woman urging her to rise.

She couldn't see her, but the woman whispered in her ear, "Welcome home," as Ingrid shifted from sleep to wakefulness, and arrived at a new sensation of quiet contentment.

She carried this feeling with her downstairs, where Roger was already waiting by the door, eager to share—as he put it—a real Spanish breakfast out in El Palo.

"How did you sleep?" he asked once they were sitting across from each other at La Peña, a simple restaurant three blocks up from their beach-front pensión. Although nothing fancy, it was known throughout Málaga for its churros and dark, creamy hot chocolate.

"Pretty good," Ingrid said as the waiter arrived with a plate of the signature breakfast. "Although, I still have vines following me in my dreams."

Roger laughed. "Still? I had my first dream of them last night."

"You poor thing." Ingrid cupped the mug of creamy hot chocolate in her hands. "The sea didn't quit all night long on my side."

"Well, I can't complain of sea noise." Roger had been the gentleman to offer her the room with the view of the sea. His was on the side with traffic.

"I think you had the right idea about sleeping in," he said. "The pensión lady was chatting away this morning, telling me about everyone who has ever stayed there. Some Germans, Norwegians, a couple from Florida, oh, and a student from Russia. Imagine, the next guest will know about *us*."

Ingrid felt relieved that he had not found it necessary to tell her about his dream. She wanted to put everything about the vines behind her—at least for now.

After breakfast, they walked down streets that Ingrid found vaguely familiar, and saw tiles that covered the walls with blue-green waves, crosses, eight-sided stars, shapes that looked like evergreens and snakes along the sides of homes. What had once been humble one-story houses gifted to the local fisherman during the time of Franco were now painted in tiles of celestial blue, maroon, desert yellow, and all other shades of the rainbow.

Potted flowers hung from second-story porches. Ivy crawled along the walls, while *el árbol de amor*, the tree of love, held pink blossoms in its arms, and the *hibiscus rosa* released a perfumed scent. Ingrid had never seen these plants in Málaga before, but it appeared they now grew on almost every street corner. She felt like a sailor coming home from the sea, taking in all the new colors, smells, and sounds that had blossomed while she had been away. Roger followed, watching her.

In the soft rain, they passed old women walking with halting steps on their way to the market, stopping to talk to friends in their high-pitched voices, dropping letters to the ground, pronouncing *s* and *c* with that thick Spanish *th*. Then they moved on, to the market where the neighborhood congregated in a chorus of noise.

In the market, Roger attracted some attention because of his height but ignored it as he joined Ingrid at the fruit stand where the smell of oranges ignited her senses, bringing back memories of shopping here with her mother. She recalled the pounds of flesh that had appeared alive as they swayed from metal hooks and the watermelons with their sweet, juicy centers that rolled on top of each other like large dark-green marbles.

Ingrid spotted the nut lady with her roasted almonds, hazelnuts, and sunflower seeds and the chicken man banging on the cutting board—one, two, one, two, dropping chicken's heads, feet, pieces of excess wing to the ground. There were also the women who sold mozzarella; Manchego; and Cabral, a cheese wrapped in leaves that become bitter with age; and *queso cremoso*, which was as soft as the fat that hides under the cow's skin.

Although the stalls were quieter now, the noise and passion of the market Ingrid had lived as a child was with her now. As were the vivid colors competing with the endless shouts, the price wars, and the passion in vendors' voices as they tried to outshout one another. Everyone had been seen and heard—the shepherd with his pieces of lamb, its shanks, arching ribs, hooves still carrying the soil of the landscape; the cow herders with their hanging meat; and the chicken farmers with their eggs.

Now, the sounds dissipated into the afternoon. Shoppers carrying netted bags through town walked down narrow alleys to their homes as Ingrid and Roger stepped outside again.

They jumped over a small puddle. Laughed. Ingrid felt lighter than she had in a while as they turned the corner to her old street, Almagro y Cardenas. Here, the smell of smoked meat drifted out the window of a second-story apartment.

"This is it," Ingrid said, the forgotten wings of her heart fluttering. "This is my old street."

Roger glanced around, emitting a few hmms and ahhs. They were standing four blocks from her old house, next to the butcher's place. Ingrid remembered walking to this corner, buying meat, bread, and cheese from the big man named Mario. Back then the trip to Mario's place had seemed like a long journey, an adventure. Now it only looked like a small, simple shop.

She still remembered how Mario used to shout obscenities about Franco and his dictatorship. Some people would line up at his shop just to hear him, while others, like Sandra, the flower lady, stationed herself across from his place, against the peeling white wall so she could counter his comments, believing as she did that Franco had brought much-needed order to her country.

Now Sandra's wall was painted the color of sunflowers, just like the ones she had once sold, but she was not there nor was the flaking wall. Instead, a sign on the building advertised a barber's shop.

From the corner, Ingrid could see the road that hooked into Almagro y Cardenas and pointed its tail toward the sea, where as a child she sought a world beyond this one.

Their old house, once a single-story fisherman's place, was farther along the street. They had been the first family in the neighborhood to build a second tier. When the family across the street had followed their lead, Ingrid had been certain they had done so so their daughter could talk to her and tell her stories from across their new second-story porch.

Now Ingrid could see the porch from the distance. It stood out like a square nose in front of her old bedroom. And in her mind's eye, her neighbor was dancing and talking, her long black hair sailing down her waist. She could see it well, the life that she had lived, the voices of the past carried by the spaces she had once inhabited.

Ingrid smoothed her hand along the wall that once peeled in the sun. Gone was the feeling of the paint crumbling below her child's fingers, but she hoped Mario, the butcher, hadn't left.

She walked with Roger across the street and slowly pushed open the door to what had been, and perhaps still was, Mario's shop. Whenever her mother had sent her here on an errand, she had run as fast as she could, eager to see the man she considered a giant. He'd stood on the other side of the counter with meat stretching on strings between them. He'd looked down at her with his big smile, rubbing his rough, bloodied hands on his apron.

Now a woman was standing behind Mario's old counter, serving a girl with large hoop earrings beneath her pinned-up hair while she ordered two kilos of chicken in her high-pitched voice.

As the clerk began to lift the chicken out of the cooler, an elderly man came out of the kitchen, prepared to wait on her. Was this Mario? Ingrid stepped up to the glass case and invented a quick order—a cheese sandwich with tomatoes. The man nodded and then wiped his hands on his apron. They were big hands, Mario-like hands, and Ingrid knew immediately that the old man was him.

Wanting to hear his voice again, the voice that once argued so passionately about politics that crowds formed in front of the store, she took a chance, and said, "So what do you make of all the tourists? Are they good for Málaga?"

Mario cut through the French bread, quick and hard, and then carefully patted six slices of cheese on top. "The tourists, the foreigners, and before them Franco," he said in a voice that had lost some of its timbre. "They're one and the same, taking from us what we got when all we need is the sea and our lives back. Our simple lives."

Ingrid smiled at hearing old Mario again. She loved his willingness to speak his mind, wished she could be so bold.

He appeared irritated, though. Probably thought she was making fun of him, until he stopped, stood still for a moment that felt like eternity, and then looked at her inquisitively.

"Wait," he said, looking from her to Roger and then back again, "are you…"

"*Sí*. Yes, it's me," Ingrid said, realizing that she didn't know what to call herself. It felt so strange.

"You're not the… German girl, the little one who used to live—"

Ingrid nodded.

"No. It can't be," he said, looking at her strangely. "It is really you, Duende?"

Ingrid felt herself shrinking into the person she had once been. All the masks, all the faces she had become were now peeling away, flesh falling from bone. Mario's words were knives cutting through years of her forgotten self.

"Duendita, Duendita, yes, it is you… wow, look at you!"

As Mario uttered this forgotten word, Roger leaned over Ingrid, and in a whisper that came out of nowhere, repeated Mario's word. "Duendita?"

Roger's presence suddenly annoyed Ingrid. She was still listening and responding to the old man's words, which carried her backward, into the chaos of memories. He used to call her "Duendita" all the time, she remembered now. He had always made her feel smaller than she had already been.

"Duendita, Duendita." Mario used to repeat her name like a mantra. He'd then shake his head as if something were wrong. She never quite understood and didn't ask. She just enjoyed listening to the way his voice seemed to play her name with deep, hypnotic certainty. It was a big voice, like his hands and smile.

Now Mario came out with that same bigness from behind the counter, and gave her a hug. "You have grown into a beautiful woman, and me, an old man who doesn't yell like he used to. You know, all the people, they don't come and listen like they used to. They've forgotten what freedom is now that they have it."

Roger watched them, silent and clearly puzzled as they

began talking, all in a rush, about Málaga and Spain and politics and the tourists, and Ingrid about Germany and her return. When she mentioned Latia, Mario told her she was still living in the same place and that she had married Constantino and that they had three children.

Only the arrival of new customers made it necessary for them to stop talking, but not before Ingrid learned that at least half a dozen families had lived in her old home since they had left, and that most of them were foreigners. Mario didn't add much to that, other than the fact that the latest family shopped in his store, and he didn't like them much. He demonstrated his feelings by raising his head and sniffing the air to let Ingrid know that they were full of themselves.

She was less concerned with the families that had moved into their home, but was excited to know that Latia—although gone for several days—continued to live in the neighborhood.

The old man, Mario, whom she had once thought was a giant, embraced Ingrid again when they parted, and it was with mixed feelings that she followed Roger out and stood in the torrential rain that flooded her being and cleansed all of the selves she had become to the bone.

DUENDE

DUENDE

"Let's go see Mario," her father pronounced.

Duende, her face dark and freckled from the sun, had just come inside after having played with a school friend. The afternoon light bounced off the piano, where her mother softly played the notes to a Chopin nocturne.

"We need some beef for tonight," her father said with shoes on, ready to go. Before Duende had time to respond, or to even go to the bathroom, she joined him on his venture.

Out on the street, the vendors paced the sidewalk, advertising their wares: "Chumberas, palmitos, la fruta." They carried their fruit on their backs, wild fruit, like the prickly pear whose ugly exterior opened to tender, sweet fruit on the inside. In the distance, a Gypsy family performed street theater and puppetry. And, as always, little girls and boys laughed and ran along the sidewalk.

Duende and her father walked quickly toward the butcher's, past the flower lady, Sandra.

"Take a good look at her, Duende," he said as he always did when they passed by. "Look at the way she gesticulates at her customers. Watch that."

Duende looked but didn't understand her father's interest

in what seemed to be the same old Sandra with the same old gestures.

Next, her father drew her attention to a young boy who, busily picking his nose, was hanging out the window to watch a group of apron-clad mothers.

"Doesn't look too pleasant, does it?" he said, and Duende knew that, as usual, everything he saw demonstrated how not to behave.

When they finally entered the butcher's place, Mario, the butcher, called out, "Señor Jorge," as he looked up from his cutting board and wiped his bloody hands on his smock. He called her father "Jorge," even though his name was Heinrich, because it was a name he gave every German. It was a story Duende had heard Mario tell numerous times—the one about his first customer, the German tourist. His name, he'd said, was Georg, or "Jorge" in Spanish. Since then, every German man had been Jorge to Mario.

Her father had his own name for Mario. He called him "Lausbub," the mischievous boy, although he had yet to translate that for Mario into Spanish. Lausbub Mario, he called him, especially when Mario started causing trouble, telling stories that incited the neighborhood's passion over what did and didn't happen during Franco's reign. Lausbub Mario he called him when Mario tried to convince her father that his meat was fresh, brought in just yesterday, when it was all too obvious that certain strips had been in Mario's cooler for as long as it took a bird to migrate from England to Málaga.

"Not too pink, not too dark, I'll take a kilo of this one, right here," her father told the butcher after close inspection of the beef on offer.

"*Sí*, señor," Mario said approvingly. "The best of the best. You know how to pick them."

Her father enjoyed an easy compliment. "Yes, I do," he was

already saying as Mario cut a kilo from the slab, wrapped it up, and handed it to him with a quick wink for the girl.

"That's a fine piece of meat I picked," Duende's father complimented himself again as they left the shop. "Now a piece like that ought to be grilled in an open-air pit, you know," he said, even though they both knew it would be cooked in the oven as usual.

Her father took a detour on the way home, down several additional streets to Paco's Restaurant, Duende walking quickly to keep up with him.

She was surprised that he invited her to join him here, where the tables were almost empty but the bar was filled with men of all ages, drinking, smoking, and talking. The smell of tobacco-laced men's clothes filled the room, while the aroma of musty cologne rubbed against the air.

There remained just enough room for Duende and her father to sit at the bar when he ordered wine for himself and soda water for her.

"Is this your daughter, señor?" the bartender asked. "She's a beautiful girl."

Duende's father nodded with pride, and then, when the bartender left them to serve other customers, Duende stared at the mirror at this man she called father with his light-blue eyes that seemed so gentle, yet mysterious to her. His graying blond hair pulled back from his face, so close to his skin, and his strong jaw and constant certainty seemed to attract people.

"So," he said, clearly amused. "Who's better looking? You or I?"

"Me," Duende dared to respond. She sat up taller on her stool, looking at herself in the mirror. She liked her long brown hair, the way it parted in the middle, pulled back behind her ears.

"That's because all you see is my nose."

Her father's Roman nose, long with a slowly arching bend toward its tip, reflected back at them between a set of wineglasses. He put his hand on top of Duende's hands for a brief moment. "You have my hands, you know." He looked back at the mirror. "You have a good life."

Duende nibbled at the nuts in front of her until he pulled them away, telling her that she had to leave room for dinner.

The bartender filled his drink and winked at the girl, whose glass was half-empty. She cupped the coolness of the glass in her hands.

"I figure your mother hasn't told you the news," her father said.

Duende wasn't sure what he was talking about.

"We're moving. Not until the end of this year, but we *are* moving... back to Germany."

She wasn't prepared to hear this.

"I've done what I need to do here with the business. It's time to go back home."

Duende stared at him, puzzled. Wasn't this home, here in Málaga? She didn't know what to say because it didn't enter her mind that a new place would be any different than what she'd known. Of course, there were her friends, including Lázaro, but she hadn't seen him since the day she'd told him about her Jesus dreams. She would miss Latia, but maybe she'd have another neighbor that would stand on her porch, dancing and telling her stories. But the Gypsy, Graciela, Paco, the nights escaping out to the bar, or her journeys to the center of the earth, what would become of them? Duende had no sense of what change meant and how much this place had left its mark on her.

"Will we have a sea?" she asked.

"We will be close enough to water, but it will be different," her father told her.

"How different?"

"Well, first they don't speak Spanish there. We'll be speaking German all the time. Secondly, we will be living in a big city, much bigger than you have ever seen, with taller buildings. And don't worry. It's not like I described it during the war. You'll like it. We'll find our own house, and nearby there will be butchers like Mario and a school down the street for you to attend. And new friends. It will be good for you to have a lot more than you have here."

Duende thought of the images her father had shared with her of the war, of demolished buildings. But then she wondered what she would have there that she didn't here.

"We'll begin the New Year in Germany," her father continued. "We'll celebrate our first *big* New Year in our new home."

He lifted his glass to his lips and looked at himself again in the mirror. "Ah, now that is good."

"What if I don't want to go?" Duende heard herself saying.

"You have no choice," he said with a shrug. "We're going."

Duende frowned as an old man walked behind her and out the door. She would need to see Lázaro before she left.

"To Spain, while she lasts." Her father took another sip, and then put his drink down, paid the bartender, and led Duende out of there.

As they walked home, Duende thought of all the people she wanted to see before leaving Málaga. She would miss them, she realized. A wave of sadness swept over her.

◈

Eager to tell Lázaro the news of her move, Duende prepared to knock on his door, but then stopped. Someone was visiting him.

"Papá," she heard a visitor say.

Silence followed as Duende gulped. *¿Papá?*

She wondered if Lázaro was there as the woman continued speaking.

"I didn't know where to find you. All that *mamá* told me was that you were a priest. But I couldn't find you anywhere until some man, a priest—"

"Father Jorge?"

Duende smiled, glad to hear Lázaro's voice.

"Yes. He said he'd seen you lately and knew you were living alone… wasn't sure you were taking proper care…"

Duende made out most of the conversation.

"Said you seemed dirty, as if you hadn't showered in days."

Lázaro laughed now, but Duende wondered why. The woman wasn't very nice.

"I expected you to look worse. In fact, I was a bit scared to—"

"So I look good?"

Duende, prepared to knock, grinned at Lázaro's response. But then she heard the woman say that her mother had died a few months ago.

"I'm sorry," Lázaro said. "She left me before you were born."

Duende creased her forehead. She felt bad. What if they found her listening?

"She said she did that to protect you," the woman said.

"From what?"

"You were a priest."

"Well, she didn't succeed."

"You mean—but how did they know?"

Duende didn't want to hear any more.

"There was talk…"

She knocked. Silence on the other side of the door.

Then Lázaro appeared, stunned. A woman stood behind him.

Duende grinned awkwardly. Would he realize she had been listening?

"I—I didn't know if I would see you again," Lázaro finally said.

Duende sighed. He hadn't noticed.

A young woman in her twenties stepped forward from behind Lázaro; she seemed awkward.

"Oh, Duende, this is my daughter, Sonia," he said.

Duende shrugged and scrunched her nose. Lázaro had never told her he had a daughter, although she had just figured it out from the conversation.

"Hello." Sonia spoke first.

"Hello."

Lázaro took his daughter's hand. "This is the first time I've seen my own daughter. It's been twenty years."

"Wow" was all Duende could say. By now, she had given up on telling Lázaro about moving to Germany. Instead, she stuttered at the door, motionless.

After an awkward moment, Sonia spoke. "Why don't you come with us? We were about to go for a walk—right papá?" She looked at her father, and he nodded. "It's beautiful out."

"Okay." Duende responded without hesitation.

As they walked along the coast, the sound of the waves filled the silence—that is, until Duende couldn't hold back her news anymore and blurted out, "My father says we're moving to Germany."

Lázaro stopped. "You're what?" He looked toward the horizon where the waters smoothed into infinity. "You don't belong there."

"Papá," said Sonia. "It's hard enough to move as a kid. Don't make it any worse."

Lázaro continued looking toward the water. "It doesn't change the fact that Duende belongs in Spain... Plus, why is it when I find my daughter, I lose my little friend? When are you going, anyway?"

"My father says at the end of the year." Duende, who was closer to the water, jumped as the edge of a wave spread onto the sand.

The beach was quiet in this midafternoon since almost everyone was home eating. The summer had simmered down and was now moving into autumn, and there was no one in sight except for several fishermen dragging their nets onto the sand.

Lázaro called out to the men wrestling them to shore. "A fish for the old man?"

One man looked up and waved. He spoke through his tangled beard. "The old man is not so old!" he called. "Señor

Lázaro, when you coming out? Teach you some real fishing. Catch you a whole month's worth if it'll last you."

By now Duende, Lázaro, and Sonia had neared the boats, which smelled so strongly of fish that Duende held her nose.

The man with the tangled beard noticed Sonia and choked on his words. "For the beautiful lady... two fish. A beautiful lady will get much farther than an old man." He laughed as Duende observed the funny situation.

"The beautiful lady is my daughter." Lázaro pushed out his chest.

The fisherman appeared stunned. "Since when do you have a daughter, Señor Lázaro?"

"I've been hiding her from the likes of you, Señor Alfonso," Lázaro said, teasingly. "Sonia, this is Raúl Alfonso."

Duende watched but was surprised when Lázaro turned the conversation toward her. "And this is Duende, who will also be a beautiful woman one day. She too will need to be protected from your kind."

She grinned.

"That's hard work, my old man," said Raúl.

The two men bantered with each other for a few minutes and then Raúl placed several fish, still squirming and alive, into a bag and handed it to Lázaro, who passed it to Duende. As she struggled to hold the bag firmly, the fish pushing against its plastic, trying to escape, Duende pictured them calm and still, no longer squirming, and soon the movement stopped.

"So is that the way you get food every day?" Sonia asked as they walked away.

"He's a good man, Raúl," Lázaro responded. "He takes care of me like clockwork."

Sonia frowned. "Do you still... You know, the church... Do you still practice?"

"Practice what?"

"You know, do you still believe?"

"It's hard to know what to believe," he said.

Duende skipped alongside, keenly aware of their words.

"I don't think it is," Sonia replied in a matter-of-fact tone. "Is that why you *really* left—because you didn't believe anymore?"

"No," said Lázaro quickly. "Well, yes."

Sonia looked at him, confused.

"I had to leave. That choice was not mine. Maybe I was a wrong fit for the church all along."

"Was *mamá* the only one?" Sonia asked without looking at her father.

Lázaro remained quiet, as Duende paid close attention. She was learning more about Lázaro by the minute.

Sonia didn't push the question.

"Did she marry?" Lázaro asked Sonia. "Did your mother marry?"

"No."

When they arrived back at the house, Lázaro shuffled around to find a pan to fry the fish, and then led Sonia and Duende behind the shack to a small pit with burned black logs, which he cleaned out and added new kindling and wood to before meticulously preparing a fire.

"Duende, today you will eat your first fish straight from Raúl's net," he said as she watched him make the flames appear.

The girl dreaded the idea of eating the once-live fish, but she didn't want to leave Lázaro, particularly since, months from now, she wouldn't see him again.

"Where are you going?" Sonia asked.

"Germany." Duende frowned.

"Have you ever been?"

She shook her head.

"So you're German."

Duende nodded.

"Well then, it can't be too bad. You have family there?"

It was, Duende thought, a curious idea. If she had "family" there, she had never heard of them.

Lázaro concentrated on cooking the fish just right. Slowly, the flames bit away at the tangled smell of sea.

"You must like Spain," said Sonia.

Duende's eyes remained fixed on the flames. She hadn't given it much thought.

"She loves Spain," interjected Lázaro. "She belongs here."

Duende looked at Lázaro as he defended her love for Spain. She wasn't sure where she belonged, or what it was like being in any place but on this land by the sea.

Duende watched the flames, feeling their warmth. She breathed in the smoky fish smell. Lázaro took one last look at his catch and then quickly lifted it onto an old metal plate. "Perfecto," he proclaimed, and began cutting the fish into pieces, insisting that Sonia and Duende eat, with a small fork and their hands, while it was hot.

It was an unusually primitive way to eat—or at least it would have been for Duende under her father's watch—but she liked breaking the rules.

Lázaro hurried into his house and came out with a bottle of wine and some cups. He filled three cups, one with much less than the others, and handed them out. "A toast!" he cried. "To seeing my daughter again. And to losing Duende to Germany. What a shame."

The only wine Duende had ever had came from a few sips of her father's drink at the dinner table. The glass in her hands held several inches of wine. She tasted it and found it bitter. But after a few sips, she felt a curious and pleasant sensation. Magical. It warmed her.

"Germany is far away, you know," said Lázaro, eating the fish with his hands. "Too far away. But perhaps when you're there, you won't have those dreams. You won't have to worry about saving you-know-who. I was a bit worried about you."

Duende felt embarrassed by his words. Worried? Did Lázaro think like the Gypsy and Oma, that her dreams would come true soon? She was too fearful of the answer to ask.

Instead, the three of them watched the small fire die down. As the flames inched closer to the ground, disappearing into ashes, Sonia told a story. Lázaro and Duende listened intently and laughed intermittently. A surreal happiness held them until, lightheaded, Duende rose, knowing it was time to leave. And because she had had such a good time with her friends and expected to see them again, she turned cartwheels all the way home.

INGRID

INGRID

Ingrid tried turning her barstool to avoid Roger's pensive gaze. But it wouldn't budge.

"So *Duende*, let's have it!" he exclaimed.

She was in a world as deep and dark as the wine in her hands. The last time she had been in a place like this was when her father had told her they were moving to Germany.

Roger leaned on his right elbow, his head resting slightly on his arm while looking at Ingrid in surrendered wonder.

She glanced at him briefly. He looked *handsome*, content.

Ingrid bit the nail of her pinky while she tapped the rung of her barstool with her shoes. "What? What do you want me to say? It's another name of mine... It's been a loooooooong time since then. *She* no longer exists."

Roger grinned. "But... *Duende*?" He looked amusingly toward the bottles lined up against the bar wall. "I could see having another nice German name, like Gertrude or María or Corinna, but *Duende*?"

Ingrid shrugged as she followed his gaze to the bottles. She bit deeper into her nail and then took a sip of wine.

"I don't get it," Roger said. "You had a Spanish name and

then changed your name to a German one? But is Duende even a Spanish name—I mean, a proper name?"

"No, it's not." Ingrid spoke between her teeth. She wished she had not agreed to come back to her old neighborhood. "My grandmother gave it to me. It—"

Ingrid stopped as she felt a shiver run down her spine. It was as if the mention of her grandmother brought a familiar sensation back to her, that tingle she used to feel as a child when Oma was around.

"What?" Roger interrupted. "What were you going to say?"

Warmth spread through Ingrid. *She's back. Oma's back.*

She looked around her to see if she could sense her grandmother. Was she here now? Was it her voice, her spirit she had heard this morning, the same one she heard that morning with the grapes out in Señor Ramos's field? She shivered at the thought.

"Ingrid," Roger said. "What is it? What's wrong?"

"Roger, do you feel anything different in here, right now?"

"No." Roger lifted his beer to his mouth.

She listened for a change about her, for her grandmother's presence. "Forget it," Ingrid finally said, wondering if she was just imagining things. "It was a long time ago, Roger."

"*What* was a long time ago?"

"My name." Her words were quiet, slurred. She turned her blurred gaze away from the bottles and looked at Roger. "You wouldn't get it, Roger." She took another sip of her wine. "Duende died a long time ago."

"Try me. Plus, there's no sense avoiding it all." Roger put his drink down. "And you can't come this far and then tell me it's just the past. This so-called past you won't talk about is smothering you. Look at you."

Ingrid glanced back at the bottles and saw her reflection in the mirror behind them. Unlike the time with her father at the bar years ago, this time she looked old. Really old. And unhappy.

And tight. She wanted to cry or hit Roger. "Why do you want to know?"

"Wouldn't you want to know if you were in my shoes? What does 'Duende' mean anyway?"

"It's a spirit," Ingrid said reluctantly. "It means 'the spirit of the earth. A ghost'..."

She felt another shiver. Her grandmother had to be there.

"Your name means 'the spirit of the earth'?"Roger seemed enthralled. "What grandmother would name their grandchild that? Amazing."

"I don't know why she felt a need to name me that," Ingrid said. "All I know is that my grandmother took a train from Germany to Málaga to attend my birth. My father used to tell me that my grandmother was so determined to name me that she carried my birth name in a book."

Ingrid felt another shiver as Roger remained attentive to a story she hadn't told anyone, let alone thought of, in twenty years.

"Look, Roger." Ingrid faced him, deciding she had shared enough. "I've got the book with me. My father gave it to me at the train station, before I left. I didn't want him to waste my time with it. But I've got it. Haven't even looked at it. But you can learn all about Duende in there. You're welcome to read it later."

"Tell me more," Roger said.

"Well there's not much more to it," Ingrid replied. "Like I said, you can read the book later. For some reason, my grandmother thought the name was important."

Ingrid sipped her wine to the bottom and ordered another. She felt she was being watched by someone besides Roger.

"So if your grandmother wanted you to have that name so badly, then why do you have a different one now? I don't get it."

"It's pretty simple." Ingrid was prepared to give a particular answer that avoided telling him the real reason she changed her name. "My mother wanted to call me *Ingrid,* and since my grandmother insisted on Duende, Ingrid became my middle name. So, when I moved to Germany, I decided to become Ingrid. Duende had died for me. The girl I had been died... Plus, it would have been weird to be Duende in Germany. Everyone would have asked me what kind of name it was, what it meant. I didn't want that kind of attention."

"Okay. Maybe not. But I want to see that book. I think it could help you understand your grandmother better."

"Later," Ingrid said. "I'll show it to you later."

"Tell you what. I'll get it, if you let me."

"Now? You want to go back to the pensión to get it?"

"It's only a few blocks away. Come on. You wait here and I'll go. You don't have to do anything, and it won't be but a few minutes."

"That's stupid." Ingrid tried to quell Roger's enthusiasm.

"Come on," insisted Roger as he got up from his seat.

"I don't—"

"You just stay here. I think I know where it is... in your suitcase, right? No worries. I'll just get it."

"But—"

Before Ingrid could say any more, Roger walked out the door with all of his eagerness trailing behind him, leaving Ingrid sitting alone, looking at herself in the mirror behind the bar. She finished her second glass of wine while she reflected on twenty years ago, on the time she learned she was leaving Spain for Germany.

She felt no different now, as alone and uncertain about life's choices as she had felt then. What had happened? The fear had followed her back here, where she had chosen to walk through this door into her past. But a part of Ingrid wanted to remain the person she had become—no matter how empty—rather than confront the little girl she had left behind. It felt easier, less painful.

Before she could retreat too far with her thoughts, Roger returned with the book, and since he was breathing heavily she guessed that he must have run all the way to the room and back. *How crazy.*

"I've got it now," he said proudly.

"Well, there's not much to it," Ingrid said. "You ran for nothing."

"I'll determine that." He opened the book to a page with an old bookmark in it. "Oh, before I read, I need another beer."

Roger ordered a drink and invited Ingrid to her third glass of wine, which she accepted eagerly, knowing she would cope with this better if she were relaxed.

"Let's see," said Roger, beginning to read a passage from the book. "'Duende is the spirit of the earth one must awaken in the remotest mansions of the blood.' Seems like that's part of some speech García Lorca gave on duende. Wow!" Roger exclaimed. "That's beautiful. I love it. What a name to give a little girl!"

"Yeah, quite a name," Ingrid said, staring into her drink. She licked her finger, and with its moisture, she rubbed the edge of her wineglass, round and round.

Roger kept reading. "'It's a ghost, goblin, an imp, a quality of passion and inspiration.'"

Ingrid could see her father now, sitting on the other end of the coach in their old Málaga apartment, telling her for the first time that her name meant "ghost."

"Look at this," Roger continued. "The origin of the word comes from a contraction of *duen de casa*, from *dueño de casa*—'owner of the house.' It's like you have this spirit, this powerful, magnetic force that is as healing and life-affirming as the spirit of the earth. And it's this spirit that needs to come home, to be embodied, to live fully in all its power and force here on the earth."

Ingrid could feel how far she had come from that place of embodied power and life-force. She felt hollow inside, that spirit of duende clearly missing. She increased the pressure of her finger on the wineglass after licking it again, but Roger didn't seem to notice as he continued speaking.

"This is amazing. This spirit of duende has tremendous power like the earth does."

Ingrid jumped in her seat as the glass sung a high "C" through the bar.

Roger smiled. "You're not listening, are you?"

"I heard you." Ingrid took a deep breath. She could still feel Oma's presence.

"You've got a great name and a great story. I wonder what it all means. I mean, did your grandmother feel that you were that spirit?"

This was, Ingrid thought, a Roger she hadn't seen as much, someone who seemed interested in dealing with problems philosophically.

"Hey, all the dreams of vines... there's something to that and your name. Don't you think?"

"No." Ingrid shook her head as she finished her wine. She felt an urge to leave now before he forced her to listen to more.

"Your grandmother wanted you to be this earth spirit," Roger went on. "You might have special powers or some wild earth connection. Maybe you did make the grapes pop on those vines!"

"Stop, Roger!" Ingrid exclaimed. "I told you not to go there."

"But Ingrid... Duende. Don't you see? Maybe that's what you're scared of. That this could be true... that you could make that happen."

Oma's presence grew stronger. Heat spread throughout Ingrid's body—rage filling her. She was about to shut off. She could feel it. No room to hide, but Ingrid needed to. Now.

"I'm going back to the pensión," she said, desperate to flee his words. She emptied the glass into her mouth.

"But Ingrid!"

She walked out the door.

"I'm sorry, Ingrid," Roger called to her as she left. He hurried after her in the darkness back to the pensión.

∿

"I am always here," Ingrid heard her grandmother's spirit say the morning after a night of tears had finally lulled her to sleep.

Oma, who had held her inside her embrace all night, was no longer the stern woman her father had portrayed her as being, but calm and beautiful. "It's time for you to come home, my dear," the old woman said, her face carrying that Gypsy spirit Ingrid had seen years ago. "Don't be afraid anymore."

When Ingrid woke, her heart was light, as though she had shed years of fears in her sleep. She was experiencing a deep calm again, a feeling of peace emanating from her grandmother's presence.

Ingrid lingered as long as she could inside this feeling, but when she finally rose and walked to the window, pulling open the curtains, she discovered gloomy, gray skies that still dropped rain to the ground. Her mood sunk slightly, for she had wanted to go to the beach and feel the sun's rays beaming warmth onto her body.

"Don't worry. It will stop soon. The rain never lasts very long in Málaga," the woman inside the kiosk had told Ingrid and Roger when she had bought some sunflower seeds yesterday. The woman wasn't the only one who had dismissed the rain as a passing aberration.

Now that the rain hadn't stopped, though, Ingrid met up with Roger to decide on some alternative plan for the day. He tried to apologize profusely for making her uncomfortable the previous night, but she stopped him from doing so.

"Look. Just forget it all, okay," she said, wishing she had stayed in her room, but knowing that if she had done so, Roger would have worried about her.

Ingrid also needed to do some research for the article,

so, accompanied by Roger, she went to Málaga's municipal archives, where they rummaged through old books and newspapers to learn about the history of local wine-making and, more importantly, the people who had tended to the vineyards over the centuries.

They read about how Málaga's wine history stretched far back, before 1850, when its vineyards were damaged by powdery mildew and phylloxera, a pest that had crossed the border from France. The wine industry managed to survive the pestilence, only to be threatened in the late twentieth century by tourism. As they had already witnessed, tourism and new transplants were competing with vineyards for the hillsides overlooking the Mediterranean.

"It's the same story everywhere, I'd say. Roger, listen to this. It about summarizes it." Ingrid read:

> *What is of even greater consequence is the fact that, not only in Málaga, but throughout Spain, tourism and urban sprawl are forcing people to abandon the land. No longer are families passing down long-held traditions of caring for* la tierra, *but tourism now competes for water in much of the country where drought and desertification are threatening the very possibility of farm life. Golf courses and garden lawns not suited for Mediterranean conditions are now slurping up the remaining water.*

Ingrid found herself wondering if she was like all the rest, just another tourist longing for the warmth of the sun and a nice tan, while people like Señor Ramos struggled with maintaining the thirsty and forgotten land that so many took from and then left.

Was this what Señor Ramos had meant when he had told her that he had hoped she would understand, that maybe somebody would see this supernatural vine-bleeding and overgrowth as more than a freak show?

Roger and Ingrid looked at each other, and it was clear they had the same thought. There was no need to say anything. She closed her notebook, feeling satisfied she had copied enough valuable information for an article, and they walked out into the rain, knowing exactly where to go.

An hour later, Roger and Ingrid were sitting on the beach, alone, everyone else inside, while they watched the rain fall into the open mouth of the sea. She wondered if the sea enjoyed drinking the sky's tears.

They were only several feet from where the water kissed the edges of the sand, and now Roger's mouth was open, the drops of cloud falling into him, bit by bit.

Ingrid enjoyed watching him and his daring innocence, the quality that had made him wear his orange outfit on their first encounter at the train station.

"Look for the man in orange, tacky orange," Ingrid could hear Franz saying. She laughed because she knew now that even Roger had known it was tacky, yet chose to wear it all the same.

Her laughter was slight but enough to draw Roger's attention away from the raindrops. "Why are you laughing?" he asked. "Is it the fact that we're both crazy enough to be sitting out here in this bloody rain, getting soaked to our bones?"

His words made Ingrid giggle harder, and then, as he looked at her with wonder and surprise, laughter threw her entire body into the wet sand. She couldn't stop, and the more she tried, the less success she had. It was as if her sounds were all the broken pieces of tension that had held her life together until now.

Soon Roger was laughing with her. And then the waves too were emanating the sound of joy against the beach. The two were almost too loud to hear them, but yes, the waves slapped their hands against the sea's body and roared a long and deep sound like drawn-out laughter.

"Did you hear it?" Ingrid spoke through the small syllables of silence that remained between her fits of joy.

"The laughter?" Roger teased.

"The waves, do you hear what they are doing?"

Her words broke the spell. He stopped abruptly to listen to the waves, as if there were some serious message in them. After a few moments, he looked at her dumbfounded.

Ingrid still had difficulty controlling herself, but she tried to put on a serious face. "The waves, they're laughing too. Can't you hear them?"

Now Roger looked like a child who had gotten the wrong answers to a quiz. "No," he said. "Can't quite hear what you're hearing."

"Well, that's okay," Ingrid said, quieting down. "They must have stopped."

"Right." Roger looked toward the ground.

At that moment it occurred to Ingrid that they had been sitting out in the rain for at least an hour. She could feel a chill that had probably been with her for some time.

Roger didn't look cold, though. He just stared at her through the drops of water, beautifully still and pensive in his gaze. "May I kiss you?" he asked while barely moving his lips.

She could feel her face flush.

"May I?" he asked again.

Ingrid felt like a bird whose wings had become paralyzed by Roger's words. Speechless, she nodded ever so slightly, but enough for Roger to receive his cue.

Roger, who was half leaning on the ground, pushed himself upright and moved toward her. She was sitting, waiting, uncomfortably.

He got closer now, leaning into her. Ingrid closed her eyes and let him find her lips.

His were wet, as were hers. In the cold moisture of their lips, she felt him close, soft, and tender as a falling leaf.

Ingrid knew in that moment that the heart that had hidden inside the folds of a distant wave had reached the shore.

DUENDE

DUENDE

The waves crashed hard onto the shore as Duende stepped onto the beach. The late-summer clouds covering the once-bright morning skies mirrored the girl's heavy heart. She would be leaving Málaga soon, and yet she hadn't visited Lázaro in a while, nor had she seen her sea friend or her grandmother's spirit. And while she had spent time with Latia and her new love, Constantino, at the movies, seeing the two of them together only made Duende want to have her own love, or to feel a sense of belonging that became harder to feel the more she experienced life.

As Duende stepped into the sand, she watched a seagull glide above a woman whose pregnant belly stretched her browned skin below a polka-dotted bikini and heard a young girl scream with laughter, dipping and swooping into the water as her father spun her around. They seemed content despite the clouds that had moved in.

But not Duende. She felt alone, and especially lately, after discovering how much of a magician she really was, and how different she was from other people. She longed for a world that didn't come in gift packages, in candy wrappers or ice cream cones, and she wished to connect with her grandmother's spirit again so she wouldn't feel so alone—so she would feel less over-whelmed by what she was being shown, and what she was being asked to do.

Duende searched for a place higher up along the gravel edges of the beach, near homes that flooded every year with sea water. When she found a small rock, she sat down, closed her eyes, and waited for her grandmother's spirit to reappear after months of absence. Duende had felt her presence, but she wanted to see her again, like she had the night she went danc-ing with Graciela, when her grandmother's face appeared and made her feel safe and secure.

"Oma," she called out. "Oma. Can you see me?"

Duende closed and then opened her eyes, looking around for her grandmother's presence. She wanted to know why she kept getting these dreams and what to do about them.

At first, there was no sign of Oma. Only a small blue-winged bird arrived and pecked at the sand in front of her before flying off, its wings wide.

"You will be like that bird soon," Duende suddenly heard someone say. She turned around but didn't see anyone. "You may not see me, but I'm here," the voice continued.

Duende shook with excitement, although she wished she could see her grandmother.

"You don't need to see me," Oma said, seemingly reading her thoughts. "Just trust that I am here. And the Gypsy is right. Your dreams will take flight; they will come true after your birthday."

Duende was incredulous. Could this really be true? How would this happen?

"I can't explain what you won't understand right now," con-tinued Oma. "Just trust me. And trust the Gypsy." Grandmother began to laugh with a soft, tickling sound. "She may be scary looking, but she means well."

Duende looked out at the sea as her throat began to tighten. She sensed her grandmother preparing to leave her side, and wished at that moment that she had known her while she was still alive.

Instead, the blue-winged bird began to flutter, to fly away for now, as Oma shared her last words: "My dear little one, my dear Duende. I am *always* here. And so is the little man from the sea. He's here to help too."

⤳

Nights of calm stayed with Duende after her visit with her grandmother, and remained with her, even as an immense wave of thick, salty air entered her room, permeating her sleep.

She dreamed she was falling far into the sea, pulled by a hand no bigger than her own.

"Come with me," she heard someone whisper. "I want to show you something."

As she followed, the sea became a dense mass pushing her down. "Where are we going?" she found herself saying, although she knew she was sleeping.

"Come with me," she heard again.

A strong scent trailed behind the voice, which inched its way toward her. Her nose twitched. She opened her eyes to her room, and to the sight of the little man from the sea walking out of the wall toward her, his bones glowing as he pointed for her to join him.

Duende shook her head in disbelief. She had never seen him away from the water.

"Come," he said again, and with that a piercing sound filled her room.

Duende covered her ears, but the noise only got louder. It surely would have woken up her parents, she thought, but then realized it was coming from inside her.

Her little friend held out his hand. "It's time you see something," he said.

She sat up in bed, looking down at her pajamas. The high-pitched sound remained.

"Don't worry about those," the man said, laughing. "For where we're going, it doesn't matter what you wear."

As Duende followed her friend to the wall, the high pitch intensified. She tried covering her ears while holding his one hand, but it didn't help a bit.

"It will go away once we get through to the other side," he assured her.

The other side?

The little man disappeared into the wall with only one hand visible—the one holding onto Duende. She took a deep breath, hoping to soften the shrill tone that had now become unbearable. The sound worsened, though, as the tips of the little man's hands disappeared into the wall, followed by Duende's hand.

Then everything went dark. Duende's palm became slippery with sweat as she held onto his hand. The pressure around them intensified. Were they traveling inside a hole the size of a miniscule needle?

The farther they traveled in the darkness, the more Duende was convinced that her entire insides were hurling out of her, with all of her disappearing, until she became a long, narrow thread piercing through the needle of time.

Duende panicked as she gulped unsuccessfully for air. She had become too small, too narrow to receive any of it. How would she make it out of here?

She tried to take another breath. Again, nothing. Before she became too scared, her friend squeezed her hand, temporarily consoling her.

They moved deeper through the darkness until the high-pitched sound lessened. Were they moving closer to where they were going, or was Duende becoming smaller? She recalled her friend's whistling. Did he produce that sound because he traveled through this thin place every time he came to see her?

Before she had a chance to answer, a whirlpool of light appeared ahead of them. Duende relaxed only long enough to take in the slightest amount of air, for the light spun forward, pulling them toward it in a disorienting spiral that made the tip of Duende's head hurt. She had become small—she was sure of this—and all the water that had been inside her had been twisted and wrung out of her.

The light quickly drew Duende out of the tunnel she had been in, and she landed with a sensation of rolling onto a hard surface that softened under her. With one hand, Duende tried unsuccessfully to cover her eyes to a blinding radiance that had no beginning or end. With the other, she held onto her friend, who slowly pulled her up.

It didn't seem to do any good, though. Still dizzy, Duende couldn't stand upright. There was no up, down, left, or right in her. Just her form that had no form. She tried to feel her contours, but felt nothing. There was nothing but a dizzying experience of trying to find herself, although by now she had adjusted to the light.

"You're not here." Her friend spoke for the first time since landing in this strange place. "You're not anywhere, as a matter of fact."

Duende looked toward the little man, but she couldn't see him, although her formless hand still held his. How was that possible? How could she feel him if he wasn't there?

"Look more deeply, beyond form, and you'll see me," he said.

His words transported Duende back to the center of the earth, where she had tried to hear what she couldn't hear in that space. Was this the same, the same with her seeing?

"Just try it."

The light would have blinded her if she had been in ordinary time, but her eyes weren't the eyes she was used to. All of her formless form could see, but how, she had no idea.

Duende concentrated on the light. She felt its presence

inside her, until she expanded to become the light as she had done with sound in the center of the earth. It tickled her. She laughed, but there was no sound in her laughter.

"Where are we?" she asked.

"Nowhere."

"What?"

"The beginning of life is here."

"Where is here?"

"Just focus on the light and you'll see it."

Duende stopped trying to figure it out and felt the light explode inside and beyond her. As she did, colors glistened around her—violet, emerald green, golden, yellow, sky blue. They twirled around her, encircling her, expanding from her being, illuminating this place she was in. Was she creating these colors?

"The colors are coming from you," her friend said as he too became colors of light filling in the space. "This is who we are. We become the place we are in. Actually, we create it."

Duende smiled, and as she did so, the colors spread out, forming a rainbow that wove a tapestry of life around her. Suddenly, an entire city or village—it was hard to tell which— rose before her from nothing. Beams of light of all colors—like flames and crystalline liquid—took form, created what appeared like tall pillars, but then changed shape within seconds, into a river, or a thousand birds fluttering into slithering snakes.

"Hello," Duende said into the space. "Hello" echoed back in pliant shapes that danced all over the place.

"This is your home." Her friend encircled her with his words, and with a glow of embers.

"Home? You said the last place we were in was my home."

"We are back inside the earth, but in that city you saw in the distance. All of these colors, all of this light, is your essence made up of all those that share this place with you."

Although she had no actual form, Duende smiled at the idea of being able to create anything she imagined. Anything! She pictured buildings with lots of people in them, and with that painted them into being with her intent. They rose from nothing. All around her.

An entire city now stood before her and her intent held it so, without the forms changing as they had before. She had always been able to make things move at will, but to create a city like this was daunting—so daunting that Duende suddenly got scared.

Her own power frightened her, and with that the colors around her dimmed. Darkness returned. She couldn't understand the immensity of this place, although she soon heard what sounded like millions of people screaming. It was the same sound of discord and pain she had heard the last time she was here in the center of the earth.

"That's the sound of what humans have created," her friend said. "A long time ago, they believed in this light inside the earth and inside themselves. They knew their power, and they used it to build empires and cities with tall buildings, but they lost an important connection with the earth and with nature's balance. They created without really understanding how their own will could change the dream of the earth."

Her friend spoke through the jarring sounds that shook Duende's body, which got denser with each second. She couldn't escape the noise, although she wished she could erase the city she had created.

"Don't worry. Your city is gone. You are merely feeling the darkness and heaviness of humanity. You are feeling what the earth feels because humans have lost their way," said her friend.

"Why?" Duende found herself asking.

"Humans have forgotten the power and light within themselves and the earth… they have forgotten how to create magic in a way that honors life—all of it," he said. "Instead they've been taught to run to some promised land away from here. But it's here, all of it."

Although Duende listened intently, she felt the urge to leave this place that she had supposedly created, wished to be back in her bed.

"You carry the earth's spirit, little one. You carry her light. That's your work," he said. "Now, focus on that and you'll feel more than this place you are stuck in."

Duende didn't want to work that hard. She was only eight years old, after all.

"Go on, feel this place. Just feel it."

Although she wrestled with the darkness, she began to open her senses to something more. Listening to her friend's advice, Duende let a dim light inside her expand until she could once again see.

"Don't doubt the magic that you are."

The eternal light of the earth filled her. She let the child in her play and make magic again. Painting the world with the innocence of love, she became the city of colors, intertwining her dancing, changing form with all the eternal space before her. The girl could feel how her own light became form far beyond this place, becoming the trees, the grasses, the sand that she had earlier stepped on. She could be all of this life, and honor it as she danced through its forms.

Duende transported her light body through the earth, toward her home, where her parents were sleeping. She filled her parents' room with colors that bathed their sleep with a love she had never felt in human form. She could actually see her parents smiling as they lay asleep inside her embrace.

Duende visited Lázaro by the ocean. He appeared upset, turning a lot in his sleep. But when she whispered to him, he became more still.

"Come back now," Duende heard her little friend say, as she left Lázaro and brought her attention back into the city of lights that now shone even brighter. Before her, her parents, and Lázaro, and all those she had known stood. Even Jesus was there. They took temporary form before shifting back into transparent rivers of color and shape.

Her friend stood before her in his recognizable form. "We live in different dimensions, but this dimension can take form on the earth as well. We can be the love and the colors and the light there that you are here in this place," he said. "You just have to dream it, and believe it's possible. It begins with feeling it."

His words took Duende back to her conversation with Lázaro and to his comment about Jesus and his dream of heaven on earth.

"Your friend Lázaro was right," the little man said. "But you're the one who can make it happen. You are Duende… Duende… Duende… Duende."

Duende wasn't sure where she was as she heard her name repeated eternally. Duende, Duende, Duende.

She sensed herself moving through the dark, narrow passageway between the worlds, felt herself returning, quickly, more easily, to her room. She saw her little friend disappearing before her, waving good-bye as a large wave swept him away.

Duende. Duende. Duende. She heard another voice now. As the girl opened her eyes to her own room and to a light coming in through her window, she saw her grandmother smiling above her. "I told you your name was special, very special—like you."

Duende curled up inside the sheet that covered her. It tickled her to be back, to see her grandmother and the light coming into the bedroom.

She looked toward the wall. There was no sign of her friend, and no sign of where they had pierced through to travel to another place.

Duende felt lighter as she embraced her form. The light and the presence from the center of the earth were with her now. The two worlds seemed so different, and yet both were a part of her, as she heard Maria Callas's voice announce the end of the night.

INGRID

INGRID

I ngrid and Roger didn't expect to see each other again after this night. Like a balloon slowly releasing its air, the end of their time together was near. To celebrate, they had decided to have dinner at El Tintero, a fancy restaurant on Avenida Cortez in the heart of the city.

It was nine o'clock when Ingrid and Roger arrived there, the light of day having fallen behind buildings and ships on the waterfront. Dampness permeated the walls as they sat down at a table.

After taking off coats soaked by rain, the two warmed their hands over a candle in the middle of the table. Ingrid peered through the candle's light at Roger. She would miss him.

His soft eyes looked back at her.

He was a true gentleman, this Ingrid knew. But she wondered if he would miss her too.

"I've been thinking," Roger said after they ordered and as they looked out at the rain. "Sometimes I feel like we are reliving the great flood scene from the Bible. It feels like God is punishing people like Señor Ramos. What if it never ends?"

Ingrid turned her eyes away from the window and toward Roger. "Now that's crazy. You don't really believe that?"

"Well, suppose it's archaic in the Biblical sense," Roger said, looking up at the waiter who arrived with drinks. He and Ingrid quickly toasted to the end of their journey, before Roger continued. "Now I'm an associate professor of anthropology—like I told you—not a religious zealot or anything of the kind. But I can't help but wonder what has caused this vine-growing craze, this kind of flooding from below. And then the bleeding, and the sudden grape growth. Combine that with all of your dreams and nightmares, and your night out among the vines, and you have to wonder. What causes each event to occur, and then only on one man's land? What's at the root of all this? Don't you wonder?"

"Well, of course I do," Ingrid said. "But as punishment, that's different. That would mean that every disaster, every natural occurrence that threatens us or our lives is punishment. That seems absurd."

She found herself thinking about the morning she had woken up among newly grown grapes. "We're really looking for an answer when there isn't one," Ingrid added, realizing she had yet to find an answer to what had happened—or at least one she felt comfortable with.

"Do you think the bleeding, overgrown vines, the sudden grape growth, and all of your vine dreams will end soon?" Roger asked.

"It has to. Señor Ramos can't live like this for much longer, and the vine dreams... I'm done with them."

As Ingrid said that, she thought about her last dream—the one with her grandmother, whose presence had stripped the vines of their danger.

"Who's to say if the whole vine situation will really end? It's hard for Señor Ramos or anyone to know what to do until they understand why it's all really happening to begin with," Roger said.

Ingrid knew that what he said was true. There was, she realized, much more depth to Roger than she had first sensed.

"Well, why did God send a flood in the Bible?" he said over the sound of a large truck passing through the narrow road in front of the restaurant. It honked several times and then left fumes of exhaust trailing behind.

"I would suspect that," he said more quietly as he leaned forward, "assuming He—"

"Maybe *She*." Ingrid grinned now.

"All right, let's make God a She. Fair enough. Then assuming She *actually* sent a flood—because after all, who's to know whether the Bible is accurate or not. But assuming *She* sent a flood, I would suspect *She* did so because somehow the people weren't listening. Listening to what God had to say, you know. And since Noah did listen, he was warned and could save a few pairs of animals and his family. I think that's reasonable. No?"

"Well, then it's not punishment."

"I guess not. I guess it's more like God bringing some kind of balance where there's an imbalance. She's bringing a flood because we've created this imbalance by not listening to the earth or places within ourselves. We're not listening to how to live according to our true nature," said Roger.

"That sounds good."

He gazed up at the waiter, who arrived with their meals, and then at Ingrid's meal. "Never seen squid so big."

She took her first bite. It was tender and soft. "So what specifically didn't we hear?" she said. "If that's what it is?"

Roger busied himself tasting his food.

"What didn't we hear?" Ingrid asked again.

"Oh, I heard you. But I wouldn't just say we *didn't* hear."

"What do you mean?"

"We still don't hear it. We still aren't listening."

Suddenly, a loud crashing sound came from the kitchen, followed by a man's screams. Everyone turned their attention toward the swinging doors, where someone swept broken dish pieces together. "What don't we hear?" Ingrid whispered, leaning forward.

"I don't know exactly," Roger said. "But I think our deafness to this something is causing the vine growth and the bleeding and all the other insane happenings on this earth."

His words carried Ingrid to the center of the earth. She could feel again what Duende had felt through her listening body—all the noise and discord of humanity "not listening" that her little friend back then had spoken about. She could sense her body wanting to expand again with a sudden heat coursing through her.

Roger didn't appear to notice. Instead, he stroked his chin as if he actually had a beard and continued speaking. "It feels as if something has been hiding, hiding for centuries below the earth's surface, like a message, waiting for us to listen. When we don't heed its call, it emerges, seizing control. It's like the waters of a flood. The water is always there, but contained, and then suddenly, with the right factors, what once was subdued becomes a force to reckon with. I think of it like this—the vines were always there, but the vines are now rising, crawling everywhere, taking over. But why now? And why Señor Ramos?"

Ingrid thought of how her recent dreams had been invaded by vines. It was as if these dreams had always been with her, since her childhood here in Spain, and only now they were rising within her like a flood. It was as if her body couldn't ignore the truth—her true nature—anymore.

"I bet if this were happening in Australia, the aborigines would say the vines are the dreams of the earth, and they are only spreading, taking over everywhere, because nobody's listening," Roger continued. "It's like the vines had to take over for us to pay attention, just like our dreams become nightmares because we ignore them for so long and ignore our true way. But even then, it seems we still don't listen." He took a deep breath.

Ingrid shivered with a feeling of familiarity as she and

Roger sipped their drinks. She leaned forward. "You think the earth dreams?"

"Why not? We do," Roger said simply.

"So what does the earth dream?"

"Maybe the earth dreams all of our pain and disconnection—all of our not listening—and periodically floods over in the form of natural disasters for us to finally see ourselves. It's causing us to see our own dreams that have turned to nightmares."

Ingrid sat up straight. She could feel with more potency what she had experienced inside the earth as a child. The heat spread inside her, painfully pulsating against her skin like an infection trying to get out—like a disease that the earth itself has also lived, and still does. "You mean the spirit of the earth… duende. This duende dreams our dreams or nightmares. I am dreaming," Ingrid whispered.

For the first time since their journey back to Spain, Ingrid was beginning to understand what had happened to her. She didn't feel afraid of her old name, because she got that it was more than a name. It was a presence, her own essence—and the spirit of the earth within her—that had followed her here, and there was no escaping who she was.

Ingrid closed her eyes and began reciting Garcia Lorca's words from her grandmother's book. "Duende is the spirit of the earth—"

"One must awaken in the remotest mansions of the blood," Roger added, completing her sentence.

They looked at each other, smiling. They knew they were onto something.

"I suppose that's it," he whispered. "Maybe duende says it all. Perhaps it's that voice of God, or the earth, or our dreams that we aren't listening to. Maybe duende is what the aborigines mean by 'dreamtime.' Maybe it's this spirit you're carrying, Duendita, all because your grandmother wanted you to bring some message of the earth to the world. It's a call, and you have to follow it."

Ingrid nodded. She became bigger, warmer, the pain inside her dissipating. His words resonated with Oma's message.

"You have to follow the dreams, the call, Duende."

Roger's eyes held a tender gaze.

"Even if it seems absurd, crazy, unbelievable. It will lead you home. You've got this gift, Duende... from your grandmother. There's something there. I know it, and this time I'm serious."

Tears softly released their grip from Ingrid's eyes. She knew he was right.

"Maybe it's this spirit that carries the message that's been held in the earth and by our ancestors and within us for so long that we all have to listen to it. It's shared, collective, you know," Roger said.

It was, Ingrid realized, exactly the kind of conversation she, as a child, had dreamed of having with someone, someone who would take her seriously and respond to her honestly.

Ingrid sat still, reflecting on duende and what she or others needed to hear. And she wondered whether Roger's idea that she carried the spirit of duende within her was true, or if the earth was sending a message through her and if the supernatural vegetation, the bleeding vines, and her unusual dreams, both today and many years ago, were all part of that message.

It seemed impossible. Why would she be the one, and why should her grandmother be involved? Ingrid could feel some knowing—a kind of subtle knowing—in what Roger was saying, yet it still overwhelmed her to consider the role she might have played.

Roger dropped his head down, toward his glass, and allowed his finger to circle melancholically upon its rim. A high pitch rang through the restaurant. He jumped slightly, startled, until he realized he had made the noise.

"I wish I didn't have to go back to England. It wasn't my

plan," said Roger, who yesterday had learned that he would have to cut his travels short and go back to England because his mother was ill.

"You know, for so long I wanted to come here and visit places like this that weren't tamed. I thought of how different it would be from England, where the people are so stuffy and polite. I grew up expecting everything to have a place, including me. Refined."

Ingrid listened easily. Had the magic of this country touched him as it had her?

Roger sighed. "But there was something missing. The chaos. I always felt, from what I had read about Spain and farther south, that I could come here to untame the Englishman in me. But sadly, this untaming is much more difficult than I thought. It's like drinking a good bottle of wine, feeling the release of emotions, then waking up the next day, looking in the mirror, and seeing the same stuffy man from the day before."

"You aren't *that* stuffy," Ingrid whispered, feeling sad for him. "You really aren't stuffy at all."

They had, she realized, reached a new level of intimacy.

"You know," he went on, "I feel guilty saying this and probably shouldn't, but strangely I don't want this trip to end. I'm ashamed to admit it, but a part of me wants this vine craziness and all of it to continue because, for once, I'm feeling a taste of freedom. It is so strange. Still the Englishman, but here I have an excuse to be someone else. I don't know if it's the land, the people, or these unnatural events, but—"

A light from a streetlamp shone ever so slightly in Roger's eyes. The rain of his emotions moistened his hazel gaze.

Ingrid wanted to take his hand and reach over the table to touch him, but he seemed so fragile, and she was self-conscious. "I think I know what you mean," she said instead.

Roger took a deep breath as if embarrassed by his confession. "Maybe we should get the bill."

Ingrid wanted to hear him say more and watch him as he unfolded himself. But it would have been cruel to expect too much from him. He had already exposed his vulnerability, and she was too scared to admit that she also wanted to be free, that she too was afraid of being locked in the cage that had haunted her all of her adult life.

⤷

The next morning, Roger stood near the steps of the train station, on his way home. The rain had stopped, and he was now squinting in the sun. Only hours earlier, the sun had pushed its fearless face through the clouds of the past week, sending all the gray masses out to sea.

"Well," said Roger awkwardly as he looked at the time on the station clock. "Five minutes and she comes."

Roger's face wore the same sadness he'd spoken of the previous night, of having to return to England, the land of defined roles, with no excuse to stay away. But Ingrid could tell there was a part of him that was glad to have completed this strange assignment.

She smiled at him. "Think about it. It's not too late to enjoy a day at the beach."

Ingrid was hopeful, although she knew he needed to go. She, on the other hand, had to stay a bit longer, and especially now after their life-changing conversations and her encounters with her grandmother's spirit. She wanted to see Latia, and although she was scared to find out the truth, she also hoped to find Lázaro. Every night and morning that Ingrid had listened to the waves from her pensión, she had thought about the old man, as well as her little friend that came from deep inside the sea.

She was finally ready to face her past as Roger tensed up before her. "I'm afraid it's teatime again. I've got to get back."

"Maybe you can return to Spain later, with or without a story," Ingrid said.

"It may not be so easy," he responded, putting his bag down temporarily. "And you?"

She shrugged with the same uneasiness. The life that awaited her back in Germany felt surprisingly heavy now. "We'll see."

The hand of the clock passed the hour of departure. Two minutes, then three, then five.

"Well, maybe the train won't come after all and you'll have to stay," Ingrid said.

Roger looked at the clock. "Don't think so." He then turned toward the empty track. "Spain likes to take her time, I've noticed. I'll miss that. I'll think about it when I'm in a train station like this one, in England, where everything runs on time."

Ingrid hesitated to say what was on her mind.

"I'll... miss you," she finally said. The words pressed past her mouth reluctantly, each syllable a new life, a fresh beginning. She had never told anyone that she would really miss them before.

Roger blushed. "Right. Me too."

It was strange to see him go. Ingrid had a hard time imagining Spain without Roger, and now, as he stood before her, she felt sad and weak.

Her body held the memories of last night, riding back to the pensión in silence, every breath of Roger's feeling like her own. She had felt for him, and for herself, knowing that soon this would all be over.

When they had arrived at the pensión, the lady of the house was still awake, watching television on the first floor. Upon seeing them enter, she had rushed to the door and repeated "Buena noche" several times in her choppy Andaluz accent before launching into a monologue of chatter. "How was your night? Did you go anywhere special? It sure is bad weather."

Roger and Ingrid had smiled politely, but made it clear that they were not in the mood for a real conversation, and escaped upstairs as soon as possible.

"Well, I guess it's a good night," Roger had said, giving Ingrid a quick hug and kiss.

The sound of the waves invited Ingrid into her room, where she changed into a light top and slipped into bed. As she watched the moon, half-full, its other half having already disappeared, she wondered if it too was lonely.

As if answering her question, Roger soon knocked on her door, calling out, "May I come in?"

"Sure." She had pushed her hair out of her face and made sure her shirt covered her breasts before he opened the door.

Miniscule lines of light trickled down his bare chest above his white pajama bottoms.

"Would you be offended if we slept together?" Roger had asked.

Ingrid was surprised by the unusual way he put it. *Offended?*

"I'm—I'm not proposing sex or anything," he stammered. "I just, well, I just would, eh, love to hold you. It's quite lonely in my room."

Moved by his awkwardness, Ingrid told him to close the door and made room for him in her bed.

"Are you sure this is okay?" he said. "I mean, I don't want you to feel—"

"It's—it's nice to have you here," she told him as he put his hand on her breast and held her close. Yes, it did feel right. In the slight darkness, waves filling the silence between them, they looked at each other, and then when he kissed her neck and then her lips, she was breathless.

"Good night, then," he said, pulling her close to him again. "A very good night."

Now, as they looked back and forth, from the clock to the train track, Roger and Ingrid were both quiet. "Well, don't forget to get the pictures to Franz as soon as possible," she finally said.

"I'll be right on it."

Roger yelled the last words over the sound of the train that had finally pulled into the station. A wind brushed through their clothes and hair.

"I think I've got a fast train this time," Roger said loudly, although the locomotive had already stopped.

He lifted his big backpack, which, having been rained on quite a bit during his time in Spain, had seen better days. He shrugged, looking at Ingrid with a sad grin. "Do have a good time. For me at least," he said. "And don't forget *Duende*."

"I won't."

Passengers were moving by them, already boarding the train.

"Well," Ingrid said.

Roger eased himself forward, his bag pulled behind him, and leaned over to give her a kiss. They held their kiss as long as they possibly could, breathing in the last seconds of each other.

"Right," said Roger as they pulled apart. "Until next time, Duende."

DUENDE

DUENDE

Teri-Amo pulled her door shut and limped a quick pace down the road. She moved with quick resolution for three to four blocks, then crossed Plaza Celeste and bumped against chairs emptied of afternoon coffee drinkers. With hurricane swiftness, Teri-Amo arrived at a large black door, big enough to fit three women her size.

"Dónde está Marie-Teresa?" she asked a woman sweeping below the inside stairs. A line of light illuminated the dust particles peering through the door from the outside. "Marie?" The woman shrugged. "I don't know where she is, ma'am. Probably upstairs."

Teri-Amo wanted to avoid the three long flights of stairs to Marie's place, especially if she wasn't there, but unable to wait this time, she climbed them, panting, cursing herself for smoking, for not exercising, for being so lazy. And since it was only when she faced those interminable stairs that she noticed her poor health, she cursed Marie as well, until, arriving at the top, gasping and disheveled, she found her waiting.

"Come on in. You're not going to get any younger standing out there," said Marie, as if Teri-Amo had been waiting for a while.

The big Gypsy followed Marie inside and accepted a glass of water, swallowing it in four large gulps.

"Now sit down," her friend said. "I'm still waiting for the day that you can climb those steps without gulping for air. But you know, it isn't going to get much easier with age. Now, how old are—"

"Just stop right there," Teri-Amo said, raising her hand to Marie's face. "Your youth doesn't give you the right to mock me."

Used to Teri-Amo's temper as she was, Marie brushed it off with a laugh. "So then, tell me," she said. "You always bring me the good ones."

"Well, I have an interesting puzzle for you," Teri-Amo said and proceeded to tell stories about Duende that even she found difficult to believe.

The big Gypsy's hands moved through the air—up, down, left, right—making crosses, circles, and all sorts of shapes with her fingers. She took deep breaths between each sentence, rolling strange tales from her lips. Then in one final breath, she was done. Her eyes opened wide, waiting for Marie to save her from this hurling madness.

"You think it's possible?" Marie asked when Teri-Amo had finished.

"Possible? That's why I'm here, for you to tell me."

Teri-Amo watched closely as Marie closed her eyes and disappeared to a place far from this dusty apartment, this room that had seen too many fleeting lovers in the past few months.

The big Gypsy got up, familiar with the woman's ways, and placed her empty glass in the kitchen, before returning to the couch. She knew that this was a hard one that required more than herself or Marie. This was a Gypsy quest, where multiple visions met, maybe in a church, maybe somewhere else, to do something. Teri-Amo wished she hadn't needed to consult Marie, but it had finally come to this.

Teri-Amo scanned the walls. She had never liked Marie's

wallpaper. It carried a handful of angels, their bodies floating everywhere, their flying, odd-shaped shadows merging in yellow, green, and light purple. Not the colors Teri-Amo would have chosen. There was no red, no sense of aesthetic in these images.

Occasionally she glanced back at Marie, who appeared to have fallen asleep. The window was open, the air directing itself through her short bobbed hair, lifting it up in the back. But Marie didn't seem to notice. The smell of fresh autumn drifted through the window.

"Marie," Teri-Amo called out to her friend. "Marie."

Marie opened her eyes and shook her head. "Sí, sí," she said. "I saw it all. It was all happening just as your little one envisioned it... Even I was there." She laughed. "But you weren't. Couldn't find you, and I sure looked. But the dancer, you know, Graciela, she was there. You've seen her dance, haven't you?" Marie let out a sigh. "It was beautiful, Teri-Amo."

Marie went on to explain her vision to Teri-Amo in detail, telling her what it meant and what was to happen.

"It's time for Jesus to come down from the cross, you know," she said. "We've been talking about it for centuries. Remember the story of the Gypsy blacksmith who forged the nails of the crucifixion and kept the fourth nail—or at least according to legend? And that *saeta* we've been singing forever—the one about freeing Jesus from the cross? Why this little German girl is having these dreams, I don't know. But she has the capacity to do this, and we're ready to help. It's time. Let me explain."

Marie shared the details of her vision—every sound, every smell, every visual, dramatic, political, social consequence of one leaf turning over, of one action rippling into others. Pacing from the couch to the window and back again, she seemed to be carried away by her own words.

By the time Teri-Amo left Marie's apartment she was exhausted, certain that it would take time for her to assimilate what she had been told. Even she was overwhelmed at how something so surreal, so intangible, could become reality.

She moved across the plaza again, but this time was careful not to knock over any of the chairs. She walked slowly in thought, no longer carrying her previous intensity. Marie said she'd take the story from here, bring the pieces together. Maybe Teri-Amo was just a love psychic after all, not a lifesaver anymore—especially not a lifesaver of Jesus, who wasn't alive anyway.

⌘

Duende was well aware that her dreams would soon come true—according to the Gypsy—but her attention was on blowing out nine candles on the thick chocolate cake in front of her. Today was her day. All hers. Her father was on his best behavior, insisting she make a wish first.

"Now think hard and don't tell anyone," he said.

After Duende blew out all nine candles, Mutti clapped her hands.

"Too bad your grandmother can't be here," her father added, and Duende smiled because she knew that she was, but not in the way he thought.

Of several gifts that lay before her, she reached for the biggest one first. Duende carefully took off the wrapping paper, without tearing it into pieces. Her father folded the green-and-yellow paper into an organized pile.

Duende looked puzzled at the book that now lay in her hands—the book that had been in the living room for weeks.

"You may not understand it all yet, but your grandmother wanted you to have this," her father said. "There's a bookmark between two pages that she particularly wanted you to read. It's her gift to you, even though she cannot be here to give it to you."

Duende put the book aside, comforted by hearing about Oma and knowing she was by her side, and moved to open her other gifts. They included a small chemistry set "for making magic," according to her father, and a necklace with wooden beads. Mutti then proceeded to cut the chocolate cake, Duende's favorite.

"You are getting to be a big girl there, Duende," her mother said to her lovingly.

Duende glanced back at her, grinning through chocolate-covered lips. She then finished her piece of cake just in time to see Latia appear.

"Look who's here for your birthday!" exclaimed Mutti.

Latia gave Duende a big hug and kiss, and held out a gift the girl immediately unwrapped.

Inside was a doll-like figure of a Flamenco dancer wearing a bold red dress that puffed out at the bottom, its hands raised over its head.

"You like it, Duende?" asked her mother, clearly surprised. "She's a dancer. I didn't know you like dance."

"She does now," Latia said, and Duende smiled to herself, remembering Graciela again and that late night under stars when she experienced her first true feeling of freedom. She would have loved to have celebrated her birthday with another night of dancing, but knew it was unlikely.

Soon, Duende's thoughts shifted back to the Gypsy woman she had met in the bar and the day she and Latia had gone to see her. "Your dreams will come true… shortly after your birthday," Teri-Amo had said, and now the idea of turning nine carried an immense weight to it.

"What's the matter, Duende?" Latia asked.

Duende snapped out of the grip of the Gypsy's words and looked up at Latia. She pretended she was fine.

"You like the doll, don't you?"

Duende nodded and let a soft smile stretch across her lips. She actually loved the doll.

"Oh, good," Latia said, appearing relieved. "Because it's you. The doll is you."

Duende liked the sound of Latia's words and wished her friend could be with her all the time—to make her feel good. But this time, as with others, they spent too little time before Latia was out the door.

The house became quiet as Duende's birthday celebrations fizzled out. The Gypsy's words—about her dreams coming true shortly after her birthday—returned to Duende.

She hoped desperately that the Gypsy and her grandmother were both wrong. But if they weren't, at least this day and night were hers. For now, on this birthday, Duende released any thoughts of the Gypsy and her words from her mind.

INGRID

INGRID

The last time Ingrid had seen Latia was on her birthday, when her neighbor had gifted her a dancing doll. She now carried this image with her as she walked through the streets, where the smell of *pescaíto frito*, fried fish, on open-flame grills, *parillas*, along the boardwalk, permeated the air.

Even several blocks away from the sea, past Calle Ricardo de la Vega and Pedraza Paez, Ingrid took in the scent of fried fish, sizzling in oil and browning to the color of nearby sand. The smell followed her as the road narrowed and she strolled past a rose hibiscus tree and a small ice cream stand, whose umbrella shaded a cooler of frozen food from the late-afternoon sun. She arrived close to her old home and Latia's.

Now, from where Ingrid was standing, she could see the window of her old bedroom and the wall that she had once climbed down to find her way into the night. The place appeared empty, but the colors were the same. The white walls with the green door. The flowers of violet, yellow, and red that hung from the porch. One long, deep-green strand of a plant pressed against the window of the first floor.

Inside, Ingrid imagined her mother's small piano still standing conspicuously in the corner of the living room, her bed upstairs receiving the breeze of spring mornings, and the smell of her mother cooking onions until they turned to caramel. At this time of the day, a shadow would cast itself across the living room, shading her grandmother's photographs, even her silver hair.

Turning toward Latia's house, Ingrid felt her heart begin to beat harder with anticipation. What would Latia be like now? How would she feel when she saw her?

Ingrid wished Roger were here with her, so he could meet Latia. She felt his absence keenly now as she stood in the shade of her porch, knocking and then waiting to see the woman who had once been like an older sister.

But instead of her old friend, a girl about fourteen with long black hair answered the door. She had Latia's eyes and her full, bee-stung lips.

"Hello," Ingrid said with a grin. "Is your mother here?"

"Mamá," the girl called out, and while they waited, Ingrid couldn't resist asking her what her name was.

The girl turned her head and peered down the hall. Then back at Ingrid. The hall echoed with the tapping sound of high heels.

"Tatiana," the girl said shyly.

A large woman, taller than Ingrid had remembered Latia to be, stepped out of the memory of her past. Thin lines of gray streaked her black hair, which was just as long as when Ingrid had known her, and she seemed to smile the same way, with her eyes.

"Do I know you?" Latia asked with familiar zest—the kind she used to exude when dancing or telling a tale, calling Duende from her porch.

Ingrid smiled mischievously as Latia brought her right hand to her hip, pressed her lips together, and stared at her, before finally opening her eyes wide.

"Duende," she cried. "Is it really you?"

This was the second time Ingrid would hear her old name spoken by former neighbors after so many years, and now Ingrid liked that. It assured her that she hadn't changed that much.

Excitedly, Latia rushed her into the house and introduced her to her family. There was Tatiana, the girl who had opened the door, and two other children, eleven-year-old Marco and the youngest, Duende.

Ingrid was taken aback when she heard the name of Latia's ten-year-old daughter. She didn't seem much like Latia, nor did she look like the Constantino Ingrid had remembered. His features had been very narrow, unlike this little one.

Duende was short and plump. She too had blue eyes, which Latia explained was the reason she had named her as she had.

"I almost didn't give her your name because until I had met you, I had never heard of anyone calling their child Duende," she explained. "But she kept looking at me with those blue eyes, and I saw you in her so I couldn't help but call her that. Isn't she cute? She has those curls you used to have too."

Ingrid wondered if this little girl would live the same fate Ingrid's grandmother had bestowed on her. Had she already lived it?

While the children went off to play, Latia told her own tale of how she had married Constantino only months after Ingrid—or Duende, back then—had left. She had been twenty-two then and she knew that if she didn't have children soon, she would feel frustrated and incomplete. So she married Constantino, and for five years they tried to conceive. That was when she returned to the big Gypsy, "The Love Queen," whom she had sworn she would never visit again, not since meeting Constantino and since Duende's Jesus encounter with the woman.

Ingrid shivered at the mention of the Gypsy and Jesus. She looked around the room she was in, scanning the walls. After all these years, she was surprised Latia had remembered.

"There were many times I wished I had never taken you to that woman," said Latia. "What she said to you concerned me."

"It's okay, Latia," Ingrid lied. "It wasn't like it happened yesterday. I've long forgotten."

As she said these words, she could see the big woman again in her mind's eye—the way she scared her in the bar, standing in the shadow, hovering above her. She couldn't imagine seeing her again.

"I didn't want to go to her, but I needed her help."Latia shrugged with the helplessness of that time so long ago. "I told her why I had come, and she brought me inside to a back room, which was only slightly neater. There she looked at my palms, not at the ball as she used to do, but the palms, reading my lines. She told me that I may never have children, said my lines didn't show any, but then—"

Latia crossed her chest, her eyes facing the ceiling. It seemed the Gypsy who had made Ingrid tremble so had given her friend a sense of hope.

"Before I had a chance to say anything, she told me that it wasn't altogether hopeless and that she'd make me a remedy that could change all that. She said to take the potion right before making love for the next two times," said Latia, "and to make love no more than two days apart at a certain time of the day and at a certain time of the month and for a certain length of time, and on and on. She said it all so quickly, and since I didn't have anywhere to write it down, I walked home that day repeating her instructions over and over again until I had them memorized."

"Of course," Latia went on, "Constantino knew *nothing* at all about this. That night when we made love, Constantino thought I had gone mad. I clocked everything down to the second, instructed him on what to do and when, and I kept telling him it was all so we could finally make babies. He kept looking at me as though I was mad, but he could see that I was serious—mad or not—and so he kept working away."

By this time Latia was shaking with laughter.

"Poor Constantino. He was exhausted. But look, three *bambinos*. Something worked. I had the baby, the first one conceived days after the workout, and then the rest, they just happened, like that, without anything."

Although Ingrid was amused, she also marveled at Latia's persistence.

"I returned to thank the woman," she concluded, "and to finally pay her, but when I went, the place was empty, the red curtain was gone, the window cleared out. She had skipped town. Probably had the officials after her. But I do wish I could have thanked her. She saved my life. No matter how badly she scared me, she saved my life. But Duende, enough about me. What about you? It's been so long."

Ingrid, who had been staring into the space between her and Latia, shifted her gaze toward Latia. "I *can* say that it is really good to see you," she said finally. "I think I forgot what it was I had missed. It's nice to be back, back to Spain, to Málaga, back here."

Latia smiled. "It's a great gift to see you. I never thought I'd see you again. So young then and you left for another life. Do you like it there?"

"Yes," Ingrid said with slight hesitation. "I think so. But I never thought I would be back here either. It reminds me of what I don't have."

"Like what?"

"The sun, the warmth, people like you, the sea—although we have mountains and lakes."

Ingrid told Latia about life in Germany, about her love life—or lack of one—and about her work at *Die Kelter*, explaining that she had come back to Spain to cover the story of the vines.

"So you came here because of the vines?" Latia exclaimed. "I've heard about them. Did you find out anything juicy?"

"The vines were still growing out of control when we were there a few days ago," Ingrid told her. "They claim they were bleeding, but I don't buy it, although some vines did bear grapes before we left." Her chest grew heavy as she spoke. "As far as I'm concerned, I don't want to see another vine."

"You know, it's strange," Latia said. "It's like when you left here. I mean, there were vines growing like that in the church, after somebody took Jesus off the cross. It was right after you left here."

Ingrid swallowed deeply as she took in Latia's words. *Vines growing in a church?* She thought of her recent dream of the green masses sprouting from the church floor. The place had seemed familiar. "What church?" she asked, trying not to show her surprise.

"You left right when things were getting interesting around here. Málaga was big news everywhere," Latia explained. "Somebody took Jesus down off the cross at La Iglesia del Mar. It was amazing."

Ingrid felt her head heat up as she took in a deep breath.

"People everywhere were crowding around the church to see for themselves how the vines were taking over. They were kneeling and praying and calling it the devil's work or an omen from Franco's dead spirit. I didn't believe that one for a minute."

Latia sat back in her chair and rested her elbows lightly on its arms. She had, Ingrid realized, been so wrapped up in telling her story that Latia had not noticed the discomfort she was causing.

"I think it was a miracle if you ask me—a good one. I went down there myself, tried to see inside, but I couldn't get anywhere close. Priests, bishops, and cardinals were coming here to see the church for themselves—to see the vines and green plants growing everywhere. Even the Pope came. Can you imagine, the Pope in Málaga?

"Everyone was waiting to hear what the Pope would say. Funny how the rumors all stopped—the ones about Franco coming back from his grave, and Satan, and miracles. They all stopped when the Pope arrived. There were some who had their ears to the ground, others up toward heaven—wherever they thought God would be—waiting for the Pope's verdict. Ironically enough, he never gave his verdict, or at least not a verdict any of us could hear. He came and left in silence, and soon Málaga was as full of rumors as before."

How had it happened, Ingrid wondered, that the Pope had said nothing? Had it been because he had no idea what had caused Christ's descent from the cross? Or had he guessed and felt it better not to say?

"There were some people, Gypsies actually, who claimed that the green growth in the church represented the voice of Christ and all of his descendants finally expressing the lessons of Jesus from thousands of years ago. Imagine! Descendants of Jesus. That would mean that he *had* children and that the Catholic Church has been lying all this time. And get this: It would also mean that Mary Magdalene wasn't the whore the church made her out to be, but Jesus's wife, his beloved, and the mother of his children. And that all this time, Jesus was like one of us. He was a teacher who had something to say, and yet nobody was listening..."

Ingrid couldn't believe her ears. Latia's words took her back to her conversation with Roger about listening, or more accurately about everyone not listening, and then the vines... *Were those the dreams we weren't listening to? And did these dreams have something to do with Jesus and what he tried to teach, and how his descendants were coming back through the earth to teach us what we hadn't learned?*

Ingrid hoped Latia hadn't noticed the small drops of sweat rolling down her forehead. She wiped them back as she tried to get her head around her friend's words. It was all so odd, and yet... her dreams of the vines and her night in Señor Ramos's field and the inexplicable appearance of grapes were as real to her as the blue sky.

"The Gypsies were saying that the time had come to take Jesus off the cross," Latia said. "They wanted to bring back the Jesus who walked on water, the one who made miracles happen, not the one who had suffered because we weren't listening.

"Imagine, this vine, the hidden family of Jesus, rises from the grounds of the church, just because somebody takes Jesus off the cross. As if taking him off the cross frees him to finally be heard and changes our consciousness."

"What did he want to say?" Ingrid asked.

"Well, I sure don't have the answers," Latia said. "But maybe the Gypsies were right. Maybe he was trying to tell us that we, too, can walk on water, that miracles are possible every day, and that our drive toward suffering and our tendency to pray to God to deliver us from the suffering we have created isn't what it's all about, that our focus on suffering is actually an insult to the magic around us, and it stops us from listening to what's really here on this earth."

Ingrid took in every word, trying to assimilate her experiences with what she was hearing. She remained stunned by the fact that vines had grown in the church and that they may still be there now, yet she wondered what to make of Latia's comments.

As a child, she had been told that her family name, Rebe, had been important, and that it meant "vine." Was her family related to these descendants of Jesus Latia spoke of? If so, was Ingrid, as Duende, being asked to free, through her actions, an ancient truth passed down through her forgotten lineage? Was this truth the same truth Roger had spoken about—about duende and the earth wanting us to listen, maybe wanting us to listen to a different dream of abundance instead of the one of Jesus suffering on a cross for our sins?

Latia appeared to notice Ingrid's overwhelmed state, yet was oblivious to what was really going on. "Oh, poor Duende. I'm sorry I'm going on like this about something you probably don't care about. I mean, maybe the vine part is interesting for your story, but the rest… Look, I've got a great idea. Why don't we go out to that bar where you used to go dancing. Before you go back to Germany. That would be more exciting than talking about something that happened twenty years ago."

As Ingrid pulled out of her trance, she realized it was a perfect place to go. "But—but is it still there?" she asked.

"It's still there, but it's changed," Latia told her. "I don't think you'll see the Gypsies there, but it's been awhile since I last went. Years, maybe. You know a lot has changed. The tourists go to those kinds of places now. They're all cleaned up, and if they're not, they're seedy places that I rarely go to. But you never know what we'll find if we go."

"Let's go, Latia," Ingrid said, relieved to be distracted by something so down-to-earth. "I want to see what's happened to that place."

Latia was apparently as excited as Ingrid to go. "You know, I still can't believe you went to that bar at night and danced there all on your own. And so young."

Ingrid smiled as Latia played with her hair, pulling at small strands of early grays woven into the black. "This old lady hasn't been out in a while. I may not be able to keep up with you now," she said.

"You're not old at all."

Latia, who seemed content with Ingrid's comment, suggested she stay with them for a few days. "Constantino can go out with us as well. I'll even let you dance a few steps together again. But," she said, then stopped and pointed her finger at Ingrid, "never forget, he's mine."

For two nights now, Ingrid thought she could hear the dark-haired children. She heard them calling her from the streets. But instead, when she looked out the window of her room at Latia's house, she saw what seemed like a flutter of pigeons or rodents crawling in and out of dark holes along the pavement.

On one of the nights, Ingrid heard a scraping sound, which she could have sworn was her, years younger, crawling down the wall outside the bedroom. She waited for this self to jump to the ground and to hear the girl she had once been walking in the direction of the bar. But instead, the sound stopped, and by the time she rose to look out, all was still and there was no one about. She stood by the window for several minutes and began to sense her body as if waking from a dream. She was her own ghost, as aware of her double presence as that stillness that called her from her sleep.

When Ingrid awoke the next day she tried to shake that sensation of a double presence from her body. But it clung to her like the shadow of the earth itself, dancing the death of her past through her. She could feel her bones aching to move to the rhythm of her forgotten self. The sounds of the streets now haunted her, the memory of the old Gypsy movement like a dammed river inside calling her back.

That evening, Latia and Constantino accompanied Ingrid as she rounded the corner to the bar. It was a Saturday night, and people filled the streets with the sound of chatter, laughter, and drunken joy, but this time there weren't any Gypsy children running alongside.

The door to the bar was open when they arrived. Several men stood there, talking and watching prostitutes who leaned against the opposite wall, smoking, their miniskirts grazing their thighs.

The bar was full, every seat occupied by young men and women, even teenagers, some of whom, in their thin, cracked black leather jackets, looked like thugs. Latia smiled an uncomfortable smile while Constantino just looked at Ingrid, waiting to see her reaction.

She had none. Tables of young people filled the place where

the dance floor had once been. The kids smoked and talked, but the music Ingrid had remembered was gone. Gone were the Gypsies and the sound of Paquito's voice of sorrow rising like a spirit and taking everyone with him. A younger, more self-absorbed crowd now occupied this space.

With no place to sit, they wandered to the rear of the bar, where, to their surprise, they found a man playing guitar and mumbling so softly that no one seemed to be listening. Looking up at them, the man smiled a welcome, and after Constantino brought their drinks and one for the man, he joined them in a toast.

Ingrid began reminding Latia and Constantino of how this place used to be, with Paquito and his voice of sorrow, and Graciela, who lifted dust from the ground with the force of her feet, and whose shoulders grew wings as she danced, her eyes saying "follow me." She reminisced about the corner of the room where the women once danced in rivers of color, and the audience applauded as if they too were moving on the floor. And then she described the night when the bartender tried to take her home and how the Gypsy woman had come out of the shadows of the bar proclaiming she knew her, and how she had known about her dreams.

Every now and then Latia glanced over at her husband as though to gauge his reaction, but instead of disapproval, he showed interest. It was no different from the time they had met him at the intersection. Even back then it hadn't seemed to bother him that a child like Duende had visited a Gypsy bar. In fact, his own comment was "Good gracious," while waiting for more.

Ingrid suddenly wished the chairs, the tables, and the walls themselves could tell the tales of what had once been in this place, that they too could speak and hear Constantino and his "*Caramba.*"

"Do you remember how to dance, Duende?" he asked her finally.

Ingrid shook her head. "Not much, and certainly not the way I learned to dance here."

Constantino whispered something to the old man, who began to hum a softer song that was unfamiliar to Ingrid, but not to Latia and Constantino, who, grinning, began to dance. Constantino took several steps back, clearing space with his passion, and then raised his chest and hands behind his waist. With his body in position, he leaned his hips forward, bending one knee, then the other, while pressing down on the front of his foot and forcing his heel into the ground. Constantino looked beautifully elegant, and at that moment Ingrid could see why Latia had warned her not to try to take her man from her.

Latia equaled Constantino's grace. She stared at him with her head up high and then eased her body into a similar position as his, but with her hands and arms unrestrained. Arching her wrists and twisting her fingers, she moved so gracefully that a small audience gathered around them.

It occurred to Ingrid to wonder whether her friends had the spirit of duende in them. Was the wind moving through their limbs, were stones tumbling their mass of memory through their bones, or were their hearts beating mountains, rivers, and seas into the room? Or were they just dancing like all the rest of them, never stopping long enough between the pauses of movement to listen to the force move within themselves?

The two moved closer, their eyes fixed on each other for a brief moment, and then sharply, abruptly, they turned and crossed each other, Latia's hair floating around her head, staring into the distance, until she was back, facing Constantino.

He lifted his arms above him and then in front of him, clapping as he allowed Latia to dance solo to his rhythmic beat. At his signal, she lifted her skirt and began to tap her feet quickly and intensely against the floor. Constantino's clapping battled to keep up, while the music man was now sweating, his fingers breaking the tension of the strings of his surrendering guitar.

The small group of onlookers also began to clap and shout, while sweat poured along Latia's brow and down her chest. Constantino grinned with his head lifted high.

At just the right moment, he joined Latia again in dance, and the two of them played off each other until they were both exhausted and the audience in the bar had lost interest. Ingrid watched in amazement, feeling the room come alive again, just as it had once done when Graciela and Paquito were still there.

"*Ves*, Duende," Latia said, breathless after dancing. "You see, I may be getting old, but I can still dance."

Ingrid laughed. "You will never be old to me Latia, no matter how many grays you get."

Latia frowned at the reminder of her grays. "You will always be my younger little sister, you know, even after twenty-odd years."

Constantino paid, and the three of them walked back outside. Once outside, under the stars, Constantino turned to Ingrid and asked her why she hadn't danced.

"Like you do?" she exclaimed. "Your dancing was too beautiful for me to even try to match it. Remember, I was only eight then, and barely that, and anything I learned of Flamenco was in one night."

"An amazing night, though."

"Yes," Ingrid said, aware of a sudden sadness and longing to be Duende again, to be that little girl who had felt freedom for the first time.

"Well, you can't leave Spain without dancing!" Constantino said when they finally reached that part of the street that separated Latia's house and the place Ingrid had called home as a girl. "Come on. We'll dance here. Just follow me."

Ingrid hesitated, but he was already moving into place. "Okay, just follow me," said Constantino, and with that she eased into the dance, sliding into a reminiscence that had shadowed her during the past few days, the movements of this ancient dance slowly coming back to her.

Soon Latia joined them, dancing behind her so that Ingrid was embraced by their two bodies, carrying the grace of a swan she had wanted to mimic, becoming a mirror of both Constantino and Latia as they danced a three-way Flamenco. They moved with increasing ease, so much so that neighbors began opening windows, some calling out their names—that is, until the neighbor who lived in Ingrid's old home asked them all to keep it down.

Ingrid looked up at the woman's window after she disappeared from sight, and thought back to that first night when she had danced home through the streets and climbed up to where she had stood.

She could now feel the freedom of that time long ago reviving her, of having once danced to the rhythm of Graciela, of Gypsies, and of having known peace in her movement. The rhythm didn't belong to anyone. It came from the earth and it moved through every bend and twist of her body.

"It's good to have you back," said Latia.

"It's been too long," Ingrid told her, and as Latia opened her arms wide, she stepped forward into her embrace.

"If it weren't for you, Duende, you dancing in the street like this, I would never have met Latia," Constantino observed under the starlit sky.

Latia winked at Constantino while her head rested upon Ingrid's shoulder. She then reached her hand out to him and he took it, pulling her into him.

"Beautiful Latia," he said.

Constantino and Latia kissed, and then all three went inside, to bed, where Ingrid dreamed of the sea and the face of the old man, Lázaro, in the doorway of his house.

DUENDE

DUENDE

Duende had every reason for her heart to skip a beat when she walked past the doorway of La Iglesia del Mar on her way to school, the day after her ninth birthday.

She had always marveled at the way this church towered over the rest of the buildings, tall and magnificent above the narrow street, but had never dared enter. Duende had avoided churches all her life, and with her dreams about Jesus, she had even less desire to go through their doors.

But today she saw her grandmother's spirit appearing and disappearing in a white cloud in front of three wide steps leading to the church.

"Go now. Go inside," she heard Oma say.

Her grandmother, taller and larger than usual, stood in front of her in the light of day. And although seeing her today was the last thing Duende wanted, she had no choice but to stop.

"It's time," her Oma said, her arms stretching out toward the big doors of the church, her finger pointing for her granddaughter to follow. "Go inside."

Duende tried to dance around her grandmother—to the left, right, back home—but it was no use. She was spirit, after all, and the size of her ethereal body was much greater than Duende's body.

"Go," Oma insisted. "Go"

Duende stood frozen, frightened. And when she took a step, reluctantly, she looked around her to see if others had noticed. No one seemed to have. She was alone, taking another step up the stairs with her grandmother behind her, almost pushing her forward.

Duende opened a big, heavy door with mere thought and a bit of help from her grandmother. She stepped into the cool, musty interior.

The door slammed shut behind her, a loud wind knocking on the other side. "Are you sure you want to do this?" the wind called out. "No!" Duende wanted to shout. She stood in the back of the church, between pews that bordered a path to a distant altar. *Are you sure you want to do this?*

Duende caught sight of the stained-glass window to her right. Multicolored light ran down the narrow window as she walked toward the flying figures that appeared to approach her.

Duende especially liked the color blue. It wrapped a blanket around one of the winged ones. The morning glowed through it, yellow beads of light spreading like stars inside the deep blue.

She could picture her dancing doll in this window, curving itself between the deep blue and a yellow roundness that may have been the sun, or maybe the moon. How wonderful it would be to place her doll there, let her twirl around and around, melt all the colors into one gigantic kaleidoscope.

Duende momentarily forgot her fear of churches. For a brief period, she was like Lázaro, enchanted by the colors and grandeur. But then she turned away from the window, inward, and noticed, to her left, behind the altar, Jesus. Yes, that was Jesus, just as he had appeared in her dreams, hanging there almost naked, looking down at her.

Two young women stood to the left of the altar, lighting candles, praying toward Jesus, as a man, carrying no less than a century in his body, walked slowly, leaning on his cane, holding onto the pews with his other hand, while gasping for air. He was the man with the cane whom Duende had seen in her dreams; the cane that had carefully carved lines of stubborn existence into the ground; the cane that knew its way from years of walking.

Recognizing the dream within this scene made Duende sad. She felt helpless without knowing why. She had been urged into the church without knowing why. She should have been out-side, on her way to school, but instead she was in this imposing structure, one she'd never entered but felt she knew well from her dreams.

Duende turned as she heard a sound knocking against the window, and thought that perhaps it was a bird with its flutter-ing wings on the other side of the colors. Black flashes danced behind angels, birds' wings waving wildly on the outside. They too didn't know where to go, except upward and inward toward a colorful place, a landscape of images moving inside them-selves, playing off each other in an ethereal abstraction.

The girl listened for the old man's breath, but couldn't hear him anymore. She lifted and turned her head to scan the inside of the stone edifice and found him sitting three rows from the front of the church. *He made it,* she thought. *He actually made it.* His cane was propped up in front of him with his hands hidden somewhere in his lap. Duende followed the path of his eyes and saw that he was looking at Jesus. Walking closer to take a better look, resting her trembling hand on a pew as the old man had done, she concentrated on the crown of thorns, the nail pinning his feet to the cross, and the blood streaming from his hands.

Why was Jesus wearing that thing on his head? she won-dered. Duende didn't recall that part in her dream.

"Jesus," she called out with no response.

Then something suddenly seemed strange. Duende realized that she was alone, and a sense of foreboding overwhelmed her. The old man was gone, and even her grandmother's spirit, and she and Jesus confronted each other in silence.

She gazed at Jesus, whose eyes appeared to open wider and look toward the entrance to the church. Duende faced the heavy doors, saw through them and beyond them, as she was capable of doing. Moving shadows carried shouts and singing that grew louder until a throng of Gypsies pushed against the doors, and boldly announced their presence.

"Jesus. We have come to get you!" the Gypsies cried out frantically.

Duende looked back at Jesus with a strong desire to release the man whose eyes grew bigger, turning a deep color, and whose chest expanded to push off from the nails that firmly held him in place. His lips became a liquid smile. Duende couldn't help but feel he was looking directly at her, calling out to her as he had in her dreams, although now she also heard the voice of her sea friend.

"You are your thoughts, especially here," she could hear him say as she pictured her friend becoming bigger and bigger, disappearing into the crystalline structure in the center of the earth.

Duende followed his advice and let her body, with all of her thoughts and dreams of taking Jesus off the cross, expand into the church. "Now's the time," she heard as the group of Gypsies, led by Graciela, screamed and danced in circles, stomping the floor wildly. Duende's body shook with a vibration that coursed through her, and all the Gypsies' pain and longing joined with hers to take Jesus off the cross.

It didn't matter if what was happening was in her mind or not, because she could feel her own ache and that of humanity ready to be freed from the chains of their illusions.

Jesus was ready too; she sensed it. He waited on the cross, crying, as the Gypsies echoed the sound of birds banging against windows wanting to get inside. Their feet pounded the floor, storms of rhythm raging into action. Now there were hundreds of birds wanting to get inside. The sound escalated to drumming. There was nowhere to go but inside this madness, over which Teri-Amo's voice echoed, and then her laugh.

"You don't know your power, Duende. I told you. I told you so."

Duende remained strong and big, holding onto the intention of her dreams. At the same time, though, she could feel her hands tighten on the pew as, in her mind's eye, she saw Latia reaching for her, dragging her out of the fortune-teller's place. And now Constantino dancing in front of her. Then Graciela. Then the doll that Latia had given her. And then her father handing her the gift of Oma's book, and just now the sound of Oma's voice, and the louder, more strident voice of Teri-Amo saying, "Around your birthday..."

Duende watched the Gypsy's figure appear in the dark corner of the bar, limping forward to announce her name, "I am Teri-Amo." And then she saw herself, Duende, hurrying out of the bar, trying to escape the image of the big Gypsy, feeling much as she suddenly did now, the desire to escape that place she had also felt in the center of the earth with all the screaming and disconnect that happens when too much power is misused.

But the Gypsies were calling, "Here we come," as they climbed a ladder to Jesus, with Graciela at the top, pulling, prying with a hammer's head to pull the nails from Jesus and the wood. With Duende's concentration and will, she forced the old gray metal from his body while the Gypsies carefully balanced on the ladder. The first nail slipped out, moving gracefully through the air until it reached the stone floor with a loud clang. The entire church echoed with the sound of the nail. The echo of almost two thousand years.

The noise broke Duende's concentration as she followed the nail with her eyes, watching it make somersaults until it landed in front of the Virgin Mary.

The second nail, the one at his feet, fell with an equally loud sound, and then the third with a thud that shattered any stillness remaining in the church. The Gypsies carefully caught Jesus as he fell, receiving him with their hands wrapped around his wood-carved body turned to flesh.

Duende watched as the dark-eyed ones carried him away, dancing and singing saetas, ancient Gypsy verses. And then the girl turned to where, only moments ago, Jesus had been, the cross now empty. It was barren, and for some reason she felt as sad at the sight of this as she had seeing Jesus up there. She cried, feeling her dreams completing themselves, as she shrunk back into her small form.

What had just happened? What—

Overwhelmed and suddenly lost, Duende nervously approached the empty cross. A light had just gone out and only a compelling instinct led her through the darkness. She couldn't reach the cross. Too high. But then she remembered the nails. One was somewhere near the Virgin, who, Duende saw, was weeping.

"Duende." She thought Mary had spoken, but the sound wasn't coming from her. "Duende. Go ahead, take it." The little girl looked around her but couldn't figure out the origin of the voice. "Go ahead," it repeated.

She inched her hand closer to the thick metal piece lying on the ground. It was old and rusted, rubbed in red. About to pick it up, Duende heard voices approaching the church, from the side door.

"Quick, pick it up," she heard again, this time recognizing the voice as her grandmother's. "Put it in your satchel." Duende did as she was told and turned to run out the main doors. She moved swiftly as the voices inched closer. She was scared she would get caught. And for what? What had just happened?

The weight of the nail in her bag pushed down on her shoulders as Duende opened the big door. She wondered if any of this was real, if what she had just witnessed was real. She couldn't help but turn around one last time, to gaze up at the cross and see if Jesus was still there.

He wasn't. He wasn't there. It was time to wake up, to escape from this dream. But people were coming through the side door. Duende could hear them enter the church as she ran down the steps, the door banging behind her.

∽

"Niña," a man said. "Niña." His voice hovered over Duende, becoming louder with time.

The man followed by tapping her shoulders, apparently trying to shake her awake.

Duende wanted to keep sleeping. "Leave me alone," she would have told him if she weren't in too much of a trance to respond.

The man shook her even more and began slapping her face. Duende got irritated, but tried to stay asleep until he desperately cried out for her to respond. "*Niña, por Diós*, wake up!"

Duende opened her eyes to the sight of a police officer smiling. *Where am I?* she thought.

"You're on the sidewalk, young lady," the officer said, seemingly reading her mind while still smiling. "It looks like you passed out. Are you okay?"

Duende propped herself up by her arms and tilted her head to the right. The steps of La Iglesia del Mar rose from the sidewalk about ten feet away from her, and at her side, still wrapped around one arm, lay her satchel.

She panicked, wondering, for a brief moment, how she had gotten to this place. But then she remembered. The satchel. The nail. She looked down at her bag, remembering its new weight.

Duende rose abruptly and completely as the police officer tried to slow her down. All that had happened in the church came flooding back to her.

"Young lady, be careful. You could faint," the man said.

The only thing she was concerned with was grabbing her bag and running off to school before he found out what was in it. She yearned to return to her ordinary life, away from this man who began questioning her now, suspicious apparently that something had happened in the church into which, she now saw, other officers were hurrying.

Duende looked away from the officer, in the direction of her school.

"Not so quick, *niña*," he said. "I'm taking you home. Where do you live?"

She shook her head, unable to talk. She had lost a part of herself.

"I need to make sure you're okay."

Duende attempted to resist him with the weight of the guilt inside her bag, but he insisted on returning her home, and she had no option but to accompany him, to show him, without words, the way.

As they walked the route Duende had come, she anticipated her father's wrath, and the response her mother would give to her.

"Señora," the officer said when Mutti opened the door. "I found your daughter passed out on the sidewalk. She won't speak, but I figure she was on her way to school. It was near that church, La Iglesia del Mar. She hasn't said a word since I found her, so I don't know what happened."

"Duende," Mutti said in an apprehensive tone. "Are you okay? What happened?" She leaned down toward her daughter, looking carefully at her.

Duende just nodded as if to say she was fine.

"I'm sorry to have taken up your time, officer. And I thank you for bringing my daughter home to me. I'll find out what happened."

The officer nodded and left.

"Duende," Mutti said as she closed the door behind her. "You're going to have to talk at some point here. Especially when your father comes home. He's going to want to know what happened. You passed out on the sidewalk, for God's sake. And

I'll have to call the school. They'll be wondering what happened to you."

Duende looked at the floor.

"And since you're home, why don't you go change," Mutti added. "I'll wash your uniform and you can work on homework and clean your room. Might as well make use of this day off."

Duende wasn't surprised by her mother's absence of compassion. She was used to it. Taking her satchel into her room, she closed the door behind her. She found a place to hide the nail temporarily and prepared to act like nothing out of the ordinary had happened.

That didn't go over well, though, when her father came home later that evening and questioned her repeatedly about what had occurred. Duende refused to speak, which made him even more upset. He translated her silence as defiance, and sent her to her room.

She barely left her room that night or the following day, a Saturday, other than to eat or go to the bathroom. And she didn't speak anymore either, despite her father's prodding. Instead, the next night, when everyone was asleep, Duende took the nail out from under her bed, placed it in her satchel, and walked down to the sea. Her tired feet followed a familiar path to the water below stars that hovered like fireflies.

The news of Jesus and the nail had already reached her home, and every other home in Málaga. So Duende knew it was only a matter of time before authorities would come searching for this heavy, cumbersome object that she now carried in her satchel.

The only thing she had to do was remove the nail from her room, to erase its presence from her life, so she could begin to forget what had happened at La Iglesia del Mar.

Now, as Duende walked below bright stars, she stepped onto the sand. The weight of the nail intensified as her feet shuffled through the granules. She wished she didn't have the nail with her, that what had happened had merely been an illusion as she hurried by Lázaro's house, where a candle was burning inside. The last person she had wanted to tell was Lázaro. He would be angry.

In the light of a full moon, Duende could see that she had reached the spot where her grandmother had spoken to her, and feeling desperately alone, she began digging in the sand, determined not to stop.

The night air beat at her face, offering little consolation as she began removing pebbles and sand with a spoon. She was alone, digging noiselessly while sea water rolled onto the gravel in the distance.

She would bury the nail so far down that no one would find it. No one would find it, until maybe, in a distant age, an archeologist might discover it and imagine this strange object of little or no use to have come from the sea, to have been swept in by the current many years earlier. The mystery of the other day in the church would remain as such, just as the true teachings of Christ and the Apostles, and an entire lifetime of human habitation on this earth, would remain a silent past.

Finally, the hole was a foot deep, enough to place the nail inside. When the weight of the nail landed headfirst into the ground, Duende covered it with more dirt and pebbles. And then, holding her hands firmly above it, she pressed her own weight against it and marked the burial spot with a large stone. Not that she ever wanted to come back here again.

Never. Never again.

INGRID

INGRID

Never had Ingrid expected to be back. Not back here where she inched her feet into Málaga's warm sand on this late-summer afternoon, retracing the route she had traveled that fateful night with the nail twenty years ago. It was one step, then another. The gray, granular sand that had been pulled up from the seafloor millions of years ago filled her shoes as she walked several hundred feet from where Lázaro used to live.

The beachfront appeared quiet. People tanned and swam, and in the distance, beyond the thinned-out crowds, several old men sat by the sea, waiting with their fishhooks in the water. Ingrid smiled as she felt warm air rise from the chanting Mediterranean waters and smelled the suntan lotion and fish.

She headed to where Lázaro's house had once stood, but as she approached the old dry riverbed, she couldn't see his shack or, for that matter, any shack. Only a new and unfamiliar board-walk, where she found an elderly man on a park bench.

"Shacks?" he said, surprised, after Ingrid inquired about them. "They cleaned this place up, I'd say ten years ago. No shacks to speak of."

"But I think there were others too, over there," she said, pointing.

The man looked at her with pity. "When did you say you were here last?"

"About twenty years ago."

"A long time. Lady, a lot changes, you know."

The man had only lived in El Palo for the past fifteen years. He pointed toward the sea, where one of the old men was fishing, and suggested Ingrid speak to him. "If there's anyone who can help you, it's him."

Was it possible that any of these men had known Lázaro? She remembered how the sea had been crawling with fishermen when she had come to visit Lázaro years ago. She recalled the activity, the noise, the smell, as the men hauled their barrels of fish. She had been told that now the sea was empty of their presence. Too many of them had depleted the waters, and it was illegal to make a real living from the sea.

Ingrid approached the lone man who sat gazing at the horizon, waiting for the line of his fishing rod to jerk and inform him that he'd caught something. She kneeled next to him, but before she had a chance to say anything, he spoke.

"Hello, young lady," the man said, still looking straight ahead of him. "Somebody tell you to come see me?"

"I'm told you know this place better than anyone."

"I suppose that's true. Everyone else left for a better life, but there's no other life for me," he said. "I'm Antonio. There aren't a lot of old-timers like me anymore, you know. But I actually left this place when I was eighteen, got out of here during the Spanish Civil War. Communists like me weren't liked very much in those days. Went to France and then came back shortly before the old geezer, El Caudillo, died. But yeah, I know this place pretty well."

The line of Antonio's fishing rod jerked briefly, but it soon became apparent he hadn't caught a thing. "So what can I do for you?"

Ingrid asked him if he had ever known or heard of Lázaro, and to this he nodded slowly and self-assuredly. "That old man, you mean, the one who once lived in a shack right over there." He pointed toward where Lázaro had lived.

Ingrid opened her eyes wide.

"Gone. No, shack. No old man," Antonio said. "Must have been at least ten years ago when they cleared out his place. It was when they asked the locals to move their shacks out of here. They made it real nice for the tourists. Money, you know. Kind of does look better. But now that I think about it, I don't believe the old man was around when the others left. Didn't take much, you know, just a few strips of cane and metal and the like. Plus, if I recall right, something happened to the man. It had to do with that church."

Ingrid shuddered at the memory of what had happened to Lázaro. She had wanted to forget. How long had he been put away?

"Many years earlier, before they got rid of all the shacks, this young lady comes by here. Looks about your age. Well, maybe older... Pretty."

The old man grinned, reminiscing. "She comes up and, like you, asks me about the old man, if I had seen him lately. And I think about it and realize, 'No, I haven't seen the man in quite some time. Probably since that church thing happened.' I figured she knew about what had happened, but thought he'd have come back home since then. Can't lock someone away too long for that craziness."

Ingrid nodded as her throat tightened. "But the lady?"

"Well, she tells me she's the man's daughter, and I almost fall down when I hear it. Just surprised me that the man would have a daughter, and beautiful at that." He smiled again.

In picturing Lázaro's daughter, Ingrid found herself weaving the strands together. That day Ingrid had met her felt like yes-terday. She had been beautiful.

"I tell her what I can, and then she informs me that she's been trying to find him for quite some time, come down to his place looking for him, and each time there's no one," the old man continued. "She looks worried. Says his stuff is still in the place and that maybe she'll clear it out and leave a note—that way it won't get stolen. And then she asks me if I think that's okay. I nod. What was I supposed to say? Barely knew the guy, to tell you the truth. He kept to himself."

With that the man lifted his hands in the air and frowned. "That's all I can tell you. Don't know where the old man went. Could be dead for all I know."

Dead? Ingrid gulped. She would have done anything right now to see Lázaro still alive. Just to know he was okay, and that what she had done had not harmed him. The weight of her guilt, of the possibility of her worst nightmares being true, descended upon her as she walked back to Lázaro's old site.

He had been an invitation, a door that was invariably ajar, unceasingly there for her. And now Ingrid missed that, felt the loss. Everything had changed.

She looked at the space where she presumed Lázaro's house had once stood, hoping that perhaps some relic of the past would uncover itself before her eyes.

With wishful thinking but no results, Ingrid walked on, along the boardwalk and onto the sand that lay several hundred feet from the dry riverbed. It was here Ingrid believed that she had buried the nail, the nail that had fallen from the cross on that fateful day so long ago, and the nail that, when found, would unearth her past.

The better part of her hoped that she would not find it. Unearthing the nail would prove that what she had dismissed as imagination or a child's fantasy had actually been real. Real would have been the Gypsies taking Jesus off the cross. Real would have been the nail that had weighed her backpack down in the dark of night as she had carried it to its grave. Real would have been her dreams that had held their secret in the earth because she hadn't been ready to hear them.

Frightened, Ingrid dug for the rusted metal. If she found it, she would have to face a reality that would be as true to her as the earth that gathered below her fingernails. There was no turning back.

For several hours she dug, using not only her hands and feet, but stones with sharp edges to soften the sand. But in all the places she had imagined the nail would be, she found nothing. Only coins, paper, and plastic wrappers.

⤺

As nighttime arrived and the fishermen moved out to sea, marking lines in the water as they disappeared in the distance, Ingrid sat by the water's edge feeling utterly defeated.

She had no place to go but inside the prison she had created for her heart. For all she knew, Lázaro had died, and the nail she had buried was gone, never to be seen again. All that had happened—all the dreams she had been told to follow—had been for nothing, nothing but heartache and guilt.

Why had she been pushed to take Jesus off the cross? What benefit did any of the power she had possessed as Duende have? And why had her grandmother's spirit, once again, welcomed her back here, to this place, when all she felt was empty?

Ingrid wished she could be carried away by the waves, to someplace beyond here. At times she cried, hoping to feel better, but then other times she didn't have it in her to feel anything. She tried imagining Roger next to her, maybe holding her hand, consoling her, giving her a sense of hope. But her imagination didn't help. Ingrid was alone, alone with the sea.

The waters inched close to her, almost tickling her feet with each crashing wave. She listened to the ebb and flow of the liquid mass before her that never gave up. It gave of itself over and over again to become the sea that never left, that had never left her.

"We are the keepers of the earth," was what the little man had told Ingrid so long ago. She recalled how he had said it was getting harder to keep this life going, to keep growing what sometimes didn't want to grow with all the noise humans had created.

Ingrid imagined this body of water gone, the waves having given up on life as she realized she and so many others had done. *The magic is in believing,* she suddenly thought, although her thoughts seemed to be coming from somewhere beyond, or deeper within herself than she had let herself go in a while. Life was about celebrating what was here in breathtaking forms, she reflected.

Ingrid closed her eyes. Listened to the sound beneath the sound as she had done long ago. It had been so painful back then, but maybe it didn't have to be, she realized.

She took a breath, then another, with ease. All that had happened to her in the past week with Roger, and then with Latia, she took in. Ingrid listened, with all of her being, to the sea, the soft wind that cooled the air, and the few birds that still sung despite the darkness. She became profoundly still until, once again, bit by bit, she could hear the whale sounds and that primordial place within the sea where life cried itself into being. As Ingrid expanded into the sounds, she finally heard it—that whistling she used to love that sprouted from the vast waters. It approached her quickly, but this time she was ready. Ready for that sudden tap on the shoulder, her friend having returned to greet her.

Bony, yet furry fingers touched her gently. "I missed you," she heard him say.

And with her eyes closed, Ingrid responded with slow-moving tears that followed with a crackling voice. "I missed you too."

The moment held an eternal grip on her until, finally, she

opened her eyes to look at the little man. Yes, he was the friend she had known as a child. And yes, Ingrid now knew that he was the same man who had been angry with her in Señor Ramos's field.

Although, through her liquid gaze, he appeared different than the man in the vineyard and the one who had taken her on adventures as a child, there was an essence that was the same. She could see this now inside her stillness.

"I may look different," he said. "Like you, I can wear many masks, but I'm the same inside. I'm an earth spirit, a duende, just like you."

Ingrid gazed at him in a way she never had as a child. She saw herself in him, in his small, deep-set eyes. He carried a sense of home that was familiar to her.

"Come with me, before you leave again," he said.

It had been such a long time since Ingrid had traveled to a dimension beyond this one. She wondered if she still could, especially since she was no longer Duende.

But the little man took her by the hand, repeated her name as her grandmother had done years ago. "Duende, Duende, Duende. Come with me."

Hearing her name helped her believe in the person she had once been. It made it easier to trust her friend enough to follow him.

"Duende, Duende, Duende," she heard him repeat, as they traveled into the sea, carried by whale sounds and the constant rhythm of water brushing against itself. Deeper and deeper she followed, holding onto the little man's hand and trusting.

Before Ingrid could doubt what was happening to her, they were back inside the earth, as if she had never left. Her heart began to expand. A pulsing heat within her pushed out beyond the tips of her fingers and feet, shifting the very essence of the person she had become.

From this place, Ingrid took in the golden rivers and the

colors that weaved in and out of her own imaginings. She felt home. Really home.

"I see now," she said, and yet her words didn't produce sound.

Ingrid didn't mind. Her friend's eyes smiled back at her, reflecting the colors of the river. He had heard her thoughts.

Everything was possible here. The magic of her heart could dance in this place, she could feel this. She could be anyone she wished to be, and life could sprout from such love and beauty that it would only create more life. The overwhelming feeling Ingrid had felt as a child—her power, her capacity to do harm—seemed inconsequential now because her heart was too big to do anything but honor and give life. Like the sea that never quit, she understood the love that could give of itself so fully that it never gave up. It gave and gave as the entire earth did.

Her sea friend watched Ingrid, the little girl who had grown to be a woman, a woman who now stood before him, finally ready to understand the immensity of who she was. "You are Duende," he said. "You are the spirit of the earth, and as a part of her spirit, you are, like me, a keeper of the earth. You are here to take care of her."

Ingrid looked at him. His smile was big. It covered the entire earth's core with its light, melting her heart inside its love.

"But it's not the same out there," she said. "It's so hard to be Duende out there. It hurts."

Without saying a word, the little man took Ingrid's hand and pulled her toward him, embracing her. He held her for what seemed like years.

"I know it's hard. I know. You were so young back then when you discovered your power and were asked to do what any eight-year-old would consider too much," he said, maintaining her in his embrace. "You needed to know what was possible, though, just like all the children do before they forget who they truly are, before they lose their way. It is because you did come here as a child, and because you did challenge the insanity that people here on earth have created, that you can come back to this place as an adult and be the earth keeper you are meant to be."

Ingrid felt his words more than she heard them, for her friend's presence brought her home to herself.

"You are not done here in Málaga, though," he said, pulling back from Ingrid and looking into her eyes as the golden rivers held the warmth in her body. "You must return to the church before you leave Málaga. There you will finally be able to let go of the pain you have been carrying so you can be on this earth, in this body of yours."

Ingrid could feel her body tightening, even as her heart remained big. "You said *this* is my home. Remember? Can't I stay here?"

"Not now, not now," she heard her friend say as she quickly traveled along his whistle, back up to the earth's surface, to the edge of the shoreline, where the waters tickled her feet.

"Not now," was all Ingrid could hear as the stars pierced through the night sky.

DUENDE

DUENDE

After Jesus had been taken off the cross, there were as many opinions on the street as there were stars in the sky. In particular, people speculated about the third nail that was missing and made up stories about the hammer marks on the wood.

As for Lázaro, however, he had little interest in opinions and stories. He was lost in a deep sleep that carried him far into the light of day. He had nothing left in him but exhaustion.

The previous night, Lázaro had noticed Duende, had seen her pass his place. Strangely, he had expected her to be there, and it came as no surprise that she had appeared to be carrying a heavy weight.

When he had seen Duende, she looked so small, so alone. Lázaro had watched her go by his home, his eyes following her as he had done so many times before. He had felt the need to protect her from those who didn't understand. Because he understood.

Creeping out of his shed, Lázaro had seen the nail. Duende had been near enough for him to make out the shape of the object as she had pulled it out of her satchel. It must have been so heavy, he had thought, remembering the size of the nails that had held up Jesus at La Iglesia del Mar. He had felt for her, understood her confusion and desperation as she had dug into the earth and dropped the long metal weight into it.

After waiting for Duende to finish her work and leave, he had instinctively known what to do. With flashlight in hand, he had carefully walked to the place where Duende had been and shined his light onto a stone and a patch of wet sand.

Lázaro had knelt down and began digging up the very object Duende had sought so hard to hide, thinking he would find a better place for it, far away from here, where the chance of some young child playing in the sand and digging it up was small.

Lázaro had pulled the nail out of the earth, placed it in his own bag, and walked for miles into the hills of Málaga. His journey was a pilgrimage—an unplanned, yet necessary pilgrimage for not only Duende, but himself.

But why was this so important? What did he need to hide after all these years? What made him so determined to bury this weight that he now carried? Was the nail a symbol of the weight he had always carried that he wanted to finally bury far from the sea?

Lázaro had gotten tired of questioning himself, tired of asking *why* all the time. That night, he had slowly forced himself to surrender and felt a sensation of freedom unlike any he had ever felt. He was like a child saying no for the first time, and he was no longer afraid to follow his heart and trust it would lead him home.

As he climbed up the hills—or what seemed more to him like mountains—he felt himself shedding his old being so rapidly that he was afraid there would be nothing left of him when he got to the top.

But there was. He arrived with sweat falling from his forehead and his legs, weak. He was on someone's land, fields of grape arbors holding barren vines. Winter, mild as it was, was nearing.

It was late, and he knew that is must have been several hours past midnight by then. In the stillness, under the full moon, Lázaro had sought a place to bury the nail.

Several feet from the end of one of the arbors, Lázaro dropped his bag to the ground. He felt the earth in his hands, sifted it through his fingers. Not too hard, it yielded.

Lázaro began to dig with a small shovel he had brought with him. Bit by bit, he cleared the earth, and then looked up beyond him, and at the house, which lay in the distance. All was still, quiet except for Lázaro's shovel scraping against the expanding hole in the ground, until finally it was ready and Lázaro could place the nail deep inside.

"Adiós, clavo," he said, lowering the nail into the ground with a final farewell. "Adiós."

Wearily, Lázaro covered the nail with great care, his head falling to the ground for a moment. Sleep. Sleep. That was all he wanted as he stumbled down the hills. Sleep. Sleep.

And sleep was what he did, deeply, until the sun drenched his shack with light at two in the afternoon.

Lázaro had never slept so late into the day. Disoriented, he wondered where he was. In the hills, in a church, out in the sand of the sea?

Still stumbling as he had last night, he stepped into the day. It was Sunday, and people were outside, families walking and playing in the sand and on nearby streets. Suddenly, it all came back to Lázaro—last night and what he had done, and what Duende had done. No one would know what had happened. All the evidence was now gone. But he still had work to do. He needed to go to La Iglesia del Mar, the church where Jesus had been taken off the cross. He wanted to see what Duende had accomplished.

Father Jorge, his priest friend, had come to him earlier yesterday, accusing him of taking Jesus off the cross. He had thrown a newspaper down on Lázaro's doorstep, or what there was of one, and shouted, "A little girl couldn't have done this. But you could have. Oh, yes. You have proven to the world that dreams, no matter how absurd, can come true, can be acted upon. You only had to grab a hammer and pull the nails off the cross, taking one of those nails with you so you can always be reminded that you—you who were too tired, too weary of saving souls— can at least make dreams come true, that you can be the magician you always wanted to be, just once, in the most despicable way. Pretend it is the dream of a child, but you can't fool us in the end."

Lázaro had defended himself against Father Jorge's onslaught—although he wasn't able to change his mind—and was now ready to see for himself what had caused such anger. He wanted to see how Duende's dream had become reality.

Lázaro felt light in a way he hadn't for years. He felt younger. Unafraid. Maybe even foolishly, but he felt unafraid as he walked toward La Iglesia del Mar, through the pain of his tight muscles.

He was dressed as elegantly as possible, with black pants from his years as a priest, a blazer that hinted of sophistication, a hat, and his best shirt, which was wrinkled, but not enough to shock those who were now ceaselessly guarding and keeping watch over La Iglesia del Mar. He also carried with him a piece of paper that verified his service to the church many years ago.

As Lázaro approached the looming structure, a gathering of clouds began to weep.

"Sorry, you can't come in here," said the guard, who stood at the top of the steps and pointed to the people whom Lázaro had just passed. "Didn't you see all these folks," he said. "If they could, they would pass straight on through as well."

Behind Lázaro were several dozen townspeople. Some were on their knees praying. Others had risen upon seeing him, but he was not prepared to let them distract him.

"I was a priest in this church once," he told the guard. "I want to see what has happened to my Savior."

"And I am the Holy Spirit," the guard scoffed. "The next thing you'll say is that you are Jesus himself, right? Maybe we'll put you up there on the cross and then all these people will go home. What do you say? Then we'll be sure to let you inside."

The guard's laughter attracted his comrades to the scene, but Lázaro continued to argue his case. "I am telling the truth, and I have papers to show it."

"¿Qué pasa?" asked another guard who joined them. "What does this guy want?"

The first guard abruptly cut off his laughter but remained with one hand on his belly. He pointed at Lázaro. "This man says he used to be a priest here. Just look at him! I told him the next thing he'll say is that he is Jesus Christ himself." He waited for the cue to resume his laughter, but the second guard failed to find humor in his words.

"I don't think this is a good time to laugh about such things, Esteban," he said with rigid authority. "Let us see your papers."

The second guard looked closely at the slightly crumpled paper that Lázaro handed him. "This was a long time ago. What brings you back here after all this time?"

"I'm here to see for myself what has become of our Savior," Lázaro told him. "I tended to him years ago, and it is important that I see what has happened."

Lázaro made an effort to look inside, past the guard, but the doors were impossible to see through. They might as well have been protecting a tomb, not the church Lázaro knew so well. "I would like to speak to the Father."

The second guard took a deep breath. He looked at Lázaro with pitying eyes. "This better be good," he said and walked away to get the priest.

After what seemed an eternity, Father Ignacio Telumbre appeared. Lázaro recognized him immediately as a boy he had once known who used to pray next to him and ask for advice on becoming a priest. Back then Lázaro often held back from encouraging him, not wanting this boy to give his life to the priesthood unless he was completely certain. Now, he appeared in front of him, no older than thirty-five, speaking with a serenity that assured Lázaro he had made the right choice.

"You are familiar," the priest said. He scanned Lázaro, who was glad that he recognized him.

"I have come here, as I mentioned to the guards, to see for myself what has happened in our beautiful church," he told him. "It is important that I see what has happened."

"But it is not for anyone to see at this moment," said Father Telumbre. The guards stood back a few feet from the priest, watching with curiosity. "And how can it be of *such* great importance when it is *you* who left the church so long ago?"

"I know it has been a long time, but… I must see it."

"You give me no reason and yet you insist upon entering. What am I supposed to make of this? Why should it be so important that you see this spectacle? What do you know that I don't?" Father Telumbre asked.

Lázaro seemed unconcerned for the way Father Telumbre stared at him suspiciously. "What do you think caused this anyway?"

"That is not for me to tell," the young priest said. "Only God knows. Isn't that right?"

"I suppose God knows everything, but aren't you curious?" asked Lázaro. "They call it blasphemy. What if it's a miracle?"

"Stealing Jesus from La Iglesia del Mar is not a miracle," Father Telumbre said, seemingly losing patience. "Do you believe that God's only son, who died for our sins, who chose to be crucified for the benefit of mankind, did so only to be stolen off a cross in southern Spain almost two thousand years later? Do you suppose it was all a mistake—that God made a mistake?"

"No, but maybe *we* did," Lázaro said, slipping the words

in without noticing the dramatic effect they were having on the priest.

Father Telumbre looked carefully at Lázaro and then at the guards, communicating to them a message that required no words. Soon, one of them took Lázaro by the arms and escorted him to follow the priest inside. Relieved that he would finally see the miracle for himself, Lázaro followed.

Behind him, the other guard was laughing, enough for Lázaro to hear, but not enough to warn him that he was being carried away to a place other than the inside of La Iglesia del Mar.

᷈

"There's no time for daydreaming. Let's get packing," Duende's father said, temporarily pulling Duende out of the dark cloud she was in.

The girl packed the few remaining items from her bedroom into a big box.

The movers had already cleared most of the house, taking the piano, the sofa, the dinner table, and filling a large part of the truck parked in the street. Now they waited to carry out the final boxes.

Although Duende still wouldn't speak, she did as she was told, moving through the house like a ghost, disconnected from reality.

When her father had first told her about going to Germany months ago, she hadn't known what to make of the news. Duende had felt she'd miss Lázaro, the sea, her little friend that came from there, and her neighbor Latia. But as the New Year and her moving date drew closer, the reality of leaving the only place she had really felt was home truly hit her. She would *really* miss her few friends and her walks to the sea.

But now, despite her love for Málaga, Duende was prepared to go. She was ready to leave behind the dreams of Jesus—which had stopped after her incident in the church—and the nail she had buried in the sand. She felt glad to move far away from the big Gypsy, that big church, and all the other places and people of Málaga that reminded her, in one way or another, of Jesus and his cross.

Teri-Amo's words—"You do not know your power"—still haunted her, along with the city she had been able to create inside the earth, as she packed the last of her belongings.

She also carried the latest news she had heard from her mother, who had followed the events at La Iglesia del Mar. Just yesterday, Mutti had announced to Duende that the authorities had finally sent the man responsible for taking Jesus off the cross to prison. It was over.

"They say the jury found this one man guilty of taking Jesus off that cross," her mother had said as she walked into the apartment with newspaper in hand. "They say he had been a priest. Imagine that."

At that moment, Duende, who had been drawing in her sketchbook at the kitchen table, was afraid to look up.

"The man's name is Lázaro," her mother had said. "Former Padre Lázaro."

Duende's hand had shaken, but she forced herself to keep calm and continue scribbling something, anything, as her mother spoke.

"They say he left the priesthood awhile ago. Not clear, though, why he'd take Jesus off the cross. Strange... and they still don't even know where Jesus went. One nail went missing too."

By now, Duende had become nauseous. She felt temporarily paralyzed, unable to move or speak. The lead of her pencil had broken in her hand. She got up from the table and, without drawing too much attention from her mother, walked as quickly as she could to the bathroom, where she released her disgust into the toilet.

Now, as Duende packed, she carried the same deep sadness and paralysis. She pictured Lázaro as she had last seen him.

He had been frying fish for her and his daughter. She couldn't believe Lázaro was now taking the fall for her or the Gypsies. It was unfair, wrong. Waves of guilt coursed through her body. She wished she could have stayed in the bathroom and released all of her dreams, the whole experience in the church, and the news of Lázaro into the toilet.

But instead, Duende pretended she knew nothing about what had happened and filled her box with meaningless possessions, all the time picturing Lázaro—not down at the beach but behind a cell door of some prison.

She wanted to scream out her protest, but she had become lifeless. Packing and packing was all she could do, and she hoped that somehow, in leaving this place, she could leave behind all of this—every bit of it.

Duende closed up her box. One of the moving men came to pick it up and carry it away. She sat, alone, feeling as empty and soulless as the blank walls surrounding her.

Time to go. Time to leave for Germany, for the cold winter snows that could, possibly—with time—cover up any memory of the guilt and pain Duende felt upon leaving behind Málaga and all that had happened at La Iglesia del Mar.

INGRID &
DUENDE

INGRID & DUENDE

Two decades later, Ingrid was back at La Iglesia del Mar. Its towering presence still cast a long shadow along the cobblestone streets and reached as close to heaven as possible, up and up, beyond the steeple, narrowing to a fine tip. Only this time, it was entirely covered in the green of the earth. The church had become a lush rainforest.

With the same trepidation she had once had, years ago, when her feet were small, Ingrid carefully pushed open the heavy, weathered doors. She stepped inside.

Here before her, ivy and branches crawled along the walls and over stained-glass windows that sprayed yellow, red, and indigo among the leaves. Ingrid's mouth dropped open as she stood there frozen, marveling at how this grandeur of manmade stone had been transformed into a rich, vibrant jungle.

Upon the altar, where Jesus had hung, lay more green, green moss, green vines, green leaves like open palms to the sky. Grapevines pushed their way through the cracks of the floor, dragging their sentient force upon the floors and walls, curling their limbs around the cross. Ingrid could hear their call, the voices of their chorus pouring their spirit of plenty into words. "Drink my blood," they cried. "Drink my blood."

The pulpit looked like a moss-covered stone, standing elegant and tall, as though prepared to make a speech. And beyond the candles used to light prayers for loved ones were miniscule flowers with their own seeds of nectar wanting to be tasted and touched. Mary, the Virgin of many faces, had grown a beard marked by a twisted branch turning upward.

Ingrid was surprised to see Mary Magdalene standing next to the Virgin, not in form, but in spirit—and she was amazed that she could, once again, see such spirit form as she once had with her grandmother. It was as if she were in the Garden of Eden sprouting new life—without sin and guilt—among the vines that had reclaimed this church.

The church was empty of people, except one man sitting about five rows from the altar. Ingrid walked to the front, letting her eyes wander up and down the cross and toward the ground where she had once picked up the nail. There was nothing there other than new growth pushing through the ground. She sat in the first pew and, in the silence, closed her eyes.

It was then that Ingrid heard disembodied voices from all directions, weaving their sentences in and out of the verdure, welcoming her home.

"What took you so long?" someone said.

When Ingrid tried to answer, there was silence kissing her lips.

In the darkness of her closed eyes, she saw faces, spirits, many of them, circling along the walls of this place, smiling.

"We've come back because of you, Duende. Because you and the Gypsies took down a false symbol of suffering… because finally the spirit of the earth can reclaim its place, and can be heard… because the miracles and abundance of this earth that Jesus spoke about can be ours to celebrate and live."

Whose voices were these? Were they the voices of the earth, the dreams—our dreams—carried by its body and shared with all? Were they the vine, the voices of the vine, her ancestors' voices, or did they belong to Jesus and Mary Magdalene? Were these one and the same?

Ingrid shivered, briefly trying to make sense of what was happening around her, before surrendering to the incomprehensible that filled the spaces.

"You know," someone from behind her suddenly said, "you should have seen what this place once looked like."

Heavy breathing broke the words of this voice, a voice that seemed so much more human than the spirit sounds she was hearing. It was deeper, more contained by form.

With her eyes closed, Ingrid heard an old man in his final words. The in and out of his breath was a grandfather clock, ticking a singular, audible rasping, inhaling the dense air of prayers gone unanswered inside these walls.

She pictured the voice as coming from the old man seated several rows behind her. His words were spoken low and with longing. Yes, she thought, smiling, she knew what this place had looked like years ago.

"I was once a priest here," he said.

He seemed old, very old.

"Watched the colors change all the time, like colors of the wind moving through this place, through me, until it was time to leave."

Ingrid could see the colors, see the stained-glass windows, the glints of glass sparkling through the greenery.

"Since that time, a lot has changed," he went on. "A lot of industry, tourism, people moving so quickly. But you know, I come in here…" He paused, and in that moment, a small dove with a thin, iridescent blue line above the top of a tuxedo-like tail flapped its wings in front of Ingrid before flying to the top of the cross.

"I come in here to remind myself of Duende," the old man said, gasping, as though he were about to surrender. "She never left us, never has. *Nunca, nunca.*"

Upon hearing her name spoken, Ingrid turned abruptly, but she could not see the old man. She looked toward the doors and either side of her. But saw nothing. La Iglesia del Mar was empty, except for her, as it had been twenty years ago after the Gypsies had carried Jesus out of the church. She was alone and confused. How had this man known her name? Had he been talking about the spirit of the earth?

Ingrid stood up, still looking for any sign of change around her. Where had this man gone? How could he have moved so quickly out of here? Nothing made sense.

Uncertain of what to do, Ingrid walked to the pew where the man had sat. She moved between the narrow wooden benches to the exact place he had been. There was something lying on the pew, a heavy metal object covered in earth and loose strands of vine. It was the nail—the one Ingrid had buried in the ground, the one she'd been unable to find again, until now.

Her hands trembled as she drew herself closer. Was this what she had feared for so long? Picking up this relic of the past, this single nail she had carried from La Iglesia del Mar and buried in the sand twenty years ago, Ingrid held it cautiously in her hands. *How? How is this possible?*

Ingrid felt this nail throb, and a new life sang into her, as if reclaiming the nail and the memories it contained opened a door she had held shut during her life and for generations before her. It vibrated to the sound of a hundred wineglasses, old chalices, resonating against each other in a celebration that sounded like laughter. Paco's voice also slid in, raising the earth's core through the ground as Graciela tapped her heels to an eternal heartbeat.

Was it, Ingrid wondered, because she could finally acknowledge what had occurred years ago—Jesus having been taken off the cross, his suffering brought down from the altar, and all of our unnecessary suffering with it—that a celebration of this earthly paradise could take place?

She looked up through tear-filled eyes to where Jesus had once been, tracing the path down the aisle to the doors through which he had been carried. He had been like a bird that day, released from the confines of the church, his destiny, and mankind's expectations.

Trembling, Ingrid pulled the rusted nail to her heart and held it there. Could it have been so? *Could I really have done this?*

In her mind's eye she saw Lázaro now, and herself as a girl, as little Duende, wanting to tell him what she had done. Duende could see him now. She imagined him standing inside the doorframe of his house, above her, his eyes like cold steel, looking down at her.

"How? How did it happen?" Duende heard him saying.

"I didn't do it," she answered, lying.

"But your dreams," he said. "It's just like your dreams."

Duende stood below him, a small girl trying to be an adult. But she couldn't. She couldn't do it anymore. She began to cry. A little, and then, once the entire truth caught up with her, she wept and hugged herself to the ground.

Lázaro kneeled next to her, held her. "It's all right," he kept saying. "It's all right."

"I saw them take Jesus off the cross. I saw it," Duende cried. "I saw it. I saw it. I saw it."

Lázaro pulled back and looked at her. "What did you see?"

"Jesus, he was looking at me. He was smiling, and then, then they came, through the big doors, dancing, making lots of noise. They had hammers. They pulled the nails off. It was all so loud. The nails fell to the ground. And then they carried Jesus out of there. He was smiling. He was so happy, I swear. He was so happy, just like in my dreams."

Lázaro looked at her intensely. "They... Who are *they*?"

"They... you know, the Gypsies, Graciela."

"And where were you?"

"In the church. I was standing there and I imagined the

whole thing, before it even happened. And then it happened. Like that." Duende was amazed to hear herself describing what seemed so magical, yet real.

"It was like my dreams, but this time I—" She stopped. She didn't want to mention the nail. But it was too late.

"This time, what?"

"There was the nail. When they all left with Jesus, I picked up one of the nails and took it with me."

Surprisingly enough, Lázaro did not seem upset, but only listened intently as she told him where it was buried.

"Why did you take it, anyway?" he asked after getting up and walking around on the sand.

"My grandmother told me to."

"So she saw you through to the end with the dream, then?"

Duende nodded, crying. It was her fault everyone in town was upset about what had happened—and that Lázaro had been blamed for it all. She couldn't forgive herself. She couldn't. She couldn't!

"Were there any angels?" Lázaro asked suddenly. "Was there a light or some other type of illumination above Jesus's head? Did it look real?"

"It looked real until they carried Jesus out the door," Duende told him.

"And then?"

"The nail was very heavy. It was in my satchel until I buried it."

"Were you happy, like in the dream? Were you happy when you saw Jesus being carried out of there?"

"He was happy," she told him, remembering how the wood that Jesus had been had turned to flesh.

"But were *you* happy?" Lázaro repeated.

"No. I was scared."

"Did you help make it happen, Duende? Did you help them?"

"Yes. Yes. Jesus wanted me to."

"Where do you think *He* is now?"

Duende felt torn between her guilt for Lázaro and the miracle that had taken place in this church.

"I didn't mean it," she said, weeping. "I didn't mean to do it. I didn't mean to do any of it."

Lázaro knelt down and, taking her in his arms, rocked her like a child.

"Duende, don't worry about me," he whispered. "You made a miracle happen because you were called to do it. You followed your dreams and your truth."

She looked up at Lázaro through her tears. How could he be so kind after what she had done to him?

"I'm okay. Really," Lázaro said, continuing to rock her. "What happened had to happen, Duende. You had to awaken to the earth, to her magic inside you, so you could find your true way in this heavenly place. It's what we all need to do. It's time."

As Duende listened to her old friend, she felt herself becoming lighter, the weight of the guilt she had carried releasing itself until she relaxed into Lázaro's arms.

"I have to tell you something, though, Duende," Lázaro said. "I saw you bury that nail. I dug it up again that night… took it to the mountains, to a vineyard where I buried it in the ground."

"You what?" she cried, stunned.

"I buried the nail again… in the mountains."

Ingrid couldn't believe what she was hearing. "But why?" she demanded.

"So no one would ever find it."

Ingrid tried to take in Lázaro's words, but it all seemed too much. Instead, images flashed before her of Señor Ramos and his vines, of the miraculous grape growth where she had touched the stems.

Could it be that she had actually brought the grapes to life—that she was capable of producing miracles, that her homecoming to the nail's resting place allowed for the message of the earth to be released? Was she truly carrying within her the spirit of the earth, the duende that is within all of us, that is capable of sprouting new life and abundance when we accept our natural place here?

Ingrid cried now. Inside this grandiose church, this Garden of Eden, where thousands of others have cried for decades, centuries, and millennia, she cried.

Could it be that she was home, that she was finally home, with her ancestors, their message, and this heavenly garden on earth?

Ingrid breathed heavily now, felt a surge of lightness in her chest. Pulsing vines ascended her legs, pumping new life into veins that had lived centuries of sleep. She was becoming the spirit of the earth once again, with its rivers of blood converging into the larger ocean of life.

Green masses and their tendrils wrapped around and through Ingrid's body. She was becoming the vine, expanding toward the edges of the earth, truly free and alive inside this magic jungle of earth called home.

That night Lázaro had a dream. The old man dreamed that he had seen Duende dancing down by the sea where he had once lived. Her hands were the wind moving in circles, her body the sun, and her feet those of mankind and all the creatures that left footprints in the sand. And in the sky was the face of an old woman, a Gypsy spirit, smiling.

La Saeta

*¿Quién me presta una escalera para subir al madero, para quitarle los clavos
a Jesús el Nazareno?*

—Saeta popular de gitanos

Sacred Song

*Who will lend me a ladder to climb the cross,
to remove the nails from Jesus of Nazareth?*

—Popular Gypsy sacred song

Excerpta de *La Saeta*

*!No puedo cantar, ni quiero
a ese Jesús del madero
sino al que anduvo en el mar!*

—Antonio Machado

La Saeta Excerpt

*I cannot sing, nor do I want to
to that Jesus on the cross,
but rather to He who walked on the sea!*

—Antonio Machado

Acknowledgements

The journey of writing my novel was a long one, as is the list of those I wish to thank.

I give thanks to Archie, the man I met on the plane whose story inspired mine to be written. I thank Carl Hyatt, Paul Hoogeveen, and count-less others (including more people I met on planes) for their inspiration and for the seeds they offered that sprouted into stories. I give special thanks to my sister, Nicole Normansell, who was my first full-fledged, highly dedicated editor; and to subsequent editors, Mary Linn Roby and Lindsey Alexander; to my earlier book agent, Moses Cardona; and to my designer, Damonza, and illustrator, Jenna Kass.

I am so grateful for all those who took their time to read *Child of Duende* and give me feedback before publication: Angela Rennilson, Aurora Lindquist, Mallory Burnett, Roberta Fotter, Susan Gretchen Schulte, Nora Hickey, Christina Florence, Ann Paden, Jean Pedrick, Barbara Adam (my mother), and so many more. Thanks to Janet Prince and Peter Berg for opening their place in the mountains for me to write; to my parents in their support of my publishing venture; and of course, to Greg Polk and Rebecca Black, whose *Monsoon Memories* home became my place of residence during the final writing stages of my book.

Finally, I give special thanks to my guiding spirits, to mother earth, and to the spirit of my grandmother. Without any of them, *Child of Duende* would never have been written.

About the Author

Michelle Adam's story didn't start as a novel. It began as a hunger, as a journey she could never have dreamed of. It came from a place far beyond her—from her grandmother's spirit, and from a collective unconscious, one we tap into when we have nowhere left to run to, when we're ready to listen.

Born in Switzerland to an American mother and Argentinean father, and raised there and in Spain and the United States, Michelle grew up without borders. She obtained a bachelor's degree in communications and international relations at the University of New Hampshire and then proceeded to work as a photojournalist, a newspaper and magazine writer, and a teacher, while pursuing a love for dance. But no matter what path Michelle pursued, she retained a strong desire to return to Spain and relive her deep connection to its land.

Michelle didn't return to Spain to live for any length of time, and instead, in her late twenties, traveled west with a spiritual longing following her. On her journey, she became injured, and spent years struggling to walk. Unable to dance, she began a few sentences of her novel, then a few more, until, years later, a story unraveled itself. She followed dreams and guidance, and only later discovered that parts of her fiction existed in reality:

like the sacred song the Gypsies would sing about wanting to take Jesus off the cross; and the story of the Gypsy girl who ran off with the nails; and a church, Saintes-Maries-de-la-Mer, in southern France, where the Gypsies make a pilgrimage every year, that has a similar name to the one in her novel.

Today, Michelle lives in New Mexico, where she leads groups in song, sound, and a journey of connecting with the land and our sacred place on this earth. She is committed to awakening, and helping others awaken their soul's longing and the child of *duende* that is in all of us, waiting to be lived.

Made in United States
Troutdale, OR
10/11/2024

23598553R00192